The girl he had known in Kansas had been wild enough to bed a drifter.

He didn't doubt for a minute that she had matured into a passionate woman who knew her own whims.

'A marriage in name only is a perfect solution. My heart's right, Abbie. I want to help you.'

She was standing on the edge of the pond as still as the deer. The sun had dropped in the sky, casting shadows through the branches so she seemed to be standing in a cage. He could sense the tug in her soul. John pulled out his best argument.

'Say yes, Abbie. Do it for our daughter.'

Praise for
Victoria Bylin

'…an author who writes with heart,
and articulates well a clear understanding
of human feelings and frailties that
readers should totally enjoy.'
—*Historical Romance Writers Review*

'These bad-boy western romances
aren't to be missed.'
—*RT Book Reviews*

West of Heaven
'The hero, definitely alpha male
and code-of-the-west cowboy, provides
wonderful appeal, as does the heroine
and her orientation to family values.
This story proves that love is salvation
from death and its worst griefs.'
—*RT Book Reviews*

Of Men and Angels
'An uplifting tale of a spiritual woman,
who's deeply human, and the flawed man
she loves. It's evident that Ms Bylin
writes from her heart.'
—*Old Book Barn Gazette*

'*Of Men and Angels* is the perfect title
for a perfect book. The characters are
wonderfully human and well rounded, and
the story is an exciting, heartwarming and
spiritual tale with a magnitude of emotion.'
—*Romance Reviews Today*

ABBIE'S OUTLAW

BY

VICTORIA BYLIN

First published in Great Britain 2006
by Mills & Boon, an imprint of Harlequin (UK) Limited,
Large Print edition 2011
Eton House, 18-24 Paradise Road, Richmond, Surrey TW9 1SR

© Vicki Scheibel 2005

ISBN: 978 0 263 22394 1

Harlequin (UK) policy is to use papers that are natural,
renewable and recyclable products and made from wood grown in
sustainable forests. The logging and manufacturing process conform
to the legal environmental regulations of the country of origin.

Printed and bound in Great Britain
by CPI Antony Rowe, Chippenham, Wiltshire

Victoria Bylin has a collection of refrigerator magnets that mark the changes in her life. The oldest ones are from California. A native of Los Angeles, she graduated from UC Berkeley with a degree in history and went to work in the advertising industry. She soon met a wonderful man, who charmed her into taking a ride on his motorcycle. That ride led to a trip down the wedding aisle, and brought two sons, various pets, and a move that landed Victoria and her family in northern Virginia. Magnets from thirty states commemorate that journey and her new life on the East Coast. The most recent additions are from the Smithsonian Museum of American History and a Chinese restaurant that delivers—a sure sign that Victoria is busy writing. Feel free to drop her an e-mail at VictoriaBylin@aol.com or visit her website at www.victoriabylin.com

To Michael…
Beloved husband, you are mine!

Chapter One

Midas, New Mexico
June 1887

When the Reverend John Leaf saw Abigail Windsor standing at the top of the train steps, dressed in black and shielding her eyes from the noonday sun, he knew that all hell was about to break loose. He'd made a million mistakes in his life and had made amends for all of them—except one. Now that mistake was coming to light in a way he had dreaded for years and deeply feared.

His eyes stayed on Abbie as she scanned the crowd. Lord, he thought, she looked awful in black. The girl he remembered had insisted on wearing pretty colors in spite of the gloom in her life. He remembered her best in a coppery dress that brought out the highlights in her hair. He also remembered her wearing nothing at all, which was a problem for a man who'd sworn off women entirely.

He'd never been inclined toward marriage or children of his own. The Leaf family curse ran thick in his blood, and he'd rather die than pass it on to an unsuspecting child. Certainly not to a son who would grow up filled with hate or to a daughter who would go through life lonely and crazed like his own mother had.

But if the letter he'd received from a girl in Virginia was true, he'd done exactly that. The hairs on John's neck stood on end as he remembered opening the envelope with Silas's handwriting on the front. On a single sheet, his friend had written, "This came for you. Godspeed."

Along with Silas's note, John had removed an expensive linen envelope addressed to him in a schoolgirl's cursive. The address was brief: "Mr. John Leaf, Bitterroot, Wyoming." Beneath the two lines she had written, "Please forward." John had peeled off the wax, unfolded a sheet of stationery and started to read.

Dear Mr. Leaf,
My name is Susanna Windsor. If you are the same John Leaf who left the Wyoming Territorial Prison in April of 1881, please write to me at my school. I believe I am your daughter.
    Regards.

John had stared at the words in a fog. The girl had said just enough to scare the daylights out of him without revealing anything about herself. The address she had supplied was for a girls' academy in Virginia. He'd never been east of the Mississippi and didn't know a soul who had, at least not someone who could afford a fancy private school. The original postmark was two months old. He figured the envelope had been sitting in the Bitterroot post office for weeks before Silas went to town where the postmaster must have given it to him.

John had spent a wretched night remembering dozens of women he'd barely known and one he'd almost taken to Oregon. He'd also sat at his desk with his head in his hands, praying that the poor girl had made a mistake. He was obligated to reply to her letter, but who was she?

He'd gotten his answer the next morning when Justin Norris had delivered a telegram from the girl's mother.

We have urgent business. Will arrive in Midas on the California Ltd. on June 3rd. Abigail Windsor nee Moore.

It had taken him a minute to put the pieces together. The stuffy-sounding Abigail Windsor was Abbie Moore, the girl who had threatened to shoot out his kneecaps, then fed him supper because she'd felt bad about it. They had spent two weeks together, alone on her grandmother's farm, and nature had taken its course.

John's stomach tied itself into a knot. He wanted a drink, but he had consumed his weekly shot of whiskey the previous night in a vain effort to forget about what had happened on their last night together. To his shame, John had ridden off and left Abbie alone to clean up the mess.

Now that girl was a woman and standing in the doorway of the train, scanning the crowd from beneath the brim of her black bonnet. Needing to greet her but not ready to face the needs of the day, John watched as she pressed her lips into a tight line and scoured the crowd with her eyes. Her chest swelled as she took a breath and then blew it out in irritation. That gesture gave him comfort. She was probably upset with him for not meeting the train. They'd both be better off if she stayed that way, so he rocked back on one heel and waited.

To his surprise, her eyes locked on someone in the crowd and turned murderous. Following her line of sight, he saw a boy with the gangly posture of adolescence pushing through the throng. The kid had a bigger head of steam than the train and was barreling straight at Emma Dray, the mayor's daughter and a member of John's congregation. The matrons in his church had picked this young and pretty woman to be his wife, much to John's irritation and Emma's ill-concealed delight.

Emma was waving at someone across the platform when the human cannon ball clipped her elbow and knocked her off balance. John had no desire to catch Emma, but what choice did he have? With two quick strides, he came up behind her and clasped her arms until she was steady on her feet.

When the boy glanced back, John gripped his thin shoulder and hauled him up short. Keeping his voice neutral, he said, "What's your name, son?"

"I'm not your son." When the kid's voice cracked from bass to soprano, John held in a grin. He remembered those painful days between boyhood and being a man, and this young fellow had a face full of pimples to go with his resistant vocal cords.

John took the boy's attitude in stride. He liked bratty kids. Some of them spelled real trouble, but most were either neglected or mad at the world, feelings he understood. Knowing that too much kindness made angry boys even more rebellious, he made his voice as grim as charred wood. "It's most definitely my business, *son*. You owe Miss Dray an apology."

Emma looked down her nose. "He certainly does. He wrinkled my dress."

Leave it to Emma to carp about nonsense. The boy's conduct needed to be addressed, but any fool could see he'd been cooped up on the train and needed to blow off steam. Ignoring Emma, John said, "So what do you have to say?"

The boy managed an arrogant scowl. "She's fat and slow. She should have gotten out of my way."

"Well, I never!" huffed Emma.

"Trust me," John said pointedly. "In about five years, you won't think Miss Dray is fat."

When a blush stained Emma's cheeks, John wished he'd been more careful in his choice of words. He'd meant to remind the kid that he was still a boy. Instead John had reminded Emma that he was a man. If he knew her mother, he'd be paying for the slip with unwanted invitations for the next six months.

Before the boy could reply, the crowd shifted, revealing Abbie hurrying in their direction. She was lugging a satchel with one hand and using the other to hold her skirt above her ankles to allow for her angry stride.

At the sight of her high-button shoes, John felt his heart kick into double time. If it hadn't been for another pair of boots, they might never have met. His gaze rose to her face where he saw her high cheekbones and small nose. Her hair was pinned in a stylish coiffure but slightly disheveled, as if it were rebelling against the black hat holding it in place. Her cheeks had flushed to a soft pink, and her eyes were glued to the boy in John's grip.

"Robert Alfred Windsor! Don't you *dare* take another step!"

Because of the feathers poking up from Emma's hat, Abbie hadn't seen John's face. She focused on Emma as she dipped her head in apology. "I'm so sorry. We've been on the train for twelve days and he's—"

John stepped into her line of sight. "Hello, Abbie."

"Johnny?"

"I go by John now," he said. "Or Reverend."

"Reverend?" Her gaze dipped from his face to his clerical collar.

The only thing John liked better than fighting was shocking people, and Abbie's gaping mouth said he'd done just that. But her expression also made him aware that time had marked him. His nose had been broken twice, and he had a scar below his right ear. He also had a lump on his jaw from the saloon brawl he'd broken up last night.

Young Robbie wasn't the only male who liked to fight. Right or wrong, John enjoyed knocking sense into men who deserved it. Last night that man had been Ed Davies. The fool had lost his pay in a poker game and then gone after the winner with his fists. John had given him a "do unto others" lesson and then stuffed a sawbuck into his pocket so he could take care of his new wife until payday.

When Abbie realized she was staring, she jerked her gaze away from his. "It really has been a long time."

All those years ago, he had heard her voice before he'd seen her face. It had been whiskey-warm and it still was, but her eyes had changed. Instead of a girlish curiosity, her gaze had an edge. Maybe it was worry for her daughter that made her irises flash, or perhaps she, too, was reliving the afternoon they'd met.

He'd found her sitting in the dirt with a twisted ankle, leaning against a broken wagon wheel and aiming a pistol at his kneecaps from beneath the buckboard.

"Put your hands over your head and stand where I can see you," she had ordered.

With a devilish grin, John had complied, then he'd raked her body with his eyes one glorious inch at a time.

As the memory of that day hit hard and fast, Judas-down-there began to stir, demanding to know if Abbie's lips were still as soft as the rest of her. A trickle of sweat ran down John's back, soaking the white shirt he wore beneath his preacher's coat. A man couldn't help his bodily reactions, but he had a choice about what came out of his mouth. Trying to lighten the mood, he fell back on the words he often used when old friends discovered that Johnny

Leaf, hot-shot shootist and ladies' man, had turned into the good Reverend John Leaf.

With a wry smile, he said, "Don't let the collar fool you. I'm as low-down as ever."

"Somehow I doubt that." As her eyes softened with the caring he remembered from Kansas, she raised her hand as if she wanted to touch him, perhaps to make sure he was real. John avoided her hand with a shrug, but their gazes stayed locked and held tight.

Before he could figure out what to say, a delicate cough called his attention to Emma. He had hoped to keep his meeting with Abbie private, but Emma's presence ensured the entire town would know the details by nightfall.

Nodding in Abbie's direction, he made the introductions. "Emma, this is Abigail Windsor. She's visiting from Washington. You've already met her son."

Emma's eyebrows arched. "It's a pleasure to meet you, Mrs. Windsor."

"The pleasure is mine," Abbie replied with a warm smile. "Please, call me Abigail."

Emma had an annoying habit of fluttering her eyelashes and she did it now, looking straight at John. "Mother and I would love to have you all for supper." Turning to Abbie, she asked, "How long will you be here?"

John was curious as well.

"Just a few weeks." With a dip of her chin, Abbie indicated her mourning clothes. "The Reverend and I have an issue to settle concerning my husband's estate, and then my son and I will be going home."

"Maybe we could plan for Sunday?" Emma said.

Or maybe next year, John thought, after Emma had found a husband. Shaking his head, he said, "Thanks, but I doubt Abbie is ready to socialize."

When Abbie gave a demure smile, Emma excused herself, leaving John and Abbie alone in the crowd. They were both dressed in black and seemed cold to each other, but John wasn't fooled. The coals in his kitchen stove had looked dead this morning, but they were banked and smoldering on the inside. If he poked them, they would flare to life. John couldn't stop himself from remembering that he and Abbie had started a fire in Kansas. All sorts of things had burned between them, including the bed sheets.

Damn, he needed a smoke. But first he had to get Abbie and her son settled at the Midas Hotel. He was about to suggest they retrieve her baggage when she glanced at Robbie who was watching steam billow from the locomotive. It rose in clouds that dissipated to nothing, a reminder that fires burned themselves out.

Seeing that her son was distracted, she turned to John. "Do you know why I'm here?"

"Not exactly." Keeping his voice level, he stuck to

the facts. "Your daughter wrote to me at an old address in Wyoming. A friend forwarded the letter."

Abbie blinked to hold back tears. At the same time, she squared her shoulders. "Susanna ran away from home. I know from her best friend that she's looking for you, but the train ticket she bought went only as far as St. Louis. The detective I hired said you lived in Midas, but he didn't tell me anything else. I was hoping she'd already arrived."

John's blood turned to ice. "Judging by the letter, she thinks I'm in Bitterroot. It's a hellhole."

"Dear God," Abbie gasped. "That must be where she went."

The terror in her eyes sent a knife through his gut. Needing to offer comfort but afraid to touch her, he jammed his hands into his pockets and looked for a shred of hope. "Who's she traveling with?"

"No one," Abbie said in a shaking voice. "I'm scared to death for her."

John knew how she felt, not because he'd ever been a parent, but because he'd been on the wrong side of the law. Not all men were honorable and neither were all women. "I'll do everything I can to help," he said.

Surprised by the depth of his worry, John sucked in a lungful of air and ended up with train exhaust coating his throat. Abbie's gaze locked on his face. She had a way of willing people to feel things and

John had that sensation now. Was she hoping he'd want to be a father to the girl? God, he hoped not.

Or maybe she'd assume he'd want to hide his sinful past. Given his calling, that guess was reasonable but miles from the truth. The whole town knew he'd lived on the wrong side of the law. He'd done time in the Wyoming Territorial Prison in Laramie for his part in the Bitterroot range war, and he was still roundly hated, especially by Ben Gantry. As for thieving, whoring, gambling, drinking and other manly what-not, well, what could he say? A long time ago he'd done it all—to the best of his ability and as often as possible.

Those days were long past, but they had left habits he couldn't change. He still had an edgy need to see around corners and through walls. It was as much a part of him as a hungry stomach, and he had that need now. Keeping his voice low, he said, "I have to know, Abbie. Is she mine?"

Her eyes turned into gentle pools. "Does it matter?"

"No," he replied. "I'll help you no matter what. I just thought I should ask. If I have an obligation—"

"You don't," she said firmly.

John knew a half-truth when he heard one. She hadn't denied his blood ties to the girl, only his responsibility for raising her. He wasn't inclined to let lies fester, but he wanted to believe what Abbie had implied. As the circumstances stood, Susanna was the daughter of a congressman, not the bastard child of an outlaw. For Susanna's sake and his own peace of mind, he decided not to push the issue right now.

"It's best for everyone that she's not mine," John said. "I'll send a wire to a friend in Bitterroot. In the meantime, let's collect your baggage and get you settled at the hotel."

He lifted the carpetbag from her hand. The suitcase wasn't heavy, a detail that surprised him considering the length of her journey, but Abbie grimaced as the weight left her grasp. Trying to appear casual, she rubbed her shoulder.

John knew about old injuries. He'd gotten tossed off a mustang and twisted his knee. It still pained him in cold weather. "Are you all right?"

She dropped her arm to her side as if he'd caught her stealing. "Of course. I'm just stiff from the trip."

Maybe so, but most people didn't groan after toting a valise. To escape John's perusal, she turned to her son just as the train whistle let out a blast. She jumped as if the warning had been for her.

"Robbie?" she called. "It's time to go."

The boy stepped to his mother's side, giving John a chance to think as he guided them across the platform. Children didn't run away from home without cause, and women didn't travel cross-country with featherweight luggage unless they had nothing to put in it. And how had she gotten a bum shoulder? She had secrets, he was sure of it.

As the sun beat down on his back, he felt the heat of the summer day building inside his coat. But more than the noon sky was making him sweat. Abbie Moore was as pretty as he remembered. They possibly had a child together—a troubled girl who had been as desperate to escape her life as John had once been.

Like father, like daughter. The thought gave him no comfort at all.

Damn it! Abbie never cursed out loud, but she had learned that anger made her strong and tears didn't fix a blasted thing. Never mind that she had good cause to cry her eyes out. She had been praying for days that Susanna would already be in Midas. She had even dared to hope that Johnny Leaf had welcomed his daughter into his life.

But that hadn't happened. Instead Abbie's hopes had been dashed to pieces. Susanna was still hundreds of miles away, and the Reverend John Leaf clearly loathed the idea of fatherhood. Judging by the aloofness in his eyes, he wasn't going to change his mind. That coldness hadn't been there when they had met in Kansas, but the command in his voice was all too familiar.

Let me take off your boot.

No, I'll do it.

He'd gripped her foot and worked the laces, peeling the leather down her calf without a care for her modesty. He had inspected her ankle with tender fingers, announced that she couldn't walk on it and scooped her into his arms. The memory fanned embers that had long since died, reminding Abbie that her heart had turned to ash—except where her children were concerned.

Thoughts of Susanna and Robbie made her pulse race with another worry. A Washington attorney intended to turn Robert's estate over to Abbie's father. If Judge Lawton Moore controlled her finances, he'd force her back to Kansas. The thought was unbearable. She didn't care about herself, but her father would scorn Susanna because of her birth and favor Robbie because he was a boy. Abbie clamped her lips into a line. Damn Robert for his deathbed confession. Abbie had learned from her daughter's friend, Colleen, what he had said. *I'm sorry, Susanna, but I couldn't love you. You're not mine…*

That was true, Abbie thought. But neither did her precious daughter belong to John Leaf, at least not in a way that mattered. Blood meant nothing if it didn't come with love.

I love you, Johnny...
Don't say it.

Abbie swallowed back a wave of anxiety. They had been rolling on a blanket in tall grass, feeling each other through their clothes. He'd cut her off and rightly so. She hadn't known a blasted thing about the ways of men. But she did now. Hell would freeze before she'd marry again. The attorney had given her that option, but it didn't bear consideration.

As they neared the baggage area, the Reverend's baritone broke into her thoughts. "Do you see your trunk?"

"Not yet," she replied.

He fell silent, giving her a chance to count off the days of the trip. She had paid dearly for the express, but the train had been delayed twice, leaving her twenty-six days to find Susanna and arrive in Kansas as expected.

She had so much to lose—her home, her friends, a decent upbringing for her children. Since Robert's death, Abbie had been renting rooms in her town house. One of the benefits was a houseful of friends, including Maggie O'Dea who gladly shared her wisdom. The other reward was money for Susanna's education. Robbie had a trust fund, but Susanna had nothing. More than anything, Abbie wanted to give her daughter the choices she herself never had, and that meant having an income of her own.

At the thought of Susanna, Abbie glanced at John. He was standing tall with his hands in his coat pockets, chatting with Robbie about locomotives. Still trim and loose-jointed, he'd changed very little over the years, at least on the outside. His eyes were still piercing and dark, and though he wore his hair shorter, he still had the look of a man who resisted haircuts. Abbie couldn't help but notice the shaggy strands brushing past his collar. The slight curl matched the bit of Susanna's baby hair she kept in a locket.

Whether the Reverend liked it or not, one glance would tell him he had a daughter. Abbie was thinking about John's reaction when Robbie pointed to the baggage car. "I see our trunk. It's in the back corner."

"That's it," she replied. For her son's sake, she tried to sound cheerful, but the sight of that battered case filled Abbie with an old rage. As a bride-to-be, she had packed her things in a shiny new trunk and left home to marry a man she had never met. Today the trunk had as many scars as she did. And instead of new clothes, it held garments that belonged in the rag bag. She hadn't bought a new dress in years and her underthings were pathetic.

Sealing her lips, she prayed that John wouldn't notice her shabby clothing. It shamed her as Robert had intended. Her husband had pinched pennies until the Indian heads screamed, and so had Jefferson Hodge, the executor of his estate. As the porter carried her trunk down the gangway, Abbie relived the day she had asked Hodge for an increase in her household allowance.

"I'm sorry, Mrs. Windsor," he had replied. "Your husband stated you weren't to be involved in financial matters. I'd be pleased to transfer authority to your father or you could marry again. A woman with your sensitive nature needs a husband."

Sensitive nature? Abbie had nearly called the man a pig. A long time ago she'd been softhearted about life, but Robert had brutalized that hopeful girl until she'd shriveled to nothing. At the thought of her marriage, Abbie wanted to snort.

Duty...honor...obey...

Her father had used those words when he'd put her on the train to Washington to meet her future husband, but the only promise that mattered now was the one she had made at his grave. She had endured her last beating, told her last lie about bumping into doors and put up with a man in her bed for the last time. God spare the fool who dared to touch her now—she'd cut off his manhood with rusty scissors.

As the porter dropped her trunk into the pile of luggage, Abbie caught a whiff of the Reverend's starched collar. She hadn't missed the heat in his

eyes, as if he knew what she looked like naked.
Which he did. Or more correctly, he knew what she
used to look like.

As the porter walked away, John stepped to her
side. At the same time Abbie turned. As her skirt
brushed his pant leg, an old friction rippled down
her spine. The scent of bay rum filled her nose as
well, shooting her back in time to a dusky Kansas
sunset. With a gleam in his eyes, he had matched his
mouth to hers. When she'd stood there like a fence
post, he had brushed her bottom lip with his thumb
and grinned.

You've never done that before, have you?
I have so.
With who? Some kid with pimples?

Rakish and hungry, he'd kissed her again, long and
slow, until she had clutched at his back and arched
into him. He'd been twenty-one years old and looking for a good time. She had been seventeen and
more naive than a baby chick. She'd also been angry
with her father and aching with awareness, and she'd
loved every rebellious inch of Johnny Leaf.

Until her brother barged in on them.

Until she discovered she was carrying his child.

Until her father had bribed Robert Windsor to
marry his ruined daughter.

The jingle of coins called her gaze back to John
who had extracted a quarter from his pocket and was

pressing it into Robbie's hand. "Ask the kid in the red shirt to take the trunk to the hotel. His name's Tim Hawk. You can ride with him if it's okay with your mother."

Robbie jumped at the chance. "Can I, Ma?"

"Sure," she replied.

Abbie watched her son with mixed emotions. She loved him dearly, but Robert Senior had spoiled him rotten. At best, his behavior these days was unpredictable. At worst, it bordered on criminal. A conductor had caught him stealing an orange on the train. To fill the silence, she turned to John. "He's had a hard time since his father died."

"It has to be rough for you, too. Losing a husband is hell on earth."

Abbie sealed her lips. What would the good Reverend say if she told him that she had come to believe in divorce and thanked God every day for her husband's death?

When she didn't reply, John took her gloved hand in both of his. "I'm truly sorry, Abbie. Death is always hard, but it's worse when it's sudden."

She felt his fingers through the black silk, warm and strong against the bones of her hand. She understood that he was a minister now, and that holding a widow's hand was second nature to him, but that same hand had once touched her breasts.

The memory brought with it a surge of heat, a

melting she hadn't felt in years and never wanted to feel again.

Being careful to hide her traitorous response, she withdrew her fingers from his. No way was she going down that road again.

"Thank you for your concern." Stepping back, she stared at her trunk. If the good Reverend came any closer, she'd use those rusty scissors in a heartbeat.

Chapter Two

Calling himself a fool, John ran his fingers through his hair. What the devil was he doing holding Abbie's hand? She wasn't an elderly widow with gray hair and wrinkles. Touching her stirred up thoughts he didn't want, and if her eyes were as honest as they had been in Kansas, she had wanted to slap him.

And with good reason. Just as he remembered, her fingers were strong and slender, perfect for kneading bread or massaging a man's tired shoulders. She had done him that favor after a day of apple picking.

I'm beat. My arms feel like old ropes.

You worked so hard... Let me rub your shoulders.

He had slumped over the kitchen table, resting his head on his forearms as she'd massaged his neck. Her fingers had worked magic, and he'd offered to return the favor. Wisely she had turned her head, but not before he'd seen the discovery of desire in her eyes. Fool that he'd been, he'd taken it as a challenge.

Now, with the precaution he should have taken in Kansas, John kept the carpetbag between them as he led the way down the platform steps. He hated to ask questions about Susanna, but he needed information. "Do you know when your daughter left Washington?"

"About three weeks ago," Abbie replied. "She was staying with her best friend in Middleburg. Apparently the girls cooked up the scheme together. They told Colleen's parents that Susanna was going home, and Susanna wrote to me that she was staying through June."

John nodded. "I've used that trick myself. It's a good one."

"Too good, I'm afraid. I wouldn't have known she'd run away if I hadn't sent a wire asking the Jensens to send her home early. We have plans to meet my father."

"We'll send him a wire, too, saying you might be delayed."

"No!" Abbie's voice carried above the street noise. John turned and saw that she was trying to appear relaxed. "He doesn't know Susanna's missing. I don't want him to worry."

"Is there any chance she's been in touch with him?"

"None at all. They aren't close."

As they approached the telegraph office, he asked

the question he'd been dreading. "What does she look like?"

For the first time since leaving the train, Abbie smiled. "Probably like a boy. She just turned four-teen, but she stole clothes from her friend's brother and chopped off her hair. The disguise won't be con-vincing for long, but right now she's a beanpole and about my height."

John had to admire the girl's spunk. "What color is her hair?"

"Dark and straight."

Like mine, he thought. He wondered if Robert's coloring had been dark, but it seemed unlikely. Robbie's hair was the color of sand.

"What about her eyes?" John asked.

"They're brown."

He'd been hoping to hear "blue like Robbie's," not that it mattered. Brown eyes were as common as mud. At least half the folks in Midas had brown eyes. John lifted a piece of paper off the counter. "Is there anything else I should know?"

"Only that she doesn't have much money. If she went to Bitterroot, the train fare cost more than I thought."

At the mention of the town where he'd been con-victed of murder, John stifled a frown. He remem-bered every building, every alley, but especially the courthouse where he'd been convicted for the deaths of Ben Gantry's sons. If anyone had cause to hate John, it was Ben. Without knowing it, Susanna was spitting on the graves of his sons.

Seeing the worry in Abbie's eyes, John looked for consolation and found it in the presence of his old friend. Silas had knocked sense into John when he'd been dumped in prison, kicking and shouting obscenities at the guards. "There's a bright spot in this mess," he said to Abbie. "I have a friend who'll look for her if I ask."

"Who?" she asked.

"His name is Silas Jones. We met in prison, but don't judge him for it. He's an ex-slave with more scars on his back than skin. He talked me through some terrible times."

Silas had known how to get along with the guards. He'd also known how to pray. After John had taken the beating of his life, he'd been begging God to let him die. Instead the good Lord had sent Silas. Thanks to that wise old man, John could sleep at night, alone and usually without dreams. Never mind that he woke up lonely and lustful. He'd made that choice for a reason and he'd be wise to remember it, especially with the scent of Abbie's skin filling his nose.

After jotting the telegram on a notepad, he asked the clerk to send it immediately. The rustle of Abbie's dress dragged his gaze to her reticule where she was digging for coins. "How much will it be?" she asked the clerk.

John interrupted. "I'll take care of it."

"No, I insist. She's *my* daughter."

Maybe so, but judging by her worn-out clothes, Abbie didn't have a lot of money. He'd assumed that Robert had been well-to-do, but the man could have gambled away every cent. For all John knew, he'd left Abbie in debt with two children to feed. It would explain the air of secrecy about her. Before she could find her coins, he opened his billfold and slapped a greenback on the counter. "Take it out of this," he said to the wire operator, a man named Bill Norris.

"No!" Abbie looked at Bill. "How much is it?"

The operator named an amount that would have made a Rockefeller grumble. From the corner of his eye, John saw Abbie pale as she extracted two small bills.

At the sight of her tense fingers, he realized more was at stake than money. She was drawing a line between his responsibilities and hers, but he couldn't let her pinch pennies. The train fare had to cost a hundred dollars each, and lodging would be expensive, too. Since the telegram was the least of her worries, he surrendered with a smile. "Want to flip a coin to see who pays?"

"Absolutely not," she said. "And please don't argue with me. I get enough of that from Robbie."

"All right," John said easily. But the conversation wasn't over. If he asked his housekeeper to live in, Abbie and her son could stay at the parsonage. It wouldn't cost her a dime. They'd be able to talk in private and get to know each other again. He'd have company at meals, even at breakfast. *Hellfire!* What was he thinking? Privacy was the last thing they needed, especially with Judas-down-there wanting to share more than toast and scrambled eggs.

John slid his billfold into his coat pocket. He'd be wise to get Abbie and her son settled at the Midas Hotel as soon as possible. As for the bill, he'd pay it. He owed it to her, and probably more in view of her description of Susanna. But he'd face that problem later.

As she stepped into the lobby of the Midas Hotel, Abbie inhaled the cool air with gratitude. The accommodations were modest by Washington standards, but the hotel had a lived-in charm. A side table held glasses and a pitcher of iced tea, and four petit point chairs were arranged in the center of the room. She was about to approach the counter when the whistle of a canary called her attention to an iron cage near the window. With the sun streaming through the bars, the little fellow puffed up and sang his heart out.

Abbie loved birds. She fed dozens of them in her backyard in Washington, and she missed the way they calmed her worries. From the cage, her gaze traveled to a doorway that led to a café where she and Robbie could take their meals if it wasn't too expensive. Overall, things could have been worse. With a little luck, she could take a bath and a nap before supper. At the sight of her son waiting politely at the hotel counter, she smiled her approval.

"Can I look around?" he asked.

"Sure. Just don't leave the lobby."

With John standing at her side, she rang the bell on the counter. A chubby man in a white shirt ambled out of the back room and smiled at them both. "Howdy, Reverend. What can I do for you folks?"

"Nate, this is Abigail Windsor. She's a friend of mine. She and her son need a suite for a few weeks."

"A single room will be fine," Abbie said. She craved the luxury of private space, but she couldn't afford it.

When Nate glanced at John, she suspected a message was being passed. She ached for a bed of her own, but she didn't want to owe John any favors. "How much will it be for just a room?" she insisted.

"Same as for the suite," Nate said. "The singles

are all taken, so I'll give it to you at a discount. The windows face the alley, but the beds are soft."

At the thought of a feather mattress, Abbie no longer cared about owing favors to anyone. "That's kind of you. I'll take it."

As the clerk turned to the wallbox holding keys, she reached for the pen and signed the register. "Is it possible to order a bath?"

"Sure thing, ma'am."

She was imagining steamy water when the casual scuff of her son's shoes caught her attention. Robbie had just stepped back into the lobby with his hands jammed into his pockets and a sly look in his eyes. Abbie's stomach lurched. The last time she'd seen that expression had been on the train when he'd stolen the orange. Needing every advantage, she straightened her spine to gain a few inches on the boy who could almost look her in the eye.

"I told you to stay in the lobby," she said firmly.

"I did."

"No, you were in the restaurant."

"Isn't that part of the lobby, Mother?"

His tone made her grit her teeth. Up until Robert's death, she'd been "Ma" and sometimes even "Mama." Abbie was stifling her frustration when she heard a cynical chuff from John. The good Reverend was leaning casually against the counter and giving Robbie the toughest stare she had ever seen.

"Son, you have a choice," he said. "You can put back the money you just stole, or you can make your problems worse by lying."

John's eyes were rock-hard, but below the intensity she saw the hope that Robbie would tell the truth. Unfortunately her son had no such compunction. Just as she expected, Robbie screwed his face into an arrogant scowl. "I'm not a thief!"

"Sure you are," John replied. "You took money that wasn't yours."

"Mother!" Robbie hooked a thumb at John. "He's *insulting* me."

Abbie arched an eyebrow. "I think the Reverend is being kind."

John tsked his tongue. "You have a lot to learn, kid. First off, don't waste your breath on straight denials. Muddy the water with a bit of truth. If I were you, I'd say something like, 'I found some change on the floor, but that's all.'"

Robbie rolled his eyes, but John ignored it. "As for stealing, taking all the money isn't smart. In a few minutes, Mary's going to come looking for what she's owed. If you had taken half of it, she'd think her customer made a mistake and you'd be off scot-free."

As Robbie opened his mouth to argue, a woman wearing an apron stepped out of the café. "Has anyone seen Cole? He forgot to pay his bill."

Keeping his gaze on Robbie, John said, "Cole's not the problem, Mary."

Sizing up the situation, the gray-haired woman marched up to Robbie and put her hands on her hips. "Did you steal from me, young man?"

"No!" Seemingly horrified, Robbie gripped Abbie's sleeve. "Mama? Tell them I didn't do it."

Being called "Mama" made her furious. Shaking her head, she said, "I wish I could, but we've been down this road before."

"I didn't take the money! I *swear* it. Father would believe me! He cared about me. You're just a stupid—"

"Apologize."

The command in John's voice sent chills down Abbie's spine. With the intensity of hell itself, he stared at Robbie, showing the boy that he'd met his match.

Startled, her son looked down at his shoes. "I'm sorry, Ma."

Abbie put iron in her voice. "You and I will finish this discussion later."

"But, Mama—"

"Don't say another word." Abbie faced Mary and opened her handbag. "How much did he take?"

Just then a young cowboy poked his head through the doorway. "Hey, Mary, I can't find my pocket-knife. Did I leave it on the table?"

"Cole Montgomery, did you pay your bill?" asked the cook.

"Of course, I did! I left it under the sugar bowl like always."

With his cheeks burning, Robbie dug the money out of his pocket. "Here," he said to Mary. "I'm sorry."

John rocked back on his heels. "Sorry you took it or sorry you got caught?"

"Both, I guess."

"That's honest," John answered. "But to make things right, you need to pay back more than you took."

"I could use an extra dishwasher tomorrow," Mary said. "It's flapjack day and I'm expecting a crowd."

"He'll be there," Abbie replied. "What time?"

"Six a.m."

So she wouldn't be sleeping past dawn and enjoying the comfortable bed. Getting Robbie downstairs would be a battle, but Abbie gave a firm nod. "I'll be sure he's on time."

John shook his head. "You need your rest. I'll tap on your door in the morning. That way Robbie and I can have breakfast before he gets to work."

Her son glared at John. "My name isn't Robbie. It's Robert."

"I'll call you 'Robert' when you earn it," John answered. "I was Johnny for a lot of years, so I know what a name means."

Abbie froze at the memory of hearing his name for the first time. Her twisted ankle hadn't taken her weight, and he'd helped her into his saddle. Her skirt had hiked up her calf, and she'd caught him looking just before he'd climbed up behind her.

My name's John Leaf.

I'd rather call you Johnny. It suits you.

Lord, she'd been such a flirt. But a man's attention had been so exciting, so intriguing—now she knew better.

As Mary left the lobby, Abbie turned back to Nate at the counter. "I'm sorry for the interruption. How much do I owe you for the rooms?"

The clerk shook his head. "I'm sorry, Mrs. Windsor, but I can't have that boy in my hotel."

Panic pulsed through her. She hadn't noticed another hotel. Hating the necessity of it, she humbled her voice. "I promise to keep an eye on him."

Nate shook his head. "I can't risk it, ma'am. The railroad boss is staying here. He'd never come back if a thief picked his pocket. Besides, you and the boy can stay with the Reverend. Mrs. Cunningham won't mind staying over to make sure things are proper."

John shook his head. "That won't work."

"Why not?" asked Nate.

"Because it just won't," John replied.

Abbie interrupted. "I refuse to impose. Perhaps you can recommend a boardinghouse?"

Nate scratched his neck. "There's one by the depot."

"Absolutely not," said John. "The place has fleas and the plumbing's broken."

Abbie's skin crawled. She hated bugs of any kind. Facing Nate, she said, "Perhaps we could rent a room somewhere else? Maybe from another widow?"

"Not with your boy's bad habits," Nate said with a frown. When Abbie stayed silent, he gave a satisfied nod. "They sell flea powder at the Emporium. You might want to pick some up."

Noise. Bugs. Broken plumbing. She was on the verge of begging Nate to reconsider when Robbie crossed his arms over his chest. "Mother, we can't possibly stay at a *boardinghouse*."

That did it. Abbie refused to raise a snob. "We certainly can. You stole money and lied. I don't blame this gentleman one bit for not letting us stay here."

"But that other place isn't *decent*. Father would be angry—"

"He'd also be angry with your behavior." Abbie hated the lie that rolled from her lips. Robert would have made excuses for his son and raised his allowance. Facing Nate, she said, "The boardinghouse will be fine. Could you send over our trunk?"

John clasped her elbow. "You'll have to stay at the parsonage. Sally's place isn't safe."

Abbie held in a cynical laugh. Her own home hadn't been safe, either. Nor had she been safe with Johnny Leaf on her grandmother's farm.

Are you sure, Abbie?

Yes...no...please don't stop...

They'd tumbled onto a downy mattress where he'd pressed her deep into the fluff. It had been a warm night, humid and heavy with rain, and she'd been wearing her grandmother's precious silk robe... The memory faded, leaving in its wake a low-bellied fear. Never mind the comforts of the parsonage. She'd feel safer in the company of strangers than with this man who still had a powerful hold over her. With the decision made, she slid out of John's grasp, lifted the valise and headed for the door. "Robbie, let's go."

"Abbie, wait," John called.

She picked up her pace, but it didn't stop him from pulling up next to her. He clasped her arm again, more forcefully this time because she was moving. Pain shot from her shoulder to her neck, but she hid it. "Let go of me," she ordered.

He released her immediately, but she was too stunned by the pain to move. His face was inches from hers, fiery and full of purpose as he hooked his hands in his coat. "If you go to Sally's, the fleas will be the least of your problems. She rents rooms to whores and drunks who use each other for target practice."

Abbie turned to her son. "Go to the corner and stand where I can see you. Do *not* disobey me."

After a snide look, he walked to the corner and stopped, probably because the Reverend was glaring, too. With Robbie out of earshot, Abbie faced John.

"I want to be very clear," she said with deadly calm. "I have no desire to spend the night with fleas or vermin of any kind. All I want is a basin of clean water, a bed that's not moving and a bit of privacy."

His eyes burned into hers. "You can have those things at the parsonage. I promise—you'll be safe."

From me.

He'd said the last words with his eyes, but she didn't believe him for a minute. She'd never feel safe again and certainly not with Johnny Leaf. Stay angry, she told herself. Stay strong.

"I appreciate the offer, *Reverend,* but I'd rather keep company with the fleas."

His spine turned rigid, giving him another inch of height so that she felt like a sparrow looking up at one of the ravens in her backyard. The creases around his eyes deepened, telling her that she'd struck a nerve. It didn't matter. Hurting John's feelings was the least of her worries. "If you'll excuse me—"

"I'll take you to Sally's," he said. "But just for to-night. When you're rested, you and I have to talk."

"Tomorrow, then," she said. "While Robbie's washing dishes."

She pivoted and hurried down the street, keeping her eyes on her son while John followed her. The thud of his boots on the wood planks reminded her that she was in an unfamiliar town and had no idea where to go. When she reached the corner where Robbie was standing, she stopped to orient herself. Across the street, she saw a dress shop, a newspaper office and the yellow facade of the Midas Emporium. Later she'd go out for flea powder and something to read so she could fall asleep, but right now she wanted to be rid of the Reverend.

He was motioning down a street that led to the outskirts of the town. "Sally's place is this way," he said.

As she peered down the strip of dirt, Abbie saw a sign advertising baths for a nickel and a splintered storefront with the swinging half doors of a saloon. Her insides sank with dread. The Reverend had been telling the truth about Sally's clientele, but she refused to change her mind about the parsonage. Even standing on a street corner in the middle of the day, she could feel the old connection between them.

So little about him had changed. His dark eyes still had a hawklike intensity, as if he could see the tiniest secrets in her heart. At the same time, she saw a loneliness in his gaze, a reminder that each of God's creatures had boarded the ark with a mate. Abbie felt her insides twist with a mix of longing and hateful memories of her marriage. If she didn't get away from John soon, she'd be a nervous wreck.

To keep her composure, she looked him square in the eye. "I can find it from here. Just tell me what the house looks like."

"Not a chance," he replied. "I'll introduce you to Sally and get you settled. I also want to be sure you can find me if you need anything."

Abbie wanted to ignore the offer, but she wasn't a fool. Whether she liked it or not, she was in a rough part of town and Johnny Leaf was her only friend. She tapped her son's arm to take his attention away from the Emporium. "Robbie? You need to listen."

As the boy turned around, the Reverend pointed at a white steeple on the other side of town. "That's the church. The parsonage is across from it. It's a two-story house with a wide porch. That's where I live."

Confident she understood John's directions, Abbie continued down the street. The three of them walked in silence, but she couldn't block out the awareness of John matching his long stride to hers. It was like walking together in Kansas. Only now she was wearing black instead of red calico. She also had scars while he seemed more confident than ever.

Eager to reach their accommodations, she peered down the street until she spotted a sign offering rooms for rent. It was hanging in front of a box-shaped house with cracked windows, peeling paint and a yard full of weeds.

"This is it," John said.

Abbie schooled her features. "It's just fine."

John gave her a skeptical look, but she hadn't been lying. She didn't care about a comfortable bed or a fancy washbowl anymore. She just wanted to be away from the Reverend and the feelings he stirred up. As soon as he left, she'd feel safe and that's what mattered most.

Chapter Three

John pushed back in the chair on the porch that wrapped around the parsonage and lit a cigarette. He usually enjoyed the end of the day, when the sun dipped below the horizon and the air cooled, but tonight his stomach was in a knot. After leaving Abbie at Sally's, he'd renewed his promise to fetch Robbie for breakfast and had walked home.

He'd spent the rest of the afternoon trying to write Sunday's sermon, but he'd gotten as far as "love thy neighbor as thyself" and tossed down his pen. He hadn't been in the mood to think about loving anyone, so he had picked up his tobacco pouch and gone outside for a smoke.

That had been four cigarettes ago, and he still wasn't in the mood to think about love. At least not the kind of brotherly devotion he'd intended to preach on Sunday. His mind kept drifting back to Abbie, Kansas and the night he had talked his way into her bed.

What a fool he'd been. Up until then he'd only been with whores. Sex had been for sport, and he'd cheerfully gone upstairs with every woman who'd asked. With Abbie things had been different. He'd been the one to do the asking, or, more correctly, the persuading.

The smoke turned rancid in John's lungs. Seducing a virgin had been a game to him. Abbie had been an untouched girl who smelled like bread instead of whiskey. She had also been the first woman he'd been with who had known less about sex than he did.

With the sunset glaring in his eyes, he didn't know what shamed him more—that he'd taken her innocence or that he'd done such a piss-poor job of it. It wasn't until it was all over that he'd realized how clumsy he'd been. With tears in her eyes, she'd huddled against him, whispering that she hurt and was afraid.

God, he'd been an idiot. He hadn't learned the finer points of lovemaking until he'd befriended a madam named Rose. He wanted to think he would have made things good for Abbie if he'd had the chance, but her brother had barged in on them. Only her pleas had kept John from pounding the kid into pulp. Instead he had held his Colt Army pistol to the boy's head and ordered Abbie to get dressed and meet him in the barn.

John stubbed out the cigarette in a pie tin full of sand. That night had been hell. With Abbie struggling to be brave, he had felt lower than dirt as he'd saddled his horse.

You can come along to Oregon if you want.
I can't leave my mother.

She'd been wise to refuse his halfhearted offer. After Kansas he'd slid deeper into the hole he called a life, while she had married well and raised two fine children. At least that's what John wanted to believe. The other possibility was too bitter to bear. Had he left her with child? Had she been forced to marry to hide the shame?

A daughter...his flesh and blood...

John's heart thundered against his ribs. The western sky was on fire and the mountains were as black as soot. As a coyote howled in the distance, another joined in the lament. The wailing reached one high note after another, ceaseless and haunting, until the night was full of pain.

Was this how Abbie had felt when her monthly hadn't started on time? Had she wanted to hide from the facts as badly as he did now? There was no getting around the evidence. Someone had told Susanna that he was her father, and Abbie hadn't flat-out denied it. The girl was fourteen years old and, judging by Abbie's description, looked just like him.

He could only hope Robert Windsor had been a

good man who had married Abbie for love. Perhaps he'd been a childless widower who'd wanted a family. The thought gave John a measure of comfort.

Pushing to his feet, he walked to the back of the house where he lived in the guest room because it offered more privacy. He didn't even allow Mrs. Cunningham inside. Once a week he brought his laundry out in a basket, and the housekeeper left everything folded by the door. He never made the bed, and he only opened the curtains when he needed to wake up with the sun.

Thinking of his promise to meet Robbie, John pulled back the drapes. His gaze fell on the jagged pines behind the parsonage and then rose to the stars. He usually took strength from the glimmering sky, but tonight he felt sober and sad. Even the crickets sounded lonely.

Lowering his head, he looked down at the desk where he wrote sermons and kept his two Bibles. One was so new the leather creaked when he opened it. The other had been a gift from Silas and was falling apart. The rest of the furniture included a wardrobe he didn't use and a double bed he truly appreciated. Three years on a prison cot had given him a taste for soft mattresses, and this one was stuffed with feathers and down.

Turning away from the desk, John shrugged out of his coat and hung it on the back of the chair. He had a rule. He never left the parsonage without the coat, and he never wore the coat in this room. He needed a place where he could snore and belch and just be a man. For the same reason, he slept buck-naked. Sometimes a man had to let his skin breathe.

This was one of those times, so he stripped off his clothes and stretched facedown on the bed, shifting his hips to avoid a lump in the sheets. As he tugged on the cotton to smooth it, he thought of Abbie. She'd have a straw tick and the bedsheets would stink of lye. The girl in Kansas had appreciated fine things, like the satin nightgown he'd lifted off her shoulders.

"Ah, hell," John muttered.

He could still feel Abbie's lips, soft and unschooled. Her breasts had been round and tipped with rosy nipples that he'd been the first man to kiss. She had explored him, too. Generous by nature, she'd been far too brave for her own good.

As for himself, he'd just been lustful. Except fifteen years had passed, and it was still Abbie's touch he felt in dreams too personal to share. In time he'd come to believe that he loved her. John clenched the sheets until his fists ached. His thighs tensed and so did his belly. Every nerve in his body was alive and spoiling for a certain kind of fight.

It wasn't often that John wanted a woman. He'd put that need behind him when he'd put on his black coat for the first time, and he'd kept it there by focusing on women like Emma Dray. They admired his good looks and his passion for heaven. They said his sermons were brilliant and wise and told him he was a good man.

They didn't know him at all, but Abbie did. She knew he had bad dreams, and she'd understood when he wouldn't talk about them. John had changed a lot over the years. He wasn't the same kid who had seduced her, but beneath the coat he was still just a man, and a hot-blooded one at that.

Abbie had been wise to choose the fleas.

You goddamn slut!

Abbie was back in Washington, trapped in her bedroom and using her arms to protect her face from Robert's blows. *Oh, God. Oh, God.* He was ripping her hands from her face, squeezing her throat and calling her unspeakable names.

"Bitch!" Only it wasn't Robert's voice that thundered through the boardinghouse walls.

Robbie sat up on the pallet next to her bed. "Ma? Who's shouting?"

Abbie pushed to her feet and put on her wrapper. "I don't know, but someone needs help."

"No! Don't go."

Her son's worry tugged at her heart, but she had been on the other side of that wall. Tying her robe, she said, "I'm going to knock on the door while you get Sally. Her room's at the bottom of the stairs, remember?"

Robbie jumped to his feet and pulled on his clothes. As they entered the hallway, she squeezed her son's shoulder. "You better hurry."

After he raced down the stairs, Abbie tapped on the door next to hers. "Hello?"

When no one answered, she pressed her ear to the wood. A whimper penetrated the barrier, followed by a man's cursing. Abbie was about to twist the knob when the door opened a crack, revealing a young woman she had met at supper. Her name was Beth and she was looking down, trying to hide her face behind a curtain of golden-brown hair.

Abbie stuck her foot in the door. "I can help you," she whispered.

Just as Beth moved her lips to reply, someone yanked her back into the room. Shrieking, the girl tumbled to the floor as Abbie stepped over the threshold. Sweat and whiskey hung in the air as a man the size of horse grabbed Beth's forearm and tried to haul her to her feet.

"Get up!" he ordered.

"I can't." Clutching her ribs, Beth slumped to the floor.

Abbie knew from experience that provoking a devil

made him more violent, so she kept her voice low. "What's your name, sir?"

He looked over his shoulder and wrinkled his brow as if her good manners had confused him. "It's Ed."

"Hi, Ed. I'm Abigail. Are you hungry? I bet Sally has pie and coffee downstairs."

As he let go of Beth's hand, his eyes narrowed to slits. "Who the hell are you?"

Abbie's knees were knocking, but she had to keep Ed talking until help arrived. "My name's Abbie. I'm no one."

"Well, Miss No One. You should have minded your own business."

Abbie prayed Ed would take the easy way out and let both women leave, but he raked her with his eyes, lingering on her breasts and her mouth. She knew all about bullies. They fed on fear, so she swallowed hers as if it were vinegar. She was about to offer to wrap Beth's ribs when Ed curled his lips into a smirk and lifted a leather sheath off the dresser. Judging by the shape, it held a bowie knife. Weighing the threat to Beth if she ran for help, Abbie eyed the door, only to see Ed slap it shut.

Focusing on the immediate need, Abbie stepped to Beth's side and helped her to her feet. Leering at them both, Ed unsheathed the knife and turned it back and forth in the moonlight, inspecting the blade for sharpness with his thumb. Because knives left marks that were hard to explain, Abbie felt fairly certain he didn't intend to use it. The motion was meant to terrify them, just as Robert had terrified her with lit cigarettes.

As long as she and Beth weren't trapped against the wall, she could buy time. Surely Sally had sent for the sheriff. But what if he wouldn't come? What if he shrugged off a woman's bruises as a family matter? Abbie's shoulder throbbed with the tension. She'd been trapped in this alley before and she still bore the scars.

"Reverend!"

Jarred awake by pounding on the front door, John yanked on his clothes and jammed his feet into his boots. It had to be a stranger. People in Midas knew to come to the back door at night. As he fumbled with a button, the pounding turned into a drumbeat.

"It's Robbie. Hurry! My ma's in trouble."

Not bothering to grab his coat, John raced through the house and flung open the front door. "What happened?"

"She went to help a lady who was crying because a man was yelling at her. I tried to get Sally, but she didn't open her door."

The argument had to be between Ed and Beth Davies. John knew that Ed's wife had left him and moved into Sally's place this afternoon. Ed had a vile temper, but he had never used more than his fists. Nonetheless, John grabbed the Colt Lightning he kept by the front door and jammed it into his waistband.

"Let's go," he said to Robbie.

Together they ran the six blocks, stormed into the boardinghouse and raced up the stairs. After a glance to be sure Abbie wasn't in her room, John faced Robbie. "Go pound on Sally's door until she opens it. Tell her I said to get the sheriff and the doctor."

As Robbie raced down the hall, John sized up the sturdiness of the door. He preferred talk to violence, but Ed had proved he was hard of hearing. Wanting to keep surprise on his side, John hauled back and kicked down the door. In a blink he took in the sight of the two women pressed against the wall and Ed lunging at Abbie.

"He's got a knife!" shrieked Beth.

As the blade glinted, John threw himself between Abbie and Ed. The blade slashed across his belly. He leaped back and aimed his gun, but Ed had already snaked his arm around Abbie's waist and was pressing the bloody knife against her throat. In her eyes, John saw a calm so deep it chilled his blood. This wasn't the first time she had been in danger.

Bracing against the wall, he cocked the hammer

and pointed the barrel at Ed's nose. "Tell me, Ed. Have you ever heard of 'an eye for an eye'? It's the surest cure for meanness I know and it's biblical, too."

"You son of a bitch."

John held his pistol steady. "I don't believe in turning the other cheek when innocent lives are at stake, but when it's just my life, I'm a generous man. What's it going to be, Ed? You can drop the knife or I'll shoot."

When Ed squinted like a rat, John decided to give him a lesson in arithmetic. "You've got three seconds. One…two…"

"Ah, hell." Ed dropped the knife to the floor and sent it skittering toward John, letting go of Abbie at the same time. "No woman's worth dying for."

John thought Ed was dead wrong. Abbie was worth every drop of blood dripping down his side, but that was his secret to keep.

Still aiming the gun at Ed, he said, "Beth, fetch your things. Abbie, get Robbie and whatever you need for the night. You ladies are coming home with me. Ed, though, is going to jail just as soon as Sheriff Handley gets here."

"I'm right here, Reverend." The sheriff strode into the room with a pair of irons in hand. "I don't tolerate men who use knives on women."

Only their fists, John thought, but that fight had

to wait for another day. Relieved to have the ordeal over, he gave Abbie a reassuring nod as she led Beth into the hallway. As soon as Handley dragged Ed out of the room, John slid down the wall until his buttocks hit the floor.

His side was starting to hurt like the devil. Sucking in a breath, he pulled his shirt out of his waistband. He'd been a fool to leave the parsonage without his coat. The wool would have offered some protection, and Ed might have thought twice about slicing up a preacher. As things stood, the gash felt deep, but it hadn't penetrated anything vital. As long as the wound didn't fester, he'd be fine after someone stitched him up.

John stifled a groan. He wasn't keen on seeing Doc Randall. The old man still talked about the good old days when he'd used leeches. John was considering sewing the cut himself when Abbie hurried into the room. Still clad in her nightgown, she dropped to her knees and pressed a wadded-up petticoat against his side. Pale and soft, it reminded him of her skin.

"Lie down," she ordered. "Moving makes it bleed."

"I'm all right." John nudged her hand away and gripped the cotton. "I'll do that. You need to get dressed."

"I'm not going with you and neither is Beth." Abbie sat back on her knees. "If a woman is the one to leave, a divorce can cost her everything."

He wanted to ask how she knew such a thing, but first he had to convince her to come home with him. He knew better than to bark orders at her, so he appealed to her common sense. "I don't trust Handley to keep Ed locked up. You won't be safe unless I stay here."

"Then it's decided."

Her mind still worked like lightning. His was fogged with pain. "What's decided?"

"You can sleep in this room and Beth can stay with me. We can take turns looking out for you."

The plan sounded logical, except John wanted his privacy. No, that wasn't exactly right. He needed solitude like he needed air. He gritted his teeth. "I'm not staying here."

Abbie looked down her nose. "Don't be foolish. That gash doesn't hurt right now, but tomorrow you'll be crying like a baby."

"Want to bet?" He hadn't shed a tear in thirty years and he wasn't going to start over an itty-bitty cut, even if it did need two dozen stitches. And he sure as the devil didn't care for the thought of visitors. He wanted to lick his wounds in private. He also wanted to be sure Abbie and Beth would be safe, and he couldn't do that here. Half the time Sally didn't even lock her doors.

A wet cough pulled John's gaze to the doorway

where he saw Doc Randall shuffling into the room with his black bag.

"Hello, Reverend," he said. "It looks like you've been fighting again."

Abbie glared up at the doctor. "The Reverend saved Beth Davies from a beating. Her husband started the fight."

Ignoring her, the elderly man hunched forward and let his bag drop the last six inches to the floor. As he crouched, John saw his knees wobble with the effort. "Damn floor gets lower every year," said the doctor.

Abbie's brows tightened with concern. "Maybe I can find a stool for you."

"I'll manage," said Randall. "Just give me a minute."

John glanced at Abbie who looked as worried about the doctor as she was about him. New Mexico generally attracted young men looking to make their fortunes, and she'd probably been expecting someone fresh out of medical college. Instead she'd just met Methuselah.

With a grunt, the doctor dropped to his hips and pushed his spectacles back up his nose. After a hearty throat-clearing, he took a handkerchief from his pocket, wiped his nose and coughed—right over John's bleeding belly.

* * *

Abbie's stomach curdled as a mist of spit hit her face. Doc Randall had experience, but she doubted he'd read a medical article in twenty years. He'd probably never heard of Louis Pasteur and Joseph Lister, but Abbie had. She read all the time. If Randall didn't take precautions, an infection was almost certain.

"Doctor, would you like soap and water for your hands? Or maybe you have carbolic in your bag?"

When Randall didn't look at her, Abbie guessed that he was hard of hearing. If he'd had carbolic, he would have used it by now, so she raised her voice and enunciated each word. "I'll get Ed's whiskey. Alcohol kills germs."

Randall glared at her. "I heard you the first time, missy. All that germ talk is nonsense. Some folks get sick and some don't. It's the luck of the draw."

"It's not," Abbie replied. "I do a lot of reading. Cleanliness is important."

She stood and retrieved the pint Ed had been swigging. After wiping the lip of the bottle with her nightgown, she held it out to the doctor. "You should use it to clean the needle and the wound."

Randall waved it off and pulled the edges of John's skin together with his grimy fingers. Clenching the bottle, Abbie dropped to her knees. "Doctor, you have to—"

"Someone get this woman out of my way."

"Listen to her, Doc," John said. "I'd rather drink the whiskey, but what can it hurt?"

Doc Randall harrumphed. "It's gonna hurt plenty. Do you want *her* to treat this wound, or me?"

Abbie forced herself to sound reasonable. "If you don't take precautions, that cut will get infected. Even with whiskey, it might go bad."

"It's a waste of good liquor," said Randall.

John shrugged. "It's my call, Doc. Just do it."

With a disgusted grunt, the doctor took the bottle and poured the alcohol on the wound without a warning. John cried out and clutched at the floor, but there was nothing to squeeze. Abbie felt his pain as if it were her own. She had learned to tend the injuries that Robert inflicted, and she'd screamed for two days while giving birth to Robbie. She'd been torn nearly in two, but what hurt even more was never having another child. With tears rising in her eyes, she rocked forward and took John's hand in both of hers. "It'll be over soon," she crooned. "Just hang on."

His fingers tightened around hers. "Don't let go."

"I won't."

His pupils had dilated with pain. If she could have rocked him in her arms, she would have done it. She hated suffering of any kind, but especially when the victim had been struck down while protecting the innocent.

All sorts of words were pouring from the Reverend's lips. Some were the prayers she would have expected from a man of the cloth, but others were bitter. In that mix of faith and human failing, she saw both the gunslinger she'd known in Kansas and the man he'd become. She wasn't sure what to make of the differences.

As the stinging passed, John composed himself, though he didn't let go of her hand until Doc Randall took the last stitch.

"That should do it," said the older man. "I'll check on you tomorrow."

John pushed to a sitting position. "We'll be at the parsonage."

Abbie was about to renew their argument about where to stay when Doc Randall interrupted. "Sally's got room for you. It's time you let your friends take care you."

When John clutched his side and pushed to his feet, Abbie knew that Doc Randall had lost the argument. Wise or not, John was going home alone and Abbie wondered why. Did he still have nightmares, the shaming kind where he cried out in his sleep? Or maybe he couldn't stand the thought of fleas and scratchy sheets.

Abbie knew in her soul that living under his roof was asking for trouble. It wasn't just the way his eyes turned hungry when he looked at her. It was knowing she could still sense his thoughts and he could sense hers. A long time ago, they'd been that close… she'd held his hand while he'd told her how his father would beat him with a shovel and his mother had walked away. She had rubbed his back and fed him apple pie…

"Abbie? Did you hear me?" John asked.

"I'm sorry, what did you say?"

"I said Doc's going to drive me home in his buggy. I'd appreciate it if you and Beth would come with me, but I won't ask twice."

But he had asked twice in Kansas. He'd asked her for more than she had been ready to give. Would he do it again? She didn't think so, but it didn't matter. She'd be a fool to make herself vulnerable to the man with her daughter's brown eyes.

But she'd be something even worse if she didn't help him—a coward, and an ungrateful one at that. The blood on the floor would have been hers if he hadn't kicked down the door. And if the wound became infected as she feared, he'd be suffering for days and even facing death. The thought made Abbie tremble with dread. Susanna had a right to meet her father, and Abbie owed him her life.

Looking at John, she said, "I'll walk over with Beth and Robbie."

He gave her a curt nod. "The front door's unlocked. Just make yourselves comfortable upstairs."

Her whole body tensed at the thought of sharing his house, but how difficult could it be? He'd probably dose up on laudanum and sleep like a baby. At least that's what she hoped.

Chapter Four

"Sam, get that broom moving."

"Yes, sir," replied Susanna, being careful to deepen her voice.

After arriving in Bitterroot three days ago, she had been lucky to find a job in Harlan Walker's barbershop where she could listen to the customers gossip. So far, no one had said anything about John Leaf, and Susanna wasn't sure what to ask. Thanks to Mr. Walker's kindness, she could bide her time. He and his wife had insisted that "Sam" sleep in the back room, and Mrs. Walker had fed her big suppers. The home-cooked meals made Susanna miss her mother, but she wasn't sorry she had run away. She needed to meet John Leaf to be sure that she wasn't like him.

Her worry had started the night two thugs attacked Robert Windsor in front of their house. Susanna didn't know much about politics, but she'd heard rumors that he had taken bribes, and that the attack had been payback for a law that didn't pass. She had heard it all from her window, including the snap of his neck as he'd hit the brick planter. For three days he had lain in his bed, paralyzed and dying. He'd talked first to her mother and then to Robbie. As always, Susanna had been last.

You're not my daughter. There's a leather pouch in my desk. That's all I have to give you. What did a girl say to such a declaration? Susanna still didn't know.

As she pushed the broom across the floor, she wished she had asked the man who'd raised her to tell her more, but she'd been too stunned to say anything. In the middle of the night, she had retrieved the pouch and taken it to her room where she'd read reports written by a Pinkerton's detective.

Truth had a way of singing for Susanna. Sometimes she recognized it in the mournful song of the birds her mother fed on their back porch. Other times she heard it in the rattle of a window holding tight against a storm. That night, she had heard the truth in the hammering of her own heart. All her life she had been told she resembled a long-dead grandmother. She didn't fit anywhere, and now she knew why. She was the daughter of a killer—a man who had sold his gun and taken lives, including those of Ben Gantry's sons.

As she swept a wad of hair into the dustpan,

Susanna weighed the evidence against John Leaf. The Gantry boys had been her age. The oldest, Eli, had been fifteen. His brothers, Zach and Orley, had been fourteen and twelve. Susanna's knuckles turned white on the broom handle. John Leaf's blood ran in her veins, and she hated him for what he'd done. He'd hurt her mother, too. They had done the thing that grown-ups did in the dark and then he'd left.

With the smell of hair tonic filling her nose, Susanna worried that his meanness lived inside her. Why else would she have said such hateful things to her mother over an algebra exam? Susanna had gotten a bad grade, not because she couldn't do the work, but because she didn't care. Her mother had been firm.

Your schooling is important, sweetie. I want you to have the choices I didn't have.

But I don't want to be you! You're weak and stupid!

Shocked at herself, Susanna had fled to her room and beat her fists on her pillow. She felt as if she'd been taken over by a monster. When her mother had come upstairs carrying hot chocolate and saying she understood Susanna was angry about her "father's" death, the monster had roared even louder. *Who's John Leaf?* But the question had stayed on her tongue, burning like too much salt.

How could she trust her mother to tell to the truth?

Susanna had known since she was small that her mother had secrets. Sometimes she had bruises on her arms, and once she had come downstairs with a black eye and said she'd walked into a door. Had John Leaf hurt her mother like her so-called father had? Was that why her mother had left him? Or had *he* left them?

Susanna shoved the broom hard. She couldn't be like John Leaf. She liked puppies and stories about Clara Barton, and sometimes she imagined Huck Finn was her best friend. Even when Robbie acted like a brat, she put up with him. And when Amy Jessup made fun of the new girl at school, Susanna had sat with her at lunch. Surely John Leaf wouldn't do those things, but she had to be sure. That's why she had written him a letter and sent it to the last address in her pouch.

"Sam?" Mr. Walker's voice cut through her thoughts. "Take out the trash. It's by the front door."

"Yes, sir."

As she raised her head, Susanna noticed a dark-skinned man peering into the barbershop as if he were looking for someone. He'd taken off his hat, revealing a head full of wiry gray hair and piercing eyes that made her nervous. When his gaze honed to her face, Susanna stared back.

"Well, I'll be darned," he murmured.

Mr. Walker loomed behind her. "What do you want, Silas?"

"I'd like a word with your helper."

Susanna's heart started to pound. "Who are you?"

"My name is Silas Jones."

She knew that name from her research. John Leaf had left the Wyoming Territorial Prison with an ex-slave named Silas. Did this mean John Leaf was looking for *her?* She let her voice rise to its natural pitch. "Do you know my father?"

The old man's eyes turned into obsidian. "I do."

Mr. Walker stepped closer to the door and stared at her. "Just who are you?"

Silas signaled her to keep quiet with a shake of his head, but she wanted to hear what the barber knew. "I'm sorry I lied, Mr. Walker, but I needed the job. My name is Susanna Windsor, and I'm looking for my father. His name is John Leaf."

"Get the hell out of my shop!"

"But—"

"Right now!" Mr. Walker grabbed the broom out of her hand and hurled it against the back wall. "You're the devil's spawn and a damn girl besides!"

"But my things—"

"Fetch 'em and get out of my sight! That bastard killed Ben's boys in cold blood. And you, young lady, are a lyin' piece of trash!"

Heat rushed to Susanna's cheeks. It was true she

had lied, but she had also worked hard and Mr. Walker owed her four dollars. She was about to insist on her pay when Mr. Jones stepped into the barbershop and positioned himself in front of her.

"There won't be any more talk, Walker. The girl's an innocent child, and I'm here to look after her."

Wide-eyed, Susanna watched as the barber hocked up a mouthful of spit and let it fly at Mr. Jones's boot. The spittle marked the toe and dripped onto the floor, but the man ignored it. "Get your things, miss."

Susanna hurried to the back room to fetch her satchel, listening as Mr. Walker's curses thickened the air. "Your kind always wants trouble," he declared. "Wait till Ben hears about this!"

Whatever doubts Susanna had about trusting Silas Jones disappeared at the mention of Ben Gantry. She knew in her bones that he'd lash out the way she had punched the pillow when she'd been mad at her mother. As she stuffed her clothing into her satchel, Susanna whispered a prayer.

Please, God. Keep me safe.

As soon as the doctor left and John was settled in his room, Abbie invited Beth to sit in the kitchen for a cup of tea. Considering the Reverend lived alone, the room had a surprising warmth. With copper pots hanging above the stove, a pie chest and a galvanized sink, the kitchen made Abbie feel at home. So did the wraparound porch and the white siding of a farmhouse. With four bedrooms upstairs, a water closet and a bathing room, the house was well suited to a family. Only the smell of tobacco belonged to John. Abbie loathed smoking, but his bad habits were his own business.

As she measured tea leaves from a canister, she glanced at Beth who was seated at the table and holding a cold rag against her cheek. Her eyes held a glitter Abbie understood. The two women would be up until dawn, trading stories and helping each other be brave. They had already talked about Ed when Beth lowered the rag from her cheek and looked at Abbie with curiosity.

"What brought you to Midas?" she asked.

"John and I have business concerning my husband's estate." As she repeated the half-truth, Abbie realized Beth would hear Susanna's name. "I have a daughter, too. She's visiting a friend and then coming here."

She didn't mention that the friend was a man named Silas in Wyoming. Abbie hated to shade the truth, but she couldn't confide in Beth until she had a heart-to-heart with John. Whether he liked it or not, he'd have to accept Susanna as his flesh and blood, which meant Abbie needed to know more about the man he'd become.

So far, she had learned that he liked his privacy. A few moments ago she had knocked on his door and opened it a crack to ask if he needed anything. He'd ordered her to keep out, which she planned to do. He could have all the privacy he wanted, except where Susanna was concerned. Abbie lifted her teacup. "Tell me about the Reverend."

Beth set her spoon on the place mat. "I don't know him very well, but I'll never forget the first time I went to church. I didn't have anything decent to wear, just a red dress. I felt like a sideshow, but he smiled as if I belonged there."

Abbie knew that feeling. Johnny Leaf had made her feel smart and brave. After adding a dash of sugar to her tea, she glanced at Beth. "Has he been in Midas long?"

"About three years, but people talk about his past all the time. If you want to know more, you should ask him."

But Abbie wasn't interested in the past. Robert had tracked John for years, taunting her with ugly stories about her "lover." It had started after Robert's election to Congress. A conniver himself, he'd worried that Susanna's natural father would blackmail him, and so he had hired a detective. Abbie shuddered at the memory of the night she had revealed John's name. She could still smell the smoke from Robert's cigarette and see the flaming tip. She had ugly scars from that night.

As she sipped the tea, Abbie tasted sugar and a hint of orange. It took her back to having breakfast at her grandmother's table. While downing cups of strong coffee and smothering his eggs in pepper, John had talked her ear off. If any man was suited to fatherhood, it was one who woke up cheerful. Abbie set her cup in the saucer with a soft clatter. "I wonder why the Reverend isn't married."

To her dismay, Beth's eyes twinkled. "He's handsome, isn't he?"

Oh, to be young again—to see a handsome man and want his lips on yours. To imagine his children and the mysteries of the bedroom. Abbie had left those days behind her, but she could hope for her friend. "Beth, you're wonderful. Even after Ed, you still have hope."

"I'm leaving him," Beth said emphatically. "Better now than later when I'd have to worry about a baby, too."

Abbie nodded in agreement. She wished she had fled the first time Robert struck her. "You're wise to leave him now. You're young enough to make a fresh start."

"So are you."

Abbie gave a light chuckle. "Oh, no, I'm not. Besides, I already have two great children."

"But there are other reasons to get married."

"Like what? Scrubbing a man's collars and cooking his supper?" *Putting up with his hands on your breasts and being afraid?*

"Like snuggling close at night and having someone to fix things when they break."

Abbie didn't know whether to envy Beth's innocence or to pity the girl. Shaking her head, she said, "I'm done with all that."

Beth raised one eyebrow. "Then why are you asking about the Reverend?"

Trying to appear casual, Abbie stirred her tea. The rattle of the spoon matched her jangling nerves. "I'm just surprised he's not married, that's all. Maybe he doesn't like children."

Beth eye's popped wide. "The Reverend *loves* children, even babies. He tickles their tummies. It's sweet."

Abbie blinked and imagined John lifting a tiny Susanna into the air and kissing her tummy while she giggled. With a lump in her throat, she remembered both Susanna's baby smile and the fact that Robert had never held her. No wonder her daughter had gone searching for her real father.

"What about older children?" Abbie asked.

"The boys follow him around town like ducks. One minute he's laughing at their silly jokes, and the next he's telling them to shape up—and they do."

Abbie had seen that rapport with Robbie, but what about Susanna? Some men treated their daughters like brainless fools. If John was one of them, she had to know. "What about the girls? I hope he's not old-fashioned."

"Not at all," Beth said. "He tells the girls the same thing he tells the boys—stay in school and dream big."

Abbie yearned for that kind of affection for Susanna. As the lamp flickered, she wondered again why John had chosen to live alone in a big house with a well-stocked kitchen. "If he likes children so much, you'd think he'd get married."

Beth's eyes lit up. "It's not for a lack of female interest. Emma Dray's been chasing him for a year. She'll probably show up tomorrow with a chocolate cake."

Abbie recalled the pretty brunette at the train station. "I'm sure the Reverend will enjoy it."

"I doubt it," Beth said dryly. "Everyone knows he likes apple pie the best."

From now on, I'm going to call you Sweet Abbie. This is the best thing I've ever tasted.

It's just an apple pie.

But it had been so much more. He'd picked a hundred apples from her grandmother's trees, and she had baked a pie to thank him. It had been the only gift she'd had, an offering of love and an invitation to taste more than fruit, though she hadn't realized it at the time. Holding in the trembling in her middle, Abbie glanced at Beth who was hugging her ribs and frowning. "I'm going to need a job. I wish I knew how to bake."

Abbie welcomed a problem she could solve. "I'll teach you. If the Reverend doesn't mind, we can bake all day. Mary might buy pies for the café."

Beth's face lit up. "I'd like that."

"We'll start tomorrow."

When Beth yawned, Abbie carried their cups to the counter and set the teakettle on the stove. "You look relaxed enough to sleep. Why don't you go upstairs?"

"I think I will." Beth pushed carefully to her feet, holding her middle to protect her ribs as she turned to Abbie. "I can't thank you enough for what you did tonight. If there's anything I can do for you—"

"Don't worry about me," Abbie said. "Just grab the future and hang on tight."

"I will. I promise."

After the two women shared a gentle hug, Beth padded up the stairs. Still tense, Abbie poured more tea while she weighed the knowledge that John loved kids. No, she corrected herself, the Reverend loved kids. John Leaf would consider a daughter of his own an obligation. Nothing more.

With the steam curling above her cup, she stared

out the window, seeing nothing but black glass and the glare of the lamp. Lord, she missed her friends, especially Maggie. She also missed the birds in her backyard and the chipmunks that lived in the wood-pile. After one of Robert's tirades, she had often stayed up all night, listening for the first twitters of dawn.

The habit had started during the first year of her marriage when she had believed Robert would come to love her. She had even hoped he'd accept the baby as his own. After all, he'd married her knowing she was with child, in part because a bad case of the mumps had convinced him he'd never have sons of his own.

Abbie's stomach curdled as the memory of her wedding night slithered through her. Robert had gotten drunk, taken his pleasure and called her an unspeakable name. The next morning he'd given her flowers and apologized like a little boy. She had tried her best to please him, but just when her pregnancy started to show, he had given her a black eye.

Abbie had endured the shame because she had nowhere to go, but not a day had passed that she didn't think about leaving him...and searching for Johnny Leaf. As she sipped the hot tea, she couldn't stop her thoughts from running amok. What would have happened if her brother hadn't found them? What if she had followed John to Oregon?

Lowering her gaze, she took another sip. No matter what Beth thought, Abbie was long past such thoughts. She had children to raise and a boarding-house to run. Dreaming about if-onlys and what-ifs was a waste of time.

Annoyed with herself, she set her cup on the counter and stepped outside to wait for sunrise. She loved the sensations of dawn—chirping birds, cool air on her cheeks, a hush that calmed her soul even after a night of brutality. Already she could see a gray light in the eastern sky. Soon it would turn to lavender and brighten to gold. The poppies in the window box would open their faces, and Abbie would feel good.

Behold, I make all things new...

It was her favorite Bible verse, because she saw the truth of it in the past six months. Since Robert's death, she had put the ugliness behind her. She had a good life now, and she intended to fight for it. That meant finding Susanna and returning to Washington with her father's blessing.

It also meant finding out why John didn't want children. Her daughter needed a father, not a man who considered her an obligation. She wanted Johnny to love their daughter as much as she did, and that meant introducing them before Susanna arrived. Abbie had stories to tell, and John needed to hear every one. His daughter was the smartest girl in her class, but he had never seen her homework. He'd never heard her laugh or make a joke, nor had he wiped her tears and seen her climb trees.

Hugging herself against the chill, Abbie thought about the man in the guest room. While she wanted John to care for Susanna, she didn't want him to notice *her*. Nothing good could come of him re-awakening feelings in her that belonged in the past. Still, for the most part, she felt safe with him. He'd saved her life and he was a minister now. But the preacher Beth had described was nothing like Pastor Deets in Washington. That old windbag talked more about sin than he did about love. He blamed Eve for everything, calling her weak and easily tempted. Abbie thought he was full of rubbish.

A smile curled on her lips. Maybe she'd ask John for his opinion. With a little luck, she'd annoy the daylights out of him and he'd keep away from her. The notion of a debate gave Abbie a rush of wicked pleasure. On behalf of women everywhere, she rather liked the idea of making the good Reverend mad.

Chapter Five

John heard the grandfather clock chime twelve times. Shivering in his bed, he didn't know whether to welcome a few more hours of night or dread the dreams that would come if he slept. Three days had passed since he'd fought with Ed, and the fever had come at last. His bones ached, and every beat of his heart sent nails into his head. This morning the wound had been pink and hard to the touch. Now it throbbed with a burning itch that made him want to claw at the stitches.

If Abbie knew, she'd say, "I told you so."

Doc Randall had been tending John's wound, but he hadn't come by this afternoon. Abbie had offered to change the bandage, but John said no. He liked the idea of her fingers touching his skin a little too much.

Blowing out a breath, he draped his arm over his forehead. What had he been thinking when he'd given Mrs. Cunningham some time off? The older woman had wanted to visit her daughter. Seeing a chance to do some good, Abbie had volunteered to run the household in her absence. With Beth and Robbie in the house, he didn't need to worry about appearances, so he'd agreed. Though if he'd known that Abbie and Beth were going to be baking apple pies, he would have said no. As things stood, he spent half the day with his mouth watering and the other half remembering Kansas.

It's not smart for a pretty girl like you to be alone out here.

I can handle myself.

But Abbie hadn't been able to handle him. He'd taken full advantage of her twisted ankle. A gentleman would have taken an injured girl to town, but John had been road-weary and ready to hole up for a while. When she'd explained that her grandmother had died and she was going to her farm to sort through the old woman's things, John had offered to lend a hand.

Resting up on an apple farm had appealed to him, and so did the prospect of flirting with a pretty girl. She had charmed him the minute she threatened to shoot him. He'd always gone for women with spirit, and Abbie had more heart than anyone he'd ever known. John sighed in the dark as he remembered cleaning out her grandmother's attic.

Dust had covered them both, but Abbie hadn't

minded as she sorted through the trunks. From the last one she had lifted a satin gown that shimmered in the sun pressing through a high window. She had rubbed it against her cheek and he'd imagined her in it—and then out of it. He had fingered the silk and grinned.

How about putting it on for me tonight?
How about if you mind your manners?

She should have slapped him, but instead she had teased him with a smile and finished going through the clothes. She had kept a few things for herself, and he'd wondered why she would want such rags.

Lying in his bed, John closed his eyes and tried not to think about buying Abbie pretty dresses. Instead he dwelled on his own misery and realized he was thirsty. He reached for the pitcher of water only to discover it was empty. He'd have to pull on his pants and pump some in the kitchen.

Groaning, he swung his legs off the mattress, reached for the trousers he'd tossed on a chair and pulled them up, leaving the top button undone so the waistband wouldn't chafe the wound. Because he had houseguests, he put on the white shirt he'd worn yesterday and buttoned it halfway. Walking down the hall gave him a new sympathy for Doc Randall and his bad knees. Every step sent an ache through John's bones, but he made it to the kitchen where moonlight was pouring through the window.

After blowing out a breath to steady himself, he took a drink straight from the spigot and then moved the pitcher into place. As the stream of water hit the pewter, he heard a match strike. A lamp flared in the darkness.

"John? Are you all right?"

Abbie's voice sounded as soft as the silk nightgown he'd just been remembering. It had taken a week of talk, but she'd put it on for him. It had clung to her curves and been warm to his touch. He didn't dare look at her now. If she was dressed for bed, he didn't want to know.

"I'm all right," he answered, still filling the pitcher. "I just needed some water."

"Let me do that."

She came up next to him and reached for the handle. As she worked the pump, her loose hair brushed her shoulders. Backlit by the lamp, it made him think of the embers left by a dying fire. He couldn't stop his gaze from dipping downward. Mercifully, she was covered from head to toe with a robe. It had once been pink, but time had leached away the color and worn the garment to bare threads.

Why was a congressman's wife wearing rags? Even in private, it didn't make sense. He wanted to ask her if she needed money, but it wasn't any of his business. He also wanted to buy her the fancy wrapper he'd seen in the dressmaker's window last week. It was emerald silk and embroidered with lotus flowers. It would match her eyes and shimmer on her skin. *Hellfire!* How did a man stop thinking such thoughts? Irritated, he focused on the stream of water filling the pitcher. When it was full, she set it on the counter.

"That should do it," she said. "Can you carry it?"

Of course he could, but his feet seemed to be glued to the floor. This kitchen had always reminded him of the one in Kansas where she'd cracked eggs into a pan for his breakfast. He remembered watching her wipe down the counter with a dish towel, just as she was doing now. He hadn't grown up with those feminine touches, and he'd been fascinated by her womanly ways. One thing had led to another, and he'd taken her to bed both in spite of her innocence and because of it.

Knowing that some confessions were best made at night, John sought her eyes. "I'd like to talk to you."

Looking up, she said, "Is it about Susanna?"

"No, it's about us." He put his hand on hers to stop her from wiping the counter. He wanted her full attention because he had no desire to repeat the conversation. "I want you to know I'm sorry for what happened in Kansas. I had no business taking advantage of you."

He waited for her an answer, but the silence thickened until it felt like humid air, almost visible and too heavy to breathe. If she had nothing more to say, neither did he, so he released her hand. "I won't bring it up again. I just wanted you to know I'm sorry."

Anger flashed in her eyes. Good, he thought. He deserved a cold shoulder, but instead of calling him a cad, she gripped his elbow. "I'm not the least bit sorry. Do you want to know why?"

The question sent a blast of fever through John's veins. He knew the answer—he'd known since he'd read Abbie's telegram. "She's mine, isn't she?"

Abbie nodded slowly. "Very much so."

"Why did you imply otherwise at the train station?" he asked.

"I needed to think things through. Besides, you'd made it clear that being a father wasn't something you wanted."

He couldn't deny the truth of her words. "Does Robbie know?"

"Not yet. I'll tell him everything after things are settled with Susanna. You're going to love her, John. She's smart and funny and full of mischief. She's so much like you—"

"Don't say that."

"But it's true."

John hadn't told a living soul about the curse that ran in his blood. He'd poured his guts out to the Almighty and felt the touch of grace, but not even

Silas knew about the night John had left home for good. He sure as hell wasn't going to burden Abbie with the truth of that day.

John would never forget Isaac Leaf's last words. *Like father, like son.* No kidding, he thought. Ugly inclinations still burned in his blood. Given a choice, he'd be drunk off his ass right now. He'd be at the saloon smoking cigars and playing poker. He'd be undressing Abbie with his eyes and taking her to bed.

The fever ripped through him, causing his side to ache and his head to pound. If he didn't sit down, he'd fall over, so he pulled a chair out from the table and lowered himself into it. "This can't be," he managed to say.

"But it *is*." Looking determined, Abbie pulled out the chair next to his and sat down. Her eyes filled with a love that shamed him. "You're great with Robbie. Won't you give Susanna a chance?"

"I can't."

"Why not?"

Because I'm dirt. I've stolen, murdered and maimed. I've kicked dogs and stomped on ants. God forgive me, I've killed children...

How could he explain that ugliness to Abbie? She may have lost her temper a time or two, but he doubted she had ever wanted to choke the air out of a man's lungs. Nor did she have a string of enemies who wanted to see her suffer.

John gave her his hardest stare, the one he saved for his blood-and-guts sermons about Old Testament battles and the sacrifice of the cross. "I don't want her in my life, Abbie. I have my reasons."

The pity in her eyes said she was unimpressed. "What *you* want doesn't matter. I can't make you love Susanna, but I *can* make sure you don't hurt her."

He felt as if he'd been punched in the gut. He would never hurt a child, especially not Abbie's daughter. But someone else hadn't been as careful with the girl's feelings. John pushed back in his chair. "How did she find out about me?"

A shadow fell across Abbie's face. "Robert told her the night he died."

"What a godawful shock." John flattened his palm on the kitchen table. "Tell me the rest."

"After he was elected to congress, Robert thought you'd try to blackmail him. He kept a file on you. That's what he gave Susanna."

John's heart plummeted down a rabbit hole of regret. Abbie's marriage must have been a nightmare and he'd been the cause. "Did he know about the baby when you married him?"

Abbie lowered her eyes. "Yes, but he didn't know about you until later. It's not important how he found out."

John knew a lie when he heard one. It was *very* important, otherwise Abbie wouldn't have mentioned it. Later he'd ask for the details, but the night was already too raw so he focused on Susanna. "Why do you think Robert told her?"

"Who knows?" Abbie said, shrugging. "He favored Robbie and she knew it. Maybe he wanted to clear his conscience, and the truth was all he had to give."

"Guilt is an ugly thing."

"I know."

Her whisper matched the murmur in John's heart. For Abbie's sake, he wished he had been a better man when they'd first met. Where would they be today if he had charmed her into marriage instead of his bed? He could have been a lawman if they'd moved far enough west. He could have started over. He wished that he had, but what was the point? It had taken six years of hell, prison and Silas Jones to bring him to his knees.

John shifted his gaze to Abbie and saw that her eyes were shiny and tense. If she had been a member of his congregation, he would have told stories and shared a few secrets, indirectly telling her that even the worst problems could be solved. But with Abbie, talk had once led to touching, and touching had led to Susanna. Now that troubled girl was in Bitterroot, where Ben Gantry wanted to skin John alive.

If he could have climbed into a cannon and shot himself back in time to the day he'd killed Gantry's sons, John would have done it. He still wished he'd died that day. If he had, Susanna would be safe and Abbie wouldn't be sitting in his kitchen, making him want things he couldn't have. He wanted to go to the stream behind the parsonage where the rushing water would calm his thoughts, but he couldn't leave Abbie. Taking a breath, he peered into her eyes. "I have regrets, too, and I don't want any more. I'll help you find your daughter, but that's it. As soon as she gets here, the three of you are getting on a train for Washington. It's best for everyone."

The glimmer in her eye told him he'd just started a fight he didn't want to have. "What gives you the right to order me around? You said yourself you have an obligation. I expect you to meet it."

"And I will. I want to pay for her schooling, her shoes, whatever she needs."

Abbie pushed to her feet, turned her back on him and gazed out the window. The pane acted like a mirror, reflecting her sage-green eyes and determined chin as she weighed his offer. He suspected she found it sadly lacking, which it was. Needing a distraction, John took a cigarette out of his pocket and struck a match on the stove. Cupping the flame with his hand, he focused on puffing life into the tobacco. When it caught, he tipped back his head and blew a stream of smoke at the ceiling.

"Do you have to smoke that thing now?" Abbie said, fanning the air.

It was his house, and he wasn't in the mood to appease her. Almost hoping the smoke would chase her away, John watched a puff float in her direction. As soon as it reached her nose, Abbie hurried out the back door. John thought her reaction was over-dramatic, but he supposed he owed her an apology for being rude. In spite of the pull of the stitches, he pushed to his feet, doused the cigarette butt in the sink and followed her to the porch. After sitting so close to the lamp, he couldn't see. "Abbie?"

"I'm over here."

He followed her voice to the side of the porch that faced Broken Heart Ridge. The crest had been aptly named for two mountains separated by a slash of a gully. Sometimes the full moon rose over that spot like a silver locket, but tonight the sky was black.

As he strode toward her, his vision cleared in layers, revealing first her wrapper, then her ivory skin and finally a halo of starlight in her hair. Leaving a foot between them, he rested his forearms on the railing. Bending to ease the pain in his side, he stared with her into the night. The silhouette of pines turned the forest into a fence, trapping him in a patch of shadows and loss, a dark place that offered no easy answers.

Keeping his voice low, he said, "I'm sorry about the smoking. I guess I'm used to living alone."

"Your bad habits are your own business," she said. "The only issue between us is Susanna."

John's gaze drifted past the trees to the sky. The same stars were glimmering over Wyoming where Susanna was searching for something he didn't have to give. "I'll get a bank draft tomorrow. After that, I'll send you money every month."

Abbie shook her head. "Money isn't enough."

"It has to be. I'm not cut out to be a father."

The last thing he expected to hear from Abbie was gentle laughter. Tipping her head to his, she said, "This may surprise you, but I know how you feel. When my monthly didn't start, I was terrified."

Abbie had faced the fear and shame with courage, and here he stood whimpering like a kicked dog. John felt like a fool. "What happened after you were sure?"

"I knew I couldn't stay at home. My father wasn't a judge yet, but he still cared about his reputation. I made plans to run away as soon as I saved a little money, but my mother saw me tossing up my breakfast. My father was in Chicago while you and I were together, but she knew I'd been alone on the farm. She put two and two together."

"I'm surprised the judge didn't get his shotgun."

"My brother told him you were a drifter, maybe even a wanted man. He didn't know your name, and my father forbade me to talk about what had happened. He gave me a choice. Marry Robert, or have the baby in Chicago and come home without her. I took my chances on Robert."

John stared into the black night. He hated to ask the next question, but he had to know. "Did Robert have feelings for you?"

She tightened her mouth with disgust, as if she'd gotten another whiff of smoke. "He married me because he wanted my father's political endorsement. We hadn't even met when I took a train to Washington. We got married that afternoon in a courthouse and that was it."

John felt the stars plumbing the depths of his guilt. To give his daughter a home, Abbie had forsaken her own chance for love. He owed her something for that sacrifice, so he made his voice gentle. "What can I do for Susanna?"

Abbie put her hand on his forearm and squeezed. He felt all sorts of things in her touch—courage, longing and hope that made him ache. "Just be kind to her."

How could John say no? "I won't hurt her. You have my word." Needing to make the promise real, he cupped his fingers over Abbie's, offering recognition of the past and a truce for the future.

She pulled back as if she'd touched cold metal. "We can't stay long anyway. I have to get to Kansas."

"A family visit?"

"I suppose. I have to talk to my father about Robert's estate."

If Abbie needed money, John wanted to know. The trick was asking without revealing he'd noticed her worn-out clothes. He made his voice casual. "When a man dies unexpectedly, it can leave a family in a bind. I've been wondering if Robert left you with a decent income."

Abbie gave a bitter laugh. "There's plenty of money in a trust for Robbie but not a dime for Susanna. As for living expenses, I have an allowance that barely covers food and coal."

"That's just plain wrong. No matter how your marriage started, you were partners. He owes you."

A winsome smile curled Abbie's lips. "You sound like Maggie. She's running the house while I'm gone. When women earn the right to vote, it'll be because of her."

John figured they could talk politics later. Right now he needed to understand her finances. "Who's in charge of the estate now?"

"A disgusting man named Jefferson Hodge. He

thinks women are weak-minded and silly—not to mention incapable of handling money."

John shook his head. "He's a fool. Every minister in America knows that women are ten times smarter than men. If you want something done, ask a woman to do it."

"Not according to Hodge," Abbie said. "He thinks we're all incompetent—except when it comes to cooking, sewing and being pretty."

John was enjoying the game. "You left out child-bearing. I'd like to see him give *that* a try."

The joke hung in silence until an owl hooted. The mournful cry changed the mood, though John didn't understand why. Abbie took a deep breath. "It's late. I'm going back inside."

She turned abruptly and walked to the door with her wrapper fluttering behind her. John didn't want to leave the darkness, but he followed her into the kitchen where the lamplight made him squint.

"Good night," she said, heading to the stairs.

But John wasn't ready to let her go, so he pulled out a chair for her. "Tell me more about Hodge. Maybe I can help."

Abbie turned back to the kitchen, glanced at the chair and shrugged. "I doubt it, but there's no reason to hide the truth. He gave me a choice. I can find a husband to 'look after me' or else he'll turn everything over to my father. If he has a say, he'll force us back to Kansas."

John weighed the options. It made sense for a widow to remarry, especially a young one like Abbie. "Marrying again isn't a bad idea," he said casually. "You just need to find the right man."

Abbie glared at him. "You better not be offering."

"Hell, no! I'm not fit for marriage."

"I feel the same way." She lifted the dish towel off the counter and sat, twisting it into a whip that offered no protection at all.

John didn't understand her reaction. He'd never known a woman with a bigger heart or more courage. A man would be blessed to have Abbie for his wife, and he hated to think she was bitter about love. "Why not think about it?"

"I married Robert because I needed a roof over my head. It's a mistake I'll never repeat."

"That's not what I'm suggesting," John insisted. "Why not be open to the possibility of something better?"

"Are you?"

The fever shot through him as he gave his standard reply. "There's not a woman on earth who could put up with me."

"I don't think the ladies of Midas agree." With an impish gleam, Abbie walked to the pie chest and opened the door. "Let's see. We have a cherry tart from Gussie Hayes, cupcakes from the school-teacher, sugar cookies shaped like hearts—that's a nice touch—blueberry muffins and a pound cake."

John was about to tell Abbie to mind her own business when she looked over shoulder. "Oops, I forgot the chocolate cake from Emma Dray."

Every instinct told John to lighten the moment with a joke, but he was aching inside. Somewhere deep and private, he wanted a wife and the babies that would come. But not with Emma Dray or Gussie Hayes. He wanted a woman who could put him in his place, a soul mate and partner. He wanted Abbie, but he couldn't have her. He wouldn't wish his bad blood and bad memories on anyone. Grumbling, he said, "You don't know me at all."

"But I do. We're cut from the same cloth."

"I doubt that." She was softhearted and he was hardheaded. She had curves and he needed to stop noticing them. Getting back to business, he said, "Is your father that bad?"

Grimacing, she sat in the chair. "He'll spoil Robbie and ignore Susanna. I *have* to stay in Washington. It's the only way I can raise them right."

Whether it was a she-bear protecting her cubs or a mama cat nursing a box of kittens, a mother's passion always kicked John in the gut. "Your kids are fortunate, Abbie. You're a wonderful mother."

She dismissed him with a shrug. "I do my best. My biggest worry is Susanna's future. College is expensive."

Somehow they had come full circle—back to their daughter. John did some quick figuring. If he cleaned out his savings, he could send Abbie home with a decent chunk of change. "I'll get a bank draft tomorrow."

When she looked down her nose, he felt like a cat presenting a dead mouse to the queen of England. "How very charitable of you."

"It's not charity. I have—"

"An obligation, I know. I appreciate the offer, but Susanna didn't run away because she wanted your money."

"You don't want to let me off the hook, do you?"

"No, I don't," she said softly. "I want you to love your daughter."

John exhaled sharply. "I'm trying to protect her from things you don't understand."

"And I'm trying to protect her from things *you* don't understand. Do you know what it's like to live with a tyrant? My father will stifle her...and me, too."

"I know exactly how you feel," John said. "I spent three years behind bars. I'd never go back—not for anything."

He saw a change in her eyes, a softening that left

him feeling cold and alone. "That's where we're different," she said. "I'd do anything for my kids."

Lord Almighty, he admired her strength. She had the conviction of Joan of Arc and the courage of Daniel in the lion's den. When her eyes locked on his face, a tremor ripped through his body, filling him with a lonely ache he'd avoided for years. The wrapper hid her breasts, but he remembered taking the weight of them in his hands.

I want to look...do you mind?

She had swallowed hard and shaken her head. Her eyes had been as wide as they were now, only then it had been from innocence. Flames licked through him, as strong as ever. Only it wasn't just sex he wanted. For Abbie, he'd move mountains and chase away the wolves. He'd throw himself in a lake of fire for her. For Adam, God had created Eve. John wanted Abbie.

But he couldn't have her—not without passing his bad blood to their children. He prayed Susanna would be spared. Calling himself a wistful fool, he pushed to his feet. "I'm going to bed."

After trudging down the hall, he closed his bedroom door and locked it with a soft click.

Chapter Six

Abbie heard the click of the door and sighed. John was naive if he thought brass and wood could protect him from the demands of the night. She had tried it with Robert and ended up with splinters and a bill from the carpenter. Locks offered no protection at all. She didn't have the strength to kick down a door, but she could pick at the lock on John's heart until he opened up to his daughter.

Pushing to her feet, Abbie tried to ignore the scent of baked goods wafting through the room. Whether the Reverend knew it or not, he also needed a wife. Abbie could sense the loneliness in him, and she remembered the nights in Kansas where they had talked like old friends. She could almost root for Emma Dray, but she doubted the woman would understand the scars John kept hidden under his black coat.

How well did Emma know him even now? Had she seen him put pepper on all his food, even a slice of bread? Did she know he muttered in his sleep? And her baking—Abbie's apple pie was ten times better than Emma's chocolate cake.

Heat flushed up Abbie's neck as she recalled John's words. *I'm not fit to marry anyone.*

God help her, she wanted to change his mind. But men expected their wives to bear children and to warm their beds, and Abbie couldn't do either. Sighing, she walked across the kitchen to the stairwell. Her silhouette followed her on the wall, reminding her of other shadows in Kansas and a door they hadn't closed. Her brother had gotten an eyeful that night.

Put on your pants, you son of a bitch! That's my sister you're poking at!

Even as John snatched up his gun, she had felt his seed thick inside her. Lying in bed with the sheet pulled up to her chin, she had smelled his scent on her skin. In that moment of awe and terror, their child had been conceived.

As she climbed upstairs, Abbie wondered if that turmoil had given Susanna her restless nature. A superstitious woman might have said yes, but Abbie didn't think so. Surely love was stronger than fear. She'd seen the evidence in her own life. Her children had kept her strong even when her marriage was at its worst. She had survived Robert's abuse, but the fight wasn't over. Susanna needed her real father.

Please God... Bring her to Midas...

Tears welled in Abbie's eyes as she stepped into her bedroom and closed the door. If something happened to Susanna, she couldn't bear it. Her gaze drifted to the nightstand where she had set the photograph album she'd brought from home. She picked it up, climbed into her narrow bed and laid her palm on the cover. She had always planned to tell Susanna the truth, but not until she had fallen in love herself... when she was old enough to understand passion, need, the search for completion. But now she knew waiting had been a mistake.

Hugging the album to her chest, Abbie closed her eyes and imagined making snickerdoodles for her daughter. They would sit at John's table and Abbie would tell her everything...that sex with a man could be nice but that it wasn't special without love. That she had no regrets, because God had turned a naive girl's mistake into a miracle named Susanna. With the album clutched in her arms, Abbie dozed...and dreamed of Johnny Leaf.

The next morning Abbie was rolling a pie crust when she heard a knock on the screen door.

"Reverend?" The voice belonged to Justin Norris, the boy who delivered telegrams.

Abbie's pulse sped to a gallop. Maybe Silas had sent word about Susanna or, God forbid, maybe her daughter was in trouble and Maggie had sent bad news. Whipping off her apron, she hurried to the door, pausing only to take a few coins out of a candy dish for a tip. She flung the screen door open and stepped onto the porch.

"I'll take it," she said, reaching for the yellow paper in the boy's hand.

He pulled it back. "I'm sorry, Mrs. Windsor. My father told me to hand it to the Reverend myself."

Abbie didn't want to wait even thirty more seconds for word of her daughter. She pinched the coins together and held them out to the boy. "The Reverend's still asleep. I'll be sure he gets it."

Justin eyed the money but didn't take it. "I can't. My pa's real particular about keeping things private."

Abbie wished her own son had as much integrity. "In that case, come inside. I'll wake him."

She hadn't been near John's door since the first night when he'd told them all it was off-limits, but she didn't hesitate now. After pacing down the hall, she rapped hard with her flour-dusted knuckles. "John?"

No answer.

She knocked harder and called him again. Still she heard no reply. Had he slipped out the back door? He'd skipped breakfast this morning. Maybe he'd limped to the café to avoid seeing her after last night's talk. Or maybe the fever had worsened and he was lying unconscious behind the door. Abbie gripped the knob. It turned a quarter inch and stopped. She knocked with more force and called his name again.

As a groan slid from beneath the door, panic welled in her belly. She didn't care for Doc Randall's methods, but he'd been checking John's wound since the fight. Ill-informed or not, he had medicines she didn't possess. Abbie hurried back to Justin. "I can't wake him," she said. "Would you get Doc Randall?"

The boy's eyes widened. "The Reverend *has* to be okay."

"I'm sure he will be," Abbie said, trying to sound reassuring.

The boy held the telegram out to her. "I guess it's okay to leave this with you. I'll hurry."

As soon as she took the yellow paper, Justin left. Abbie stepped out to the porch, unfolding the telegram and reading it as she hurried to the back door to John's room. The words blurred in front of her eyes.

Am bringing your daughter home. S.J.

Weak with relief, she whispered a prayer for Silas Jones and Susanna. As she put the wire in her pocket, the words rang in her mind. *Your daughter.*

No wonder Justin's father had been careful with the message. Abbie was grateful for that respect. The town would be asking questions soon enough, but right now John had other needs and privacy wasn't one of them. She passed his closed windows, turned another corner and pounded on the door. "John, I'm coming in."

Silence.

She jiggled the knob hard, but it didn't budge. Instead she heard a deep-throated groan followed by something heavy thudding to the floor. Abbie knew delirium when she heard it. She had to get inside. The windows were her best hope. After racing around the corner, she tensed her fingers on the frame and lifted. The wood barely budged, but that half inch let her grip the sash.

She pulled with all her might, but layers of paint made the window stick. When was the last time the fool man had aired out his room? She was about to give up and break the glass when the wood screeched upward, giving her just enough room to squeeze inside. Gripping the sill, she swung her leg through the opening and planted her foot on the floor. As she pulled herself into the room, she stood straight and looked toward the double bed where John lay sprawled on his back—as naked as the day he'd been born.

Abbie caught her breath. She'd expected him to be wearing a nightshirt as Robert had. Instead she had a plain view of a broad chest and long legs lightly covered with dark hair. His face was tilted upward and his left arm was dangling off the mattress, palm up as if he'd surrendered to the fever.

Abbie refused to notice the narrowness of his hips and the taut skin on the sides of his belly. Apart from the wound, his body held no interest for her, not even the part of him she'd sworn to cut off with rusty scissors, though she couldn't help but notice the thickness of him.

Averting her eyes, she walked to the foot of the bed, lifted the sheet off the floor and covered his legs and hips, leaving the wound exposed. How long had it been red and oozing? She didn't need to touch his forehead to know he was burning up. Heat rippled from every inch of him.

She was about to go to the kitchen for water and bandages when he took a shuddering breath and looked at her with fever-glazed eyes. "Oh, God," he cried. "Don't—don't—"

"Don't what?" she said, lifting his hand in hers. "Don't come in? It's too late for that. I'm already here."

He pulled out of her grasp. "Jesus, I hurt. God, cover me up."

"I did," she said. "But I need to clean the wound."

"Just get the doc."

Her heart squeezed for him. She knew how it felt to lie naked and helpless. One of Robert's cruelest habits had been to strip off her nightgown and make her sit on the bed while he smoked a cigarette. Nakedness had made her as jittery as an infant in need of swaddling.

A baby needed to feel safe and be cared for with tenderness, and that's what Abbie would do for John. He'd hate every minute of it, but someone had to help him fight the fever. The infection could spread to his blood and pneumonia could fill his lungs. Abbie refused to let those things happen. Susanna needed a father far more than heaven needed another preacher.

As she stroked his fingers, his eyes flicked open and stayed wide. To soothe him, she touched his cheek and felt day-old bristles. In Kansas, he'd shaved every day and bathed in the creek. She'd never seen him haggard, but now even his lips were cracked. She'd ask Beth to buy some glycerin so she could coat them.

He swallowed hard. "I need water."

"I'll get some."

Crouching, Abbie reached for the water pitcher that had skittered under his bed. Along with dust wads the size of cannon balls, she spotted a shot-gun, stacks of sermon notes and a dog-eared copy of *Huckleberry Finn*. Blinking, Abbie saw Susanna under the dogwood in their backyard, reading the book for the third time.

After grasping the pitcher, she hurried to the

kitchen where she checked the reservoir for hot water. It was empty, so she lit the stove and filled a kettle. She was covering the pie crust with a towel when Robbie came through the back door. She needed to get back to John, but her son needed attention, too.

So far, she'd been pleased with the change in his behavior. He'd finished his dish-washing assignment without too much complaining, and he had made friends with Tim Hawk. Abbie hoped her son had learned his lesson. "How was your morning?"

Robbie grinned. "Pretty good. Mrs. Brewster offered me a real job doing dishes. Can I take it?"

"Sure." Abbie loved the idea.

"So can I spend the money on anything I want?"

She wanted to teach Robbie to plan for the future, but she also wanted to reward his efforts. "How about if you save half and spend half?"

"All right," he said. "I'm going with Tim to buy licorice. Is that okay?"

"Just be back for supper," she said. As quick as a flash, her son raced out the door.

Where had all this cooperation come from? The kettle let out a whistle, matching the suspicion in Abbie's heart. She wanted to believe Robbie had learned a lesson about stealing, but she refused to be fooled. Robert had thought nothing of fibbing about small things. Unfortunately he'd taught Robbie to do the same.

Breathing a sigh, she took a washbowl out of the hutch and filled it. If John had been well, she would have asked him to speak to Robbie. The two of them had become friends, with John talking about locomotives and Robbie bragging about having a telephone.

As the water steamed in the bowl, Abbie thought about the ways of men. They spent hours talking about their work and telling the same jokes. They were all alike in that way. But in other ways they were as different as sand and granite. A sniffle had turned Robert into a baby, while John was burning with fever and too prideful to ask for help.

Abbie draped a towel over her arm and lifted the bowl. Men were just plain strange and that was a fact.

Susanna looked at the passengers waiting to board the stagecoach out of Bitterroot and wondered which one would complain first. Probably the old lady who smelled like garlic, though the man with the case of patent medicines had a sour look on his face. Susanna hated the thought of sitting with them all the way to Cheyenne. She knew from her first stage-coach ride that the rocking would be unbearable and people got sick.

Silas had already been told to ride on top. Susanna thought prejudice was deplorable, but she envied him the chance to ride in the open air. Since she was still dressed as a boy, she turned to him. "Can I ride on top with you?"

He pursed his lips. "It could be a long day."

"I wouldn't mind. I like the sunshine."

She also liked listening to Silas's stories. The week at his ranch had been one of the best in her life. He had dozens of books and Susanna had read ten of them—including a history of ancient Egypt and a guide to the stars. He had taught her how to milk a cow and shown her a valley with more cattle than she had ever seen. In turn, she had told Silas about Washington and the mummies at the Smithsonian Castle.

Susanna had been almost sorry when a neighbor led away the milk cow and Silas said they were ready to go. After boarding his horse and wagon at the livery, they had walked to the stage stop where the butter-yellow coach was waiting.

Susanna gripped the satchel containing the Pinkerton's reports. She had asked Silas about her father, but the old man had answered with stories that she didn't understand. This morning before dawn he'd taken her outside to a hill where he'd pointed to Sirius, the dog star.

"You won't see better proof of God," he'd said. "He knows all about you and your daddy."

Not sure what to say, she had told him about the

planetarium she had visited with her classmates. He'd told her how fortunate she was to have grown up in a city with museums and schools. "Your mama's done right by you. Your daddy's gonna be proud."

For no reason at all, a lump had risen in Susanna's throat as they'd stared up at the sky. "I don't care what he thinks."

"Of course not, but I bet you want to know what he's like." The coldness in her heart had sealed Susanna's lips, but Silas had kept talking. "When I first met him, he didn't care about anything. Now he cares about everything, sometimes too much."

"What does that mean?"

"Only that he feels things deep—both good and bad."

That had confused Susanna even more and she still hadn't sorted out her thoughts. She was about to ask Silas again if she could ride on top when she saw a bony old man staring at her from across the street. With his close-cropped hair and sallow skin, he looked old, but Susanna guessed he was in his forties.

Without breaking his stare, he strode toward them and stopped a foot away from her. His wiry shadow seemed to pass right through her legs.

"Well, if it isn't Silas Jones," the man said in a gravelly voice. "Who's that *boy* with you?"

The stranger stank of whiskey, just like Robert Windsor sometimes smelled.

"Hello, Ben," said Silas, not answering the man's question.

As the man stared at her, Susanna realized she was looking at Ben Gantry. With a scornful glare, he said, "I know who you are, miss. I have a message for your father. Tell him I'm coming after him and blood's gonna spill—both his and yours."

Terror snaked around Susanna's throat and cut off her air. She could feel the hate rising from the man's skin and see it in his pale eyes. At that moment Susanna wished she had never come to Bitterroot, had never been born. But the deed was done and this wasn't the time for cowardice. "I'm not like him," she said to Ben Gantry.

"Young lady, I don't give a damn about you. I lost my sons—all three of them. I want them back. I want—"

Silas interrupted. "I'm sorry for your loss, Ben. So is John, but hate won't bring them back."

"Just give him the message." Gantry sneered at Susanna, revealing a mouthful of stained teeth. "As for you, miss, it don't matter to me if you're like your daddy or not. Do you know what the Egyptians did to the phayroahs? When one of them went bad, they buried the whole damn family. Think about it," he said. Then he walked away.

Fear pulsed through Susanna. She didn't care about John Leaf and she'd brought the danger on herself, but what if Ben Gantry hurt her mother or Robbie? She looked up at Silas. "Does he know where we're going?"

"I'm afraid so. It's no secret that your daddy writes me letters. All Ben has to do is ask at the post office."

Susanna wanted to turn back the calendar and pretend she had never heard of John Leaf. She hated him for what he'd done to all of them—Ben Gantry, her mother, even herself.

The stage agent opened the door. "Hurry it up, folks. Climb in."

Silas spoke quietly. "If you still want to ride on top, I'll tell you a story about your daddy and a dog named Bones."

Susanna shook her head. She didn't want to hear any more stories—not today. And especially not one about John Leaf and a dog. She loved animals. If he loved them too, she didn't want to know.

"I'll ride inside," she said. Leaving behind the sun and fresh air, Susanna plopped down next to Mrs. Garlic Breath, clutched the satchel in her lap and stared through the window as Ben Gantry walked into the post office.

John didn't know if he'd gone to heaven or hell. It was too hot for heaven, but the bed was too soft for hell, and an angel had climbed through his window. She had been wearing an ugly brown dress. Funny, he thought, angels usually wore white. He'd seen one before, a long time ago when he'd eaten peyote buttons with a Shoshone warrior he'd met in the middle of nowhere.

"You'll see God's face," the warrior had promised.

But he'd been wrong. John had been attacked by spidery creatures with veined wings. He'd cried out, and then the angel had come in the form of a man on a white horse. The horseman had galloped across the sky, chasing away the monsters with a blast of light before he'd vanished into a mist.

This angel hadn't vanished. She had stayed with him for hours, and she smelled like bread. His mouth started to water but not from hunger. God help him, he was going to be sick. With his stomach heaving, John rolled to his side. A cool hand steadied his forehead, and a bowl appeared at the side of the bed as he retched.

Pain ripped through him, but nothing came up. It had been years since he'd had the dry heaves—not since he'd ridden with the Too Tall gang. They had spent a week in Cooper Creek celebrating a train robbery, and all he remembered was waking up with a king-hell hangover.

"Oh, Johnny. It has to be awful."

The angel sounded close to tears. She also sounded

like Abbie Moore, the girl he had almost taken to Oregon. They had talked about it.

I hate farming, but I'd make a hell of a lawman.

You would, Johnny... We could build a house and plant apple trees.

They had both been dreaming, talking as if he wasn't already a lost cause as a man and she wasn't too good to leave her ailing mother. Lying in his bed, he ached to hold her again, to be the kind of man who wanted a wife, a garden, a house full of children.

As a groan tore from his throat, the angel laid her finger on his lips. "Stay still. You're going to pull your stitches."

She was leaning over him now, wiping his forehead with a damp cloth. When she lifted it off his brow, he wanted it back and so he gripped her wrist. Instead of the cloth, he felt her palm on his forehead and her fingers in his hair. Her skin felt cool like ice on a summer day. Like Christmas... *Lord, be with me...*

Calmed by the prayer, John opened his eyes and saw that someone had pulled back the drapes. Judging by the dusky light, the sun had just set. A breeze stirred in the room and prickled over his belly. Confused, he raised his head and looked down the length of his chest to his abdomen where he saw a row of inflamed stitches.

The details of the past few days came back in a rush. Thank God, he was in his own room. Sleeping in his own bed. Naked. *Hellfire!*

Abbie was the angel, and John wasn't wearing a stitch. She had folded the sheet so that it covered just his hips, and she was wiping his calves with a damp towel, working her way up, up, up. Judas was at full salute—not that it mattered at this point. Someone had been bathing him with cool water, and those gentle hands sure hadn't belonged to Doc Randall.

"Oh, jeez," he groaned. "Cover me up."

Abbie's hand went still as she looked straight at him. "Are you cold? Otherwise it's not a good idea."

He was burning up, so he lied. "I've got chills."

It hurt like the devil to move, but he wanted to sit up. Using both hands, he dragged his hips backward and bent slightly at the waist. Abbie jammed two pillows behind his back, grazing his skin with her damp hands.

"This will help," she said, spreading the comforter from his feet to his chest, giving him the weight of the blanket to keep Judas in check. After tucking it around his ribs, she stepped back. "You've been delirious from the fever. We had to cool you down."

"You should have shot me. It would have been kinder."

She gave him a playful smile. "Be nice or I still

might. Doc Randall says you're the worst patient he's ever had. For once, I agree with him."

John groaned. He'd probably been cussing and throwing punches. His dreams had been that bad. "I didn't hurt you, did I?"

"No, but you had a few choices words for the Man Upstairs."

John wasn't surprised. He'd mouthed off to God before. For a grown man he had a real knack for pitching fits and then being sorry. "How long has this been going on?"

"A day and half."

"I bet you're dying to say 'I told you so' to the doc."

Triumph sparked in Abbie's eyes. "He apologized to me last night. He did some reading and ordered carbolic."

John's stomach rumbled. Trying for a smile, he said, "It sounds delicious."

"You must be feeling better. I have a pot of chicken broth on the stove. Would you like some?"

"Sure." John preferred food he could chew, but ailing men couldn't be choosy.

After wringing out the towel, Abbie draped it over the basin. "I'll be right back."

As she stepped into the hallway, John wondered what the past two days had been like for her. Even without the fever, he sometimes had dreams so bad he cried out in his sleep. He preferred to keep those torments private, but fever had a way of stripping away a man's pride.

Two minutes later, Abbie walked through his door carrying a tray with a bowl of broth and a cup of tea. He saw that she'd cleared the clutter from half his desk, and that's where she set the tray. When she handed him the cup, he took it with one hand, saw he was shaking and realized he was weaker than he'd guessed.

"Here, let me," she said.

Covering his hand with both of hers, she raised the cup to his lips. The honey-rich tea slid down his throat and warmed his belly. He'd never tasted anything so welcome. Nor had he ever felt a woman's hand stronger than his own. As Abbie's fingertips warmed his knuckles, her strength flowed into him along with the tea.

After he downed the last drop, she lifted the bowl of soup. She didn't ask him what he wanted to do. She just went ahead and fed him. When he'd taken several sips, she set the bowl on the desk. "If you're up to it, I have news about Susanna."

John wasn't, but he had to ask. "Is she all right?"

"Silas sent a wire. He's bringing her to us." Abbie's face glowed as she took a telegram out of her pocket and handed it to him.

Silas's voice seemed to come from the paper. *Your*

daughter. John felt a pain so deep he cringed. For Abbie's sake, he tried to be nonchalant. "This is good news."

"When do you think they'll get here?"

John did some quick calculations. "Silas will have to find someone to see to his livestock, and then it's a matter of taking the train. It'll be a few weeks."

Abbie wrinkled her brow. "It's a lot to ask of a stranger. I wish I could go myself."

John weighed the idea. He'd be sorry to see Abbie and her son leave town, but he wouldn't have to face Susanna just yet. On the other hand, he'd be worried sick that Gantry had already gotten wind of the girl's search for him. The ace in the hole was Silas.

"I'll send another wire," he said. "If Silas thinks it's safe, you could meet them halfway. You'd get to Kansas that much quicker."

Abbie shook her head. "I can't leave until you're well."

"I'm doing fine," John replied. Never mind that he couldn't stand up to pee, and the fever came at him in waves. "Your daughter's more important than I am. If it's safe, I want you to go to her."

She arched her eyebrows. "Tell me the truth. Do you trust Silas?"

"With my life."

"Then so do I. We'll wait together. It'll give us a chance to talk about her. I have so many stories—"

"I'm sure you do." John grunted, hoping Abbie would be quiet, but instead her voice picked up speed.

"I have pictures of her," she said. "Would you like to see them?"

"Not now." *Not ever.* Leaning back, he covered his eyes with his forearm. "I'm tired. I want to sleep."

"Of course."

She stood, blocking the last of the twilight from his face, and lifted the water basin. He felt like a weasel, but a bedridden man didn't have a lot of options when it came to avoiding a caring woman. And he definitely needed to hide. John couldn't stop imagining Abbie as a young mother with a baby at her breast—with her hair loose and her eyes brimming with a love that John couldn't allow himself to feel. Determined to stay away from thoughts of babies and where they came from, he decided to think about locomotives…boilers…engine rods… When Abbie didn't take the hint, he let his breathing go deep as if he'd dropped off to sleep.

After the third breath, she said, "You're a worse faker than Robbie. I'll be in the kitchen, but the door's staying open in case you need me."

He wasn't going to need her or anyone else, but he couldn't argue without proving just how much of a faker he was. Instead he added a little snore for good measure. The tap of her shoes stopped at the threshold. "Pleasant dreams, Johnny."

Her voice had a whispery edge, as if she knew that his dreams wouldn't be pleasant at all. He could hope, but he knew he wouldn't see rainbows and sunshine. He could feel the fever rising again, but he'd go up in flames before he'd ask Abbie to soothe him with that cool water. He liked her touch a little too much.

Chapter Seven

Abbie marched into the kitchen and dumped the water from the washbowl into the sink. Beth was dishing up supper and humming "Camptown Races." After the fourth doo-dah, Abbie slammed down the basin. "That fool man is an idiot!"

Beth chuckled. "What did he do?"

Desperate to talk about her daughter, Abbie made a snap decision to confide in Beth as she would have confided in her housemates in Washington. Women needed each other, especially when they had a fight on their hands. "Can you keep a secret?"

"For you, yes. What is it?"

"I knew John a long time ago."

Beth left the spoon sitting in the mashed potatoes and looked at Abbie with wide eyes. "I thought there was something between you. I could feel it at Sally's."

"It's long over," Abbie replied as she wiped the washbowl. "It lasted just a few weeks, but that's why

I'm here now. John is Susanna's father. It's up to him to claim her and say what he wants in public, but if I don't talk to someone I'll start breaking things. I'm so damn mad at him!"

"Abbie! I've never heard you swear!"

Beth's light chuckle made Abbie feel sheepish. "I usually don't, at least not out loud. It's just that John's being so reluctant. Susanna needs to know him, and he's holding back like he's going to poison her. It's just plain stupid!"

"I agree," Beth said. "I loved my pa. I remember him telling stories about dragons and giant castles."

Abbie swiped again at the already-dry bowl. Susanna was too old for bedtime stories, but surely John could talk to her about adult things. Up until the fever struck, they had all enjoyed lively supper conversations about everything from politics to Indian folklore. Even breakfast had been full of talk, an activity Abbie found annoying until she'd had her morning tea.

She hung the dish towel on a hook and put the basin in a cupboard. "I don't understand why he's being so cold about this. He's a minister. You'd think he'd want to help her."

"Maybe he thinks he is." Beth opened the silverware drawer. "He's not like other preachers. He makes the Bible sound like a mix of poetry and a dime novel because that's how he's lived. There's a sadness in him. I know, because I feel it, too. I'd change all sorts of things if I could."

The lament in Beth's voice tugged at Abbie's heart. "We *all* feel that way. It's part of life."

"Maybe. But I wish I'd never married Ed, and I bet the Reverend wishes he'd never set foot in Bitterroot."

Abbie picked up a knife and sliced the ham. "What exactly did he do? I know he went to prison, but they let him out after three years. It couldn't have been that bad."

Beth lowered her gaze as she set down the third plate. "It's not my story to tell. You need to ask him."

Abbie decided to do exactly that, but she already knew that John's past didn't matter to her. Who didn't have regrets? They were unavoidable, like the ashes from a fire that nourished the earth. Abbie had made mistakes, too. They were part of being a parent. The trick was to learn from them. A wry smile touched her lips. With his less-than-perfect past, John was more than qualified to be a father. Mistakes had made him wise and regret had made him humble.

When she finished cutting the ham, she set the platter on the table as Beth called up the stairs. "Robbie? Supper's ready."

Abbie listened for her son's footsteps. The trip to Midas had worked wonders for his character. He'd made a point of showing her the box where he kept his savings. As for his spending money, the Midas Emporium had a new best customer when it came to penny candy.

As the three of them sat, Abbie glanced at the empty chairs around the table. There were five of them—for John, Susanna and three more that made her long for more children. It was an old regret, one that passed as soon as she blinked. Bowing her head, she said grace, thanking God for the bounty in her life.

As family chatter drifted down the hall, John closed his eyes. He could feel the fever spiking in this chest like a lake of fire, carrying him to places he didn't want to go—to Kansas, wanting Abbie and the daughter he didn't want to claim.

As the hours passed, he drifted from the pain to fiery dreams. He heard himself cry out, then a lamp flared and Abbie was at his side. She put a cloth over his eyes, blinding him as she covered his chest with a damp towel. Water trickled down his sides. It felt like blood, but he welcomed the coolness and the brush of her fingers at the base of his throat.

Desire quivered through him, making him hard in spite of the fever. Mercifully the sheet covered his nakedness, but it wasn't enough to hide the betrayal of his body. A new pain built inside him and crawled on his skin like spiders escaping from a jar. John hated spiders. He hated the fear and the pictures swirling in his mind in shades of red.

Pa, don't!

He was just six years old and his pa was beating him with a shovel while his mother watched. He could feel the blade slicing his skin and the air whooshing from his lungs. It hurt, damn it! He couldn't breathe—the monster was after him.

But then he felt Abbie's cool hands on his cheeks. "It's all right. You don't need to be afraid."

But she was wrong. Ghosts were dancing on the walls—his father's twisted face, his mother's blank stare. His head throbbed and his bones ached. The evil lived inside of him. He wanted to die and be free of it. He knew his Bible. To die was gain—he'd be in heaven. Living took courage. It meant fighting for women and children in harm's way and helping men who'd lost their souls.

It also meant living in his own tarnished skin. Damn those soft hands on his chest. Sexual need stirred in his belly. Or was it something else? The hunger for love, the urge to join with a woman and be whole. Groaning, John rolled in the sheets and tried to bury himself in his bed.

"Oh, God," cried Abbie. "He's on fire."

Through the haze of his dreams, he heard Doc

Randall bark an order. "Keep those wet towels on him. We have to cool him down."

But the towels weighed a thousand pounds, and John wanted to fly. He wanted to go to heaven where his crazy mother would be picking flowers and Ben Gantry would be playing checkers with his sons—and Isaac Leaf would be nowhere in sight.

A prism of light exploded in John's mind and shot him to a knoll in Wyoming. He could smell the new grass and see it shimmering with dew. The tall blades had a tender look, and the pale green reminded him of Abbie's eyes. He wanted to flop down on the knoll and sink into the earth, but a man was clearing his throat. John blinked and saw Silas sitting on a brown horse and looking disgusted.

You damn fool! You gotta girl to raise.

But John was afraid he'd hurt her like his father had hurt him. Not with his fists—never that—but with the darkness in his heart. He dropped to his knees and told Silas he could help her more from heaven. He'd make her dreams come true. He'd dry her tears and give her a future bright with hope. And as sure as the sun rose in the morning, he'd make certain that any man who came calling on *his* daughter had the most honorable of intentions.

The next thing John knew he was aiming a shotgun at a devil with bleached hair and pale eyes, threatening to shoot him dead if he so much as winked at

Susanna. A smile played across John's lips. He rather liked the idea of being Susanna's guardian angel. Pleased with the plan, he told Silas it was time to trade his preacher's coat for a set of wings.

Gripping the saddle horn, Silas leaned low and glared at John as if he were stupid. *Forget that angel talk! Your daughter needs you now.*

But John had nothing to offer except a shameful past. He wanted the curse to end, and that's what he told Silas.

If you die now, boy, so help me God, I'll climb off this horse and tan your sorry white butt.

John told Silas he'd like to see him try.

Oh, no, you wouldn't. She needs you, son. I'm bringing her home.

The face of a dark-eyed girl with chopped-off hair shimmered in John's mind and then split apart like ripples in a pond. Even when the face was gone, he heard the solitary cry of her heart. She thought that no one understood her, but John did. They had the same need to seek out the truth and live big. And from her mother, she had no doubt inherited a good heart and the rebellion that had sent her running from home.

At the thought of Abbie, John flashed back to the first time he'd unbuttoned the front of her dress. It had been a game to him—how many buttons would she let him undo? All of them, he'd discovered. He'd been the one to stop, only because he'd realized she didn't want him to. Later that night, they had gone to bed and made Susanna.

John saw Silas scowling at him. *You owe Abbie, too.*

Yes, he did. He'd give her every cent he had.

Silas spat on the ground. *You know that's not enough.*

But it had to be. John had nothing else to give.

Yes, you do. You've got love in you now. Show it to Abbie.

A moan tore from John's throat. Why couldn't Silas understand? Of course, he loved Abbie. He wanted to buy her pretty dresses and make her laugh. He wanted to bury himself inside her and feel the wholeness of their love. But loving her meant keeping her safe—from Ben Gantry, false hopes and babies with his bad blood.

As the fever spiked through him, he shivered inside a cloak of cold sweat. Abbie was better off in Washington, but first she had to go to Kansas. In his dream the Wyoming grass withered to straw and the sky turned black. John had never laid eyes on Judge Lawton Moore, but he felt the man's heartlessness in the sudden chill. Abbie was the grass. She'd die without the sun. Rising to his feet, John looked for Silas and found him on top of a stagecoach.

You know what you have to do, son.

No, he didn't. He had no idea. Silas raised his voice as if he were shouting at a mule.

Do right by her, boy! Give that woman your name.

A blast of light plastered John against the bed. He felt the fever-soaked sheets clinging to his legs like a shroud and kicked them off. As a breeze rippled over his skin, he saw what he had to do. He'd marry Abbie. He'd give her his name, his possessions, his heart—everything but the union of their bodies. It was time to right a past wrong. That meant giving Abbie the benefits of marriage without taking advantage of the privileges.

As he opened his eyes, he saw her face close to his. He wanted to tell her that he'd keep her safe, but his throat was too dry. Seeing his need, she lifted his head and raised a cup to his lips. As the first drop brought relief, he gulped for more.

As soon as he felt better, he'd talk to her about everything he wanted to do for her—and the things he couldn't. He'd ask her to be his wife and he wouldn't take no for an answer.

As soon as John calmed down, Doc Randall left for the night and Abbie collapsed in the chair at his bedside. She hated seeing him lashing out like a terrified boy. Doc Randall had been close to tying him up, but she had refused to let him do it.

She knew how it felt to be trapped in the dark with a monster. The fear stripped away reason and turned a woman into a pleading child. In the first years with Robert, she had bargained.

Please don't hit me. I'll make things nice for you.

But her pleas had only inflamed him. Holding in tears, she recalled fighting with her fists, but he had flipped her to her belly and taken her from behind. She had struggled like a wild animal, only to end up bleeding and too terrified to ever resist him again.

The old terror welled in her belly now, spreading to her chest and up her throat. Pressing her hands to her cheeks, she forced herself to breathe slowly. If the panic struck, she'd be sobbing for hours. The sadness would come like a smothering heat, and she'd be trapped in it for days, even weeks.

Damn! Damn! Damn!

She had to stay angry. If she let her guard down, the sadness would come back in a rush. But how could she stay angry when her heart was burning with John's pain and she ached to comfort him? He had taken a knife meant for her. He'd befriended her son. And though he hadn't opened his heart to Susanna, he was helping in the search.

With tears pressing behind her eyes, Abbie took his hand in both of hers and kissed his fingertips one at a time. As his breathing quickened, so did hers. The rasp took her back to another night when her breath had come hard and fast. She was running to her grandmother's barn, where Johnny Leaf had just saddled his horse. He had wiped away her tears with his knuckles.

Come with me, Abbie. You don't belong here.
I don't belong with you, either.

As she remembered his matter-of-fact nod, her heart ached just as it had that night—for herself because it hurt to see him leave and for him because it didn't seem to hurt at all. She had reached for his hand.

I'll never see you again, will I?
Probably not.

She had wanted to say something more, but he had lashed down his rifle and climbed into the saddle. Looking down at her face, he had run his fingers through her hair, letting it fall a strand at a time. A wistful smile had curved on his lips, and he'd given her another halfhearted invitation to Oregon.

Looking at him now, Abbie felt the ache of that choice all over again. Would she have left with him if she had known she was pregnant? Probably not. She loved her mother, and Dorothea Moore had been fighting the breast tumor that had taken her life. Abbie had made the right decision, but sometimes— when she looked at Susanna and saw John—she tasted a regret so thick she couldn't swallow. If her mother had known what the future held, she would have given her money and shipped her things, just as Abbie would do anything to protect her own children.

Blinking back tears, she counted the specks of silver in John's beard. Fifteen years ago she had loved a young man without a line on his face. In the presence of the adult he'd become, she felt those seeds of love stirring to life, like the tulips she planted in autumn and forgot about until spring.

She loved walking into her garden and discovering the first green blades had emerged from the moist earth. It gave her a little thrill, and she had that feeling now—a warmth in her middle that made her feel alive. It was spreading through her chest and down to her womb, as if the seeds John had planted in Kansas were opening inside her.

Could she really be feeling this way? The evidence was moist between her legs and tingling in her breasts. Even her breathing had changed from something she never noticed to a rasp escaping from her throat. She ached to open her garden gate and invite John inside. She wanted to bloom and flourish with this man who had planted the first seeds of love in her lonely life.

Keeping her eyes open to hold back Robert's ghost, Abbie bent low and kissed John sweetly on the lips. She saw his brows arch with surprise, but he didn't open his eyes. Instead he tilted back his head and matched his lips more fully to hers. The silky glide turned moist and warm like a spring afternoon. She flashed on her snow-covered garden, the first burst of the April sun and the melting in her womb.

She had kissed John this way in Kansas, leaning over him with her weight on her hands and only their mouths touching. It hadn't been enough then and it wasn't enough now. She bent her elbows until the tips of her breasts grazed the hardness of his chest. A pulse-pounding shock ripped through her. At the same time, John tangled his hands in her hair and held her tight, deepening the kiss with all the passion of a virile man.

Abbie pulled back, but he didn't let go. Instead he moaned and pulled her close with a need of his own. For closeness…for love…for sex… Her breath caught in her throat. The muscles cinched tight, choking her like a man's hand. As her eyes popped wide, so did John's.

"Abbie—"

Gasping, she ran for the back door, slamming it behind her. What had she just done? She'd kissed him as if… She couldn't stand the thought. She raced down the steps and through the garden, past the moonlit rows of strung-up tomatoes and into the pines. Her toe caught on a rock, but she didn't slow until the path ended at a rushing stream.

Dropping to her knees, she knotted her hands in her lap and wept. Why did she want things she couldn't have? Her marriage had left her crippled. She could no more make love to John than a woman with a limp could climb a mountain. The only difference was that her scars didn't show as long as she kept her clothes on. Raising her eyes to the heavens, she searched for solace and found it in the faces of her children. She loved them and that was enough. It had to be.

As Abbie fought her tears, an owl hooted and took flight. The shadow of its wings crossed her face, filling her with a longing to follow the bird into the darkness.

Instead she was destined to live like a cooped-up chicken in Kansas. Unless her father had changed, he'd give her a withering look and order the sale of her house. She'd be dependent on him for every bite of food. He'd make her wear mourning for four more years and then she'd be doomed to navy blue.

Abbie could have endured the emptiness for herself, but Robbie and Susanna deserved better. Raising her eyes to the heavens, she searched for another answer. She longed to fly into the dark like the owl, but she didn't have wings. She ached to love again, but she didn't have the heart. Never mind that she had kissed John and her lips were still tingling. With a little luck, he would think he'd dreamed it. Her heart swelled with longing as she wished on the stars, but then a train whistle cut through the stillness, reminding her that soon she'd be living in Kansas and dining on chicken feed.

Chapter Eight

John maneuvered one leg into his trousers, took a deep breath and wrestled with the other one. He didn't have his strength yet, but spending another day in bed was out of the question. He wanted a cigarette in the worst way, and he needed to speak to Abbie in private.

Between Beth's pie business and Robbie's chatter, the parsonage was a beehive of activity. John didn't want to be interrupted when he presented Abbie with his plan. That's why he had asked her to take a walk with him this afternoon. He'd also asked her to bring a picture of her daughter. He wanted to see Susanna to confirm that she was the same girl in his dream.

Those images had lingered in his mind like smoke. Common sense told him to dismiss them as feverish wanderings, but it had all felt real—everything from Silas's bossy tone to Abbie giving him a kiss that left him aching. John didn't believe in dreams per se, but he did believe in signs and wonders. If the photographs of Susanna matched the face in his dream, he'd know for sure that marrying Abbie was the right thing to do.

A light tapping on the partly open door interrupted his thoughts.

"John? Are you ready?" said Abbie.

"I'll meet you on the porch."

A few days ago she would have walked into his room at will and why not? She'd seen him naked and raving, but that time had passed. Since the fever, she had become reserved. John appreciated the courtesy, especially since he thought about her all the time. When the kitchen floor creaked, he imagined her making supper. The ripple of female laughter told him when she was with Beth. Abbie even haunted the silence as he imagined her upstairs in her room, napping or writing letters.

John's plan called for formality, so he selected a starched shirt with a preacher's collar. After shrugging into it, he put on his coat, opened the desk drawer and retrieved a dried-up pack of Duke's Best cigarettes. He thought about lighting up while they walked to the creek, but he didn't think Abbie would appreciate it. Instead he put the pack in his pocket and walked out to the porch where he saw her.

Dressed in gray and wearing a floppy straw hat, she was standing in the yard, holding a picnic basket and a blanket, staring down the lane that led to town. Puffs of steam from the one o'clock train were rising over the buildings. It wasn't hard to discern her thoughts. Ambling down the steps, John said, "She'll be here soon."

Abbie turned and smiled. "I won't relax until I know she's safe."

John felt the same way. His heart wouldn't be at ease until Abbie and her children were back in Washington. He eyed the wicker basket and held in a grimace. He wanted to transact business, not share a picnic. "What's all that?"

"Just some sweet tea and apple pie." Abbie looked sheepish. "Beth packed it for us. I'm afraid she's a bit of a matchmaker."

With a grunt, John took the blanket from Abbie and guided her down the path that led to a creek about a quarter mile from the parsonage. With a hint of mischief in her eyes, she looked up and smiled. "Beth should have packed the basket for you and Emma Dray. She'd make a fine preacher's wife."

"Oh, no, she wouldn't. I like my privacy."

Abbie chuckled. "We've turned your life upside down, haven't we?"

"I don't mind." The understatement was close to a lie. He'd enjoyed every minute of her company and would miss her terribly. As they neared a stand of pinyons, he breathed in the heavy scent and listened to the squawk of a scrub jay. John hoped his proposal would come out with a bit more finesse, though it had been a long time since he'd needed to charm a woman.

"There's a spot up ahead where we can talk," he said.

"You're probably craving quiet after this morning's visitors." Abbie chuckled, but John hadn't been amused by Emma Dray and her mother. The old woman had followed Abbie into the kitchen, leaving Emma alone with John. Why did women think that being cow-eyed made them charming? John preferred a woman with spirit, someone who'd take him to task for his own stupidity. Someone like Abbie. Pushing back that thought, he joined in her teasing.

"Someone needs to tell Emma to bake cakes for Harvey Miller. He's been looking for a wife for years."

"And you're not?" Abbie teased.

Only in name, but that conversation had to wait. John kept his voice light. "Like I said before, there's not a woman in the world who could put up with my bad habits."

"We really are cut from the same cloth," she said lightly. "There isn't a man who'd want to put up with me."

But through the teasing, John heard a note of wistfulness and wondered why. She wasn't seventeen anymore, but she'd only grown more beautiful. Today her skin had a rosy glow, and the sun brought out the tinges of red in her hair. She had put it up in a loose knot, revealing her slender neck and a tiny mole just below her ear. He remembered kissing that exact spot. They had been lying hip to hip under an apple tree, and she'd giggled because his lips had tickled. He'd nuzzled her again, harder, and the laughter had turned into a moan.

John swallowed hard and looked away. Marrying Abbie would be easy. Keeping his hands to himself was another story. He was going to need more than a touch of grace to resist the temptation to flirt with her, and that's why he had picked a special place for today's talk. Most people would have seen an oak tree, a creek and a patch of grass, but John saw a haven. He often came here to do business with God. Sometimes he dropped to his knees and prayed. Other times he skipped rocks across the stream and let his mind wander.

"This is the spot," he said, nodding at the oak.

Abbie looked up and smiled. "It's so peaceful."

John spread the blanket and sat against the trunk of the oak while Abbie opened the picnic hamper. Instead of Beth's pie, she lifted out a photograph album. "It's time to meet your daughter."

No, it was time for a smoke. But looking at Abbie's

bright eyes, John didn't have the heart to stall. Holding out his hand, he said, "Let me see."

Instead of giving it to him, she scooted to his side and bent her knees to prop up the pages. "Robert insisted on a family portrait every Christmas. He didn't know it, but I paid the photographer to take separate pictures of Susanna."

Tenderly she opened the leather cover, revealing a photograph of a young mother holding a baby in a fancy christening gown. Abbie's young eyes brimmed with love, and the baby looked like all babies looked when they were tangled up in lace. She looked miserable.

A lump pushed high into John's throat. "I bet she started screaming right after the picture."

"How did you know?"

He could tell by looking into her eyes, but that's not what he said to Abbie. "I've dedicated a lot of babies. They all fuss."

Smiling with pleasure, she turned the page to reveal two more pictures of mother and daughter. John had been prepared for a single photograph of Susanna as she was now, something like a mug shot, but instead he was staring at a toddler with eyes that matched his own. Someone had told her not to smile. At least that's what he hoped as Abbie turned page after page, bringing her daughter to life a year at time.

He heard about the pony rides at her fifth birthday

party, her first straight-A report card, her favorite colors and her friends. She liked blue dresses and hated pink ones. Lace made her neck itch, and she couldn't walk by a stray dog without taking it home.

John tried to make comments as Abbie spoke, but he couldn't manage more than an occasional nod. In each photograph he saw more of himself. At the same time, Susanna emerged with greater detail until she turned into a dead ringer for the child in his dreams.

She had put on pretty dresses and let her mother put up her hair, but John saw a wildness in her. She was a rebel at heart, a tomboy, a crusader who would do great things in life. She belonged in school in Washington, studying to be a doctor. Or maybe she'd want to study the law and lead the fight for women's rights. God, he was proud of her. And yet he had no right to a father's pride, only an obligation to protect her.

When Abbie reached the last page, she smiled up at him. "The pictures don't do her justice. She's smart and funny and brave. You're going to love her."

She took his hand and squeezed. Startled, John turned his head, putting their faces just inches apart. Her green eyes widened and her lips parted, as if she wanted to say something but didn't dare.

John felt the same yearning. He wished to God

he'd hauled Abbie off to Oregon and been there for his daughter's first step. As a sparrow chirped, he imagined singing his baby girl to sleep. He wanted to read her stories and to make her laugh with tales about Noah and his ark full of smelly animals. He wanted all the things he couldn't have, including Abbie as his wife.

Never mind that the scent of her made him hard and the touch of her shoulder burned through his sleeve. He couldn't let his mind dwell on that attraction, nor could he let himself relive the kiss that had burned through his dreams. He wanted to give Abbie so much more than his name—his heart, his love, the best of everything.

Annoyed with his foolish ramblings, John pushed to his feet, walked to the creek and lit a cigarette. After inhaling a lungful of smoke, he stared upstream at the ribbon of water. High in the mountains, a lake had filled with melted snow. The runoff had traveled miles down a canyon to this spot, curling around boulders and passing through forests filled with deer and wolves.

The flowing water matched the love spilling out of his heart, but he was just as aware of hidden dangers. He took another drag on the cigarette. The first gulp of smoke had calmed him. The second made him nauseous because he knew that a sudden storm would turn the stream into a torrent that ripped at trees and moved boulders. All hell would break loose when his past caught up with him, and that's what he was risking by marrying Abbie—torrents of longing and dangerous storms.

He already wanted her in all the ways a man wanted a woman. The force of that lust was enough to make him forget his cursed blood, but then he flashed to Ben Gantry swearing revenge outside the Bitterroot courthouse.

You're gonna suffer, Leaf, like I'm suffering…

Since there wasn't a thing Gantry could have done to hurt him, John had dismissed the man's ranting. But Susanna had changed that landscape. Blinking, he imagined Abbie dressed in black again, weeping while he preached their daughter's funeral. The picture turned his blood to ice. He had to put Abbie and the kids on a train to Washington as soon as he could.

After tapping the ash from the cigarette, he glanced over his shoulder and saw Abbie leaning against the tree with the picture album in her lap. She looked mad enough to tear him in two. The urge to charm that angry pucker off her face hit him low, but instead he took another drag of tobacco and blew the smoke through his nose. After tossing the butt into the stream, he faced her.

As if he were in the pulpit, he put his hands on his hips and rocked back on his heels. "I asked you here today so we could talk about the future. I have a plan that will secure your income without involving your father."

"How?" Her eyes widened with hope.

Tenderness welled in his chest, but he didn't dare let it show. "What I have in mind is strictly a legal arrangement. I don't want anything in return. I'm just righting a past wrong."

While he waited for his words to sink in, he watched her eyes for signs of interest but saw a scowl instead. "If you're offering what I think you are, please don't."

How could he not? He wanted to protect her—no matter the cost. John put iron in his voice. "A marriage in name only is a perfect solution. We can take a train to Raton, see a judge and be home before dark. I'll write to Hodge immediately. When the legal matters are settled, we can get an annulment."

Abbie set the album on the blanket and pushed to her feet. They were at least ten feet apart when she gave a soft shake of her head. "I appreciate the offer, but I've been down that path before. Marrying without love is a mistake I'll never repeat."

But he *did* love her. That was the whole point. He loved her enough to send her home to Washington, to protect her with his name and to deny himself the pleasures of the marriage bed. That seemed pretty damned loving to him. Annoyed beyond reason, John said, "Who says I don't love you?"

When she gasped, he had to hurry his words. "Love is more than all that romantic stuff. It's friendship. It's a commitment to put your well-being before my own. *That's* what I'm offering."

Her eyes faded from the green of dewy grass to a grayish slate. Shaking her head, she said, "Friendship is what got us here in the first place."

"Don't fool yourself, Abbie. That was lust, pure and simple."

Irked at having to explain himself, John lit another cigarette and blew a cloud of smoke. Through the haze he saw her blinking fast. Ah, hell, he thought. He'd hurt her feelings and he'd been lying to boot. "Abbie, I'm sorry. That didn't come out right. That time in Kansas was more than lust, but—"

"I know what you meant." She turned sideways to hide her eyes. "We were foolish kids who got carried away. We're not kids now, but the answer is still no."

"Tell me why not. You're a widow and I'm single. You need a husband and I owe you. It makes perfect sense."

Abbie shook her head. "I know you're trying to help, but a marriage in name only is a kind of lie. I won't let you compromise yourself."

John smelled victory. He had never been married, but he knew all about promises. "So how many weddings have *you* performed?"

She glared at him. "Not a single one, but I've taken the vows. I know what they mean."

"So do I." They were on his turf now. "I've performed a dozen weddings. People get married for all sorts of reasons."

"Of course, they do. But that doesn't make it right."

"Nor is it wrong. I've married lovestruck kids who couldn't wait to start making babies, and I've said the words for older folks who wanted nothing more than companionship. What happens in bed is no one's business but theirs. What *doesn't* happen in ours is between you and me."

Abbie turned away from him, dropped to a crouch and lifted the picture album. John hoped she was thinking about what he'd made clear—that he'd keep his hands off her no matter how much Judas complained. But he couldn't see her face. The silence was close to killing him when she set the album in the picnic hamper and closed the lid. Pushing to her feet, she said. "I won't compromise. Marriage is a vow before God. I take it seriously."

John had considered that part of his offer carefully. "I intend to keep the vows, but as a friend.

The annulment offer is for you. As long as we don't consummate the marriage, in God's eyes you're free to walk away. In fact, you'd be smart to do exactly that."

She looked at him skeptically. "That cuts both ways. Someday you'll meet a good woman and fall in love."

He already had, but she didn't need to know. Instead he made his voice somber. "I made a promise to myself the day I left prison. Marriage isn't in my future. That leaves me free to help you now."

With the cigarette dangling between his fingers, he watched as Abbie ambled down to the creek. With the toe of her shoe, she tapped a pool of water between two boulders. A dozen circles expanded like a target. When they faded to nothing, she peered downstream where a doe and her fawn were drinking. The mama stood still, staring at them with eyes full of trepidation. Oblivious to the human threat, the fawn raised its head to a branch and nibbled leaves.

Abbie whispered. "I wish we could tell her we mean no harm."

John needed to convey the same message to Abbie. "She'll have to sense it."

He had kept his voice low, but the deer still spooked. The mama bounded into the trees with the baby running at her side.

Abbie sighed. "At least she has someplace to go."

"So do you. Let me help you."

She crossed her arms at her waist. "I can't understand why you don't want a wife. She could reach out to women like Beth and organize a Sunday school. She could help with all sorts of things—even the bookkeeping."

John had thought of those things and more. Most people thought men made the best ministers, but he knew that women gave a church its heart and soul. A wife would be a full partner, someone who could share his burdens and tell him to straighten up now and then. Bending low, he picked up a rock and skipped it down the stream. It ricocheted four times and sunk. His record was five. Keeping his eyes on the stream, he said, "I like living alone."

"I don't believe *that* for a minute," Abbie replied. "You and Robbie talk all the time. I've never heard so much boring chatter about train parts."

John pulled his eyebrows together in feigned shock. "What's boring about connecting rods?"

"Everything!"

"Not when you're twelve years old. He's a smart boy."

"And you're great with him," she said. "Face it, Johnny. You have a good life, and a wife would make it better. That's why I can't marry you. I'd be in the way."

Or worse, he thought. He'd come to need her more than he did now. After tossing another rock, he looked up at the towering sky where two condors were riding a thermal. Lucky devils—the birds mated for life and didn't think twice about predators and eggs falling out of nests. But John did. That was the whole point of today's offer—to give Abbie and her children a nest in Washington. Lowering his eyes from the sky, he focused on the needs of the day. "We're not talking about me. I have no interest in marriage."

"You're lying," she said quietly. "All men want sex."

He liked the frank talk but not the angry tone. What was wrong with wanting sex? Not a thing that John could see, and he was sure the Almighty agreed. John clamped down on a smile. He'd been reading through the Bible for the first time when he'd stumbled across the Song of Solomon smack-dab between Ecclesiastes and Isaiah. His eyes had almost popped out of his head. The poetry about streams filling wells and a bride inviting the groom into her garden wasn't exactly subtle. John didn't have to read between the lines to know the good Lord wanted husbands and wives to enjoy each other.

More stirred up than he wanted to be, he considered lighting another cigarette but discarded the idea. Instead he reminded himself that he'd worn his black coat for a reason. With a wry smile, he said, "In case you hadn't noticed, I'm not a lustful kid anymore."

"That's true. You're a grown man who should have a wife. You can't tell *me* you don't have desires."

If she wanted to be direct, he'd oblige. John looked her square in the eye. "You bet I do. It's the way we're made, but men can control those urges."

John figured he'd been controlling *his* urges just fine and he'd keep controlling them. What mattered was securing Abbie's future. He watched as she dipped her toe in the water, making more circles in the pond. The motion reminded him of the girl who had hiked up her skirts and waded in. "Go ahead and take off your shoes," he said. "The water's ice-cold."

"I haven't done that since Kansas." As she stared longingly at the water, a frightening thought ker-plunked to the pit of John's stomach. The girl he had known in Kansas had been wild enough to bed a drifter. He didn't doubt for a minute that she had matured into a passionate woman who knew her own whims. And then there was the matter of children. She was young enough for more babies, and she had a mother's heart. John decided to be direct. "If you want more from a marriage than I'm offering, you should find a man who wants a houseful of children. That's not me."

Abbie shook her head. "I'm not interested in anything but raising the two kids I have."

"Then a marriage in name only is a perfect solution. My heart's right, Abbie. I want to help you."

She was standing at the edge of the pond as still as the deer. The sun had dropped in the sky, casting shadows through the branches so that she seemed to be standing in a cage. He could sense the tug and pull in her soul. She wanted to accept his offer, but she wouldn't do it for herself. Knowing he'd regret the words as soon as they left his lips, John pulled out his best argument.

"Say yes, Abbie. Do it for our daughter."

Chapter Nine

Abbie's heart fluttered against her ribs. The owl had flown over this exact spot, daring her to follow it into the dark. John was asking her to do the same thing. With his black coat snug on his shoulders and loose over his hips, he reminded her of the ravens that visited her backyard. They were confident birds, all-knowing and all-seeing. The sparrows watched the ravens, and when the ravens took flight, they followed.

Abbie wanted to be one of those tiny birds, but how could she put aside her feelings for this man? She didn't want a marriage in name only. She wanted to be seventeen years old again, walking along another stream while Johnny Leaf talked about Oregon.

But the risk… Abbie hugged herself. She didn't believe for a minute that John was dead to desire. She had seen him in all his naked glory, aroused and dreaming. She ached to make the marriage real, to touch the only places she hadn't bathed with cool water. She had even tested herself with that foolish kiss and ended up in a panic.

She couldn't be John's wife in the truest sense, and that made accepting his offer akin to walking into a burning house. She'd get singed, maybe even scarred again. But Lord Almighty, she didn't want to live like a chicken in Kansas, nor did she want to deny Susanna the chance to know her father. If Abbie accepted John's offer, she could stay in Midas as long as she wanted.

From the corner of her eye, she saw him skip another rock across the pond. She guessed that he did it often, just as she sat in her backyard and watched the birds when she needed to calm herself. The thought gave her courage.

Forcing a smile, she said, "I'm trying to figure out who's crazier—you for making this ridiculous offer, or me for wanting so badly to say yes."

"You're crazier," he said with a grin. "We decided that in Kansas."

Heat rushed to her cheeks. They had been watching a thunderstorm. John had been standing behind her with his arms laced around her waist, and she had nestled against his throat. Her clothes had been damp with humidity, sticking like a second skin as she'd dreamed of another life.

Someday I want to sail across the ocean. Maybe to Australia…someplace new and far away.

His throat had hummed against her temple. *You're flat-out crazy. Oregon is far enough for me.*

Was she still that daring girl? Abbie didn't think so. She had become practical and wise. Glancing up from the stream, she made her voice firm. "If I agree to this arrangement, we need a few rules."

"Of course," John said. "I have a few requirements of my own. Let's have some of Beth's pie while we talk."

They turned in unison and sat beneath the oak. After dropping to her knees, Abbie sliced the pie and handed him a wedge. She took one for herself but set it aside. She didn't want to talk about marriage with the taste of apples on her tongue. "First of all, I need to move out of the parsonage. Now that you're well, I shouldn't be living under your roof."

John swallowed the bite of pie and shook his head. "It's only for another week or two. As soon as Silas gets here, you and the kids can head home."

Abbie shook her head. "But if we're married, I won't have to leave. I'll ask Maggie to send my father a wire canceling the trip. We can stay all summer."

John set down the plate, leaving the wedge of pie half eaten. "That's not part of the plan. We're doing this so you can go home as soon as possible."

"That's *your* plan. *I'm* staying for the sake of my children, especially Susanna. She needs to know you."

"Staying here just isn't wise," he insisted. "One

look at the two of us and the whole town will know she's mine. The less she has to do with me, the better."

Abbie's spine went rigid. Shame had no place in her daughter's life and neither did John's reluctance. "I know you have a reputation, but I don't care what people think. Are you embarrassed to claim her?"

"Hell, no. I owned up to my past a long time ago. No one's going to be surprised I have a child."

"Then why not be straightforward? Susanna deserves that respect."

John's eyes hardened, but Abbie knew his heart wasn't dead to his daughter. She had seen tenderness in his gaze as he'd looked at the photographs. Even now, she sensed a love for Susanna behind his cold exterior. She could see emotion in his eyes—deep ones she didn't understand. As much as she wanted to break through his shell, she waited until he found words of his own.

"It's not a question of respect," he finally said. "It's a matter of her safety and yours."

Abbie lifted his plate and set it in the hamper. The stickiness of the pie clung to her fingertips, reminding her of Beth's comments about Bitterroot. After closing the lid, she said, "Why are you so afraid for us?"

His gaze honed to her eyes, then he pushed to his feet and ambled down to the creek. Bending low, he snatched up a rock and side-armed it deep into the meadow where it cracked into a tree. The sound matched the slap of Robert's hand on her cheek. Inwardly she flinched, but she couldn't take her eyes off John. In his black coat he looked like a lightning-scarred pine, charred on the outside but smoldering in places she couldn't see. She knew all about burns—the more tender the skin, the deeper the scar. Rising to her feet, she walked to his side. "You have good aim."

Disgust tightened his jaw. "Ben Gantry would agree with you. I killed his three sons. They were children, Abbie. Not much older than Robbie, and I shot them dead."

"Oh, my God."

"I know," he said. "It's horrible. I wish to God I'd been the one to die."

Sick to her stomach, she touched his sleeve. What did a woman say to such a confession? She didn't know, but she understood that he needed to talk. She also needed the facts to gauge their effect on their daughter. "Tell me everything."

John stared across the meadow. "Back then, I sold my gun to anyone. Sir Alfred Walker was a rich English thug who wanted to scare off a bunch of sheep farmers. Ben Gantry was their leader, so I focused on him—and the people he loved."

John raised his hand to the pocket with his

cigarettes but then lowered it without taking one. A hawk circled overhead while the stream rippled with music that didn't match the mood. Abbie felt a pain so deep she couldn't speak. Robert had brutalized her terribly, but he had never touched the children. If he had, she would have shot him dead in his sleep. She couldn't bring herself to think about Ben Gantry's suffering. After hooking her arm around John's elbow, she rested her cheek against his biceps. He was a new man, and she wanted him to know that the past didn't matter—at least to her.

Unflinching, he stared across the meadow. "I knew Ben had gone to town and left the boys alone, so I asked Walker's son to come along for a little fun. Pete was younger than me, and he thought I walked on water. What a damned fool."

Abbie glanced up just as John raised his face to the sky and peered through the branches. The shade dappled his face with bars, filling her with an ache as she squeezed his arm tighter.

"Pete and I stood behind a tree a lot like this one," he said. "Every time one of the kids opened the door, we fired. The plan was to scare them, but the oldest one snuck out a window and came up behind us with a Sharps rifle."

Not knowing what to say, Abbie reached around his waist. The heat of the sun had soaked into his black coat, making it hot against her hand. As if her touch were even hotter, John broke from her grasp, picked up another rock and hurled it at the same tree. It struck dead-on. "I could have fired an inch above his head and scared the devil out of him. Hell, I could have shot off his ear. Instead I aimed for his chest."

Tears pushed into Abbie's eyes. They were for the boy who'd tried to be a hero, Ben Gantry who had come home to the blood of his sons and John who had to live with himself.

Turning away from the creek, he looked straight at her. "Do you want to hear the rest?"

"I'd spare you the misery, but I need to know for Susanna's sake."

"And for yourself, too," he said quietly. "I spilled my guts to God and Silas a long time ago, but you need to know who you're marrying. I'm a child-killer, Abbie. The murdering didn't end with Gantry's oldest boy. The other two charged out the door to help their brother. One had a pistol he could barely lift and the other had a shotgun. I shouted for Pete to stay behind the tree, but he yelled something stupid and the kid with the pistol fired at him. The bullet went through his shoulder and knocked him flat. The boys were both charging at him and firing, so I shot back. One bullet each and it was over."

How did a father survive the murder of his three

sons? Abbie bit her lip, but she couldn't stifle a gasp of horror.

"Yeah, I know," John said bitterly. "I was a real son of a bitch."

"Now I know why you went to prison."

He nodded. "I should have hanged, but Pete's wound saved my life. We lied and said they fired first, and that all the shooting was in self-defense. No one believed us, but the judge took a bribe to lessen the charge. Pete and I both got out of prison three years later."

Had that sentence been an injustice to the Gantry boys, or was it mercy for a man who had changed? Mercy, she supposed, though she doubted Gantry would agree. "What did Ben do after you got out?"

"He swore to kill us both. Pete got caught in a blizzard and froze to death. After prison, I lived with Silas for a while. I wrote a letter to Ben telling him I wished I'd died in the place of his sons, but I never mailed it. It's still in the back of my Bible."

"Do you think about sending it?"

"Every day, but I waited too long. If Gantry's gone on with life, it would stir up the pain."

Abbie touched his sleeve. "And if he hasn't?"

"He'd want revenge."

He said it with such authority that Abbie knew he had more secrets. She wanted to ask, but this wasn't the time. She needed to focus on the danger to Susanna. "If Gantry hasn't come after you since you left prison, why do you think he'll do it now?"

John reached into his pocket for another cigarette. She watched as he took a drag and blew the smoke sideways, away from her nose. "As the saying goes, 'An eye for an eye.' If he hears about Susanna, he'll want revenge and he'll have a means for it. She's in danger, Abbie. I feel it in my bones."

In spite of the heat, Abbie shivered. "I feel it, too."

"That's why you and the kids have to leave."

With a sad clarity, Abbie understood why John didn't want a wife and children. His love would put them at risk and so he'd chosen loneliness. "You're afraid for us," she said.

"Damn right I am. I don't want to have to kill Gantry to protect you, but I'd do it. He can have me. I'd throw my guns at his feet and beg forgiveness, but he can't have you or Susanna."

Abbie flashed on John holding his gun on Ed at Sally's boardinghouse. No wonder he'd been so calm—he had no fear of death, only a fear of living. Her heart ached for him. He wasn't the same man who had murdered Gantry's sons and she wanted him to know it. She laced her hands behind her back. "Can I ask you something?"

"Sure."

"Beth tells me you're the best preacher she's ever

heard. She says you tell people the truth without rubbing their noses in their mistakes."

He shrugged. "That's my job."

"It's more than that. You've lived this life—both the ugliness and the kindness. Deep down you know how we all feel—even Ben Gantry. I don't know if he can forgive you, but you're not the same man who committed that crime."

John waved off her words as if he'd heard them a hundred times. "I know all about God's mercy. I'm alive because of it, but I'm still a child-killer. I figure it's the worst thing a man can do."

Was it worse than a husband beating his wife? Worse than massacring women and children of any color or letting orphans starve? Or enslaving a race of people? Abbie didn't think so. Violence and pain riddled the human landscape. If meanness was the curse, love was the cure.

Knowing that kindness would make John rebel, she said, "Yep. You're a real bastard."

The cussword startled him, but he composed himself. "That's right. I'm a lying, thieving, cheating son of a bitch."

Abbie raised one eyebrow. "Don't forget your bad language. I've heard you cuss."

John's gaze narrowed on her face. "What else do you know about me?"

"Only that you're not the evil so-and-so you're

pretending to be." She touched his sleeve. "Do you know what courage it takes to face the past? You're a good man, John. I want Susanna to know you."

He shook his head. "The past won't disappear."

"That's why we have to stay for the summer. She knows about the past because of Robert's file. You can let her think the worst or you can show her your best."

When he hung his head, Abbie knelt in front of him and tipped her face up to his. His dark eyes glowed like banked coals. She smelled tobacco smoke on him, but he needed to know that he wasn't repulsive to her so she raised her hand and cupped his jaw. The bristles of his beard tickled her palm. Did she dare kiss his cheek? She imagined the roughness of his skin against her lips and felt a stirring in her belly, soft like a butterfly wing. Closing her eyes, she rose up on her knees and kissed the tender spot in front of his ear.

Air whooshed from his lungs. "Abbie, don't."

But he was stroking her hair and breathing in the scent of her skin. As she pressed her cheek against his, she felt traces of stubble scraping her skin. Robert had worn a beard. John's skin felt wonderfully new. Feeling brave and wanting him to know she cared, she kissed the smooth skin again, staying close until he sought her mouth with a searching need of his own.

As if she were seventeen, Abbie parted her lips,

offering tenderness in place of the sorrow. This kiss was a gift to him—a rose plucked from the garden of her heart. Aching to enjoy the bloom before it withered, she etched the caress into her memory. Someday she'd pluck a rose and remember the softness of John's lips. She'd feel the sun on her back and recall the hot wool of his coat against her palm. Wanting more, she cupped the back of his head and ran her hand along his scalp. Never again would she look at a raven and not think of John's feathery hair falling through her fingers.

As she massaged the back of his head, he brushed her lips with his tongue, asking her to let him inside. Abbie knew it was risky. Deepening the kiss could set off the panic. But how could she say no? He needed tenderness and she wanted to give it. The seeds in her belly wanted to bloom and he was the sun.

When she parted her lips, his tongue found hers, daring her to give him more. She tasted apples, but then her lips started to burn with the traces of the nicotine. Her body stiffened with hate—not for John but for the taste of him and the memories of Robert's abuse. Desperate to escape the smokiness, she opened her eyes. Her gaze landed on the white scar near his ear and she flashed on Ed and the knife. John had protected her with his life. How could she not trust him to be good to her?

Fighting the instinct to push him away, she squeezed her eyes shut and kissed him harder, but his hair smelled like smoke and so did his coat. She could feel him stroking her back, pulling her closer, as if he were memorizing every curve. The caress was hungry yet tender, but dread made her tremble. If the panic struck… She couldn't bear to think about it, so she got angry.

Damn! Damn! Damn!

Choking back a curse, Abbie pulled out of his grasp. She couldn't be mad at John—she'd kissed him first. She had no one to blame but herself. Pushing to her feet, she pressed her hands to her cheeks. "That's the *stupidest* thing I've ever done. I didn't realize—"

John's face had turned to stone. "I did. You should add 'lustful' to that list of my *fine* qualities."

But he was lying. She had tasted love in his kiss and he'd held her so close because he needed her. Abbie bit her lip. "You're being too hard on yourself. I started it."

"But I finished it. It won't happen again."

John stood and hooked his hands in his pockets so that his coat pulled away from his chest. As stiff as a pine, he looked at her. "My offer stands, but only if you move out of the parsonage. I'll rent a house for you and Beth."

Abbie's heart broke at the thought of John going

back to his lonely life, but it was best for everyone. "I accept, but we're staying in Midas until I feel it's time to leave."

When John blew out a breath and looked downstream, Abbie followed his gaze to a pool that glistened with the brilliance of a mirror. The glare blinded them both and they turned to each other at the same time. John frowned at her. "I don't like it, but I'll respect your decision. There's a local train to Raton on Thursday. We need to be on it."

Abbie nodded. She'd have to time to buy a suitable dress. "We'll need to explain the trip to Beth and Robbie."

"That's not a problem," John replied. "We're going on legal business concerning your husband's estate."

And that, Abbie realized, was sadly true.

Susanna liked riding on top of the stagecoach a lot better than sitting inside. The seating change had come about on the second day of the trip to Cheyenne. Mrs. Garlic Breath had turned out to be a nonstop talker, and Susanna had changed her mind about sitting in the stuffy coach.

After she and Silas settled among the trunks and mailbags, the driver cracked the whip. For the next several miles, she reveled at the wind in her face. She loved the vastness of the West, the open grasslands, the blue sky and the rolling hills. If she squinted, she could see silver water in the Powder River. Overhead, a huge bird with brown wings was circling above a clump of trees. Susanna pointed to the sky. "What kind of bird is that?"

"A golden eagle," he replied. "The last time I saw one of those was the day I met your daddy. He was kicking against the shackles and cussing at the guards."

Silas's description matched the Pinkerton's report in her satchel. *This* was the man she'd been expecting. "That was in prison, wasn't it?"

"Yes, it was." Silas shifted his gaze from the bird to her face. "I got locked up for rustling cattle, a crime I didn't commit. Things were different for your daddy. Do you know why he went to prison?"

Susanna felt her heart rise into her throat. "He killed three boys."

"Yes, he did. He should have hanged, but instead he went to Laramie and the guard tossed him in with me." Silas chuckled softly. "He hated my guts on sight."

"Because of your color?" Susanna stiffened with outrage. She had grown up in Robert E. Lee's backyard, but her mother had taught her that *all* men and *all* women were created equal.

Silas shook his head. "That wasn't it at all. What irked your daddy was my Bible reading. He didn't want to hear it."

Susanna almost felt sorry for John Leaf. She knew how it felt to be stuck in Sunday school on a sunny day. Wrinkling her nose, she said, "Miss Pickett used to read out loud for a solid hour. It was really boring."

"Lord, child, I'm not a thing like Miss Pickett," Silas replied. "I started with the Gospel of John and then switched to the Revelation. Your daddy wouldn't say so, but he liked the parts about the four horsemen and the angels coming down with fire."

Susanna's skin prickled with understanding. Most girls didn't like stories about warrior angels, but she did. Sometimes she imagined she was one of them. As it rattled down a hill, the stagecoach picked up speed. She had to brace against a trunk to keep from sliding backward, just as she had to hold herself back from wondering what else she had in common with John Leaf. Had he read *Huckleberry Finn*? Did he think poetry was silly?

As the stage leaned into a curve, she realized she didn't know John Leaf at all. Maybe he was a rancher now or perhaps he owned a store. Susanna's stomach started to churn. He could be married with other children.

As soon as the road leveled, Silas went on with his story. "All that Bible reading made your daddy more ornery, but then a new guard started work.

He had a crippled old dog that used to visit our cell at night."

Susanna's heart clenched. Robert Windsor had bought a pedigreed cocker spaniel for Robbie. Susanna liked the puppy, but she had a soft spot for strays. Dogs, cats, it didn't matter. The more an animal needed a home, the more she loved it. She wanted to tell Silas to stop talking about dogs, but instead she said, "I like animals."

"Then you understand why your daddy started talking to that mutt. He kept calling it a low-down ugly cur, but I caught him feeding it bits of his supper. A few weeks later he named the dog 'Bones,' which was short for 'skin and bones.' I do believe that was the first time your daddy loved anything."

At the thought of John Leaf feeding scraps to a skinny dog, Susanna wanted to cry. It hurt to think about the man, so she focused on the animal. "Maybe Bones had rheumatism."

"I expect so. He sure couldn't walk very far, and that made your daddy mad." Silas looked up at the sky where the eagle was soaring in widening circles. "I'll never forget the day John asked me about God. He said, 'Silas, if your God is so full of love, why the *hell* does Bones hurt all the time?'"

Susanna hugged her knees. "What did you say?"

"I told him to ask the Almighty for himself. He didn't think I was awake, but later I heard him pray the dangedest prayer. He said, 'Okay, you Almighty so-and-so, if you're real, heal this poor old dog.' Then he growled, 'Amen.'"

Susanna's eyes popped wide. "Calling God a bad name isn't a good idea."

Silas shrugged. "God understands our anger. It's our indifference that hurts him, and your daddy was anything but indifferent after that night. He watched Bones all the time. He shared most of his food and even made a bed for the mutt by sliding his own blanket through the bars."

Susanna would have done the same thing. "Did Bones get better?"

Silas nodded. "Day by day, he moved a little easier. After a month he had a spring in his step. When your daddy and I were released that winter, the guard let Bones go with us."

The Pinkerton reports had said nothing about Bones and Silas. She had to wonder what else the detective hadn't seen. "Where did you go?"

"Back to my ranch. I had a partner who kept it running while I was locked up. Your daddy stayed for about a year, but his heart wasn't in it. Instead of working, he read all my books, especially the Bible."

"What happened to Bones?"

"He did well for about a year, but he was an old dog. He died peacefully in his sleep. Your daddy buried him on the hill where you and I looked at the stars. A few days later John decided to strike out on his own."

Susanna remembered that hill. It had felt magical to her. "Where did he go?"

"South to Colorado. He found work on a peach farm owned by an old preacher named William Merritt. I gave your daddy his first Bible, but Mr. Merritt gave him his first black coat and set him up with a church in Midas. That's where he is now."

Susanna thought of the Gantry boys and the satchel full of shame. "He's a *minister*?"

Silas's gaze burned into hers. "Yes, he is, child. When a man's spends time on his knees, he's free to stand tall. I'm proud to call John Leaf my friend."

With the satchel at her side, Susanna looked up at the sky where the golden eagle was guiding them south. The answers to her questions would come, but somehow she knew they weren't going to be the ones she had been expecting.

Chapter Ten

May I, Abbie?

If you're careful of my camisole. It's new.

He untied the ribbons and pressed his lips to the heart-shaped curve of her breasts. His mouth traveled lower, lower, to the valley between the soft mounds. And then higher, higher... Hellfire!

John jerked awake and found himself on the train to Raton where he and Abbie were seated across from each other. The half-full passenger car smelled of diesel, and it was jolting along the track about an hour out of Midas. A seasoned traveler, she had brought a book for the trip. He'd brought only his restless thoughts, and they had gotten more rebellious with every passing mile.

Last night he had barely slept because of that kiss by the creek. Somehow she had reached across the abyss of his shame and made him feel whole. He'd wanted her warmth, her heart, her hands on places they didn't belong, but he couldn't allow those feelings to grow.

Thank God she had come to her senses. He'd been back in Kansas, lying with her on a blanket on the edge of another stream.... With dusk settling, he had rested his head in her lap while she ruffled his hair.

You like the night, don't you?
Yeah, it's private.
Do you ever feel lonely?
Not with you.

He had pulled her head down to his, kissing and coaxing until she stretched her body next to his. Together they had rolled all over the blanket, exploring each other through their clothes until he'd asked to unbutton the front of her dress. John grimaced at the memory. Lust had pulled those two kids together as surely as a stone rolled downhill, but it didn't match the need he felt for her now. He could handle lust. It was wanting to love her that was making him crazy.

As the train chugged uphill, he stared out the window at a steep canyon only a bird could have crossed. It matched the distance he had to keep from Abbie. He could enjoy the beauty of the pines from afar, but he couldn't rest in the shade. He could see the river at the bottom of the gorge, but he couldn't drink the water.

John stretched his leg and frowned at his spit-shined shoes. He couldn't wear his preacher's coat today, so he'd put on the suit he'd bought in Colorado before his preaching days. He felt like a different man, and he wondered if Abbie's new dress made her feel the same way.

The bodice nipped in at the waist and showed off her curves. John thought it looked pretty on her, except for the color. The gray made him think of ash. He would have picked something in red or a coppery brown. Nor did he like her hat. The short veil hid her eyes and emphasized her pink lips, which he couldn't stop noticing. He wished he'd brought a newspaper. He was about to signal the conductor for a copy of the *Raton Herald* when Abbie chuckled.

"What are you reading?" he asked.

After closing the book, she draped the veil over the brim of her hat, giving him a clear view of her eyes. "*Huckleberry Finn.* It's Susanna's favorite."

It was John's favorite, too. He was getting used to the idea that he had a daughter, especially since Susanna carried Abbie's blood as well as his own. The photographs had played through his dreams along with memories of Abbie's apple-sweet lips on his smoky ones. Hoping to strike a casual pose, John propped his foot on his knee. "Tell me about her."

Abbie trailed her fingers over the cover the book.

"She's just like Huck, maybe even as restless. It tears at my heart because I want her to be happy."

John did, too. "What is she interested in?"

Abbie's cheeks flushed to a soft pink. "Horses, books and boys."

"Boys?" John clenched his jaw. If some young cowboy started chasing after his daughter, the fool would be answering to both the good Reverend and the ex-gunslinger. "She's too young for that nonsense."

Abbie gave him a sympathetic smile. "We don't have to worry just yet. She's wants to be a doctor."

"She must be bright." *And kindhearted like you.*

"She's brilliant," Abbie said with pride. "For a woman, that can be a burden."

Not if John had something to say about it. With the train speeding through the canyon, he realized he could give Susanna the gift he'd received from Silas. He could believe in her when no one else did. John knew all about kids struggling with broken lives—boys who were trying to be men too soon and girls who mistook sweet talk for love. He told them each to hang on for better things and to trust God for the best life had to offer. Surely he could do that for Susanna.

But the more he learned about her, the more he worried that she suffered from his black moods. Everyone had heartache, but only a select few lived with a darkness that never lifted. He prayed Susanna wasn't one of them, but the facts couldn't be denied.

"Why did she run away?" he asked. "Looking for me is just a sign of the trouble that's underneath."

Abbie nodded solemnly. "Robert resented her and she knew it. I tried my best, but we had a terrible argument before she left. I said all the wrong things. I—"

John couldn't stand her remorse. He reached across the space between them and put his hand on hers. "Don't blame yourself. You're the best mother I've ever known."

Looking into his eyes, she turned her hand so that their palms made a shelter of sorts. John didn't know what to do. He'd sworn not to touch her and yet here he was—memorizing the shape of her fingers like a blind man. He needed his black coat for distance, but Abbie needed a friend even more. As the train lurched, he clasped her hand even tighter. "Right now, Susanna's mad at the world. I know, because I used to feel the same way."

Her eyes burned into his. "She needs you so much."

But John didn't want anyone to need him. He lived inches from eternity. Hell, he didn't even own a dog. Now he had a woman and two children depending on him.

He let go of Abbie, leaned back in his seat and turned to the window. As the train slowed and rolled onto a trestle, the steam whistle blared. The click of the wheels faded as the ground dropped out from the track, leaving nothing but timber and air beneath them. The trestle felt flimsy compared to solid earth, but it was the only way to get from one end of the canyon to the other—just as today's ceremony would secure Abbie's future.

Against his better instincts, John studied her face. The glimmer in her eyes made him ache for the innocence of Kansas, which in turn made him worry about Susanna. *His daughter.* He could think it now. But what good would that do? His past burdened all of them.

As the train lumbered across the trestle, John could see only sky. They could have been on a bridge of clouds for all he knew. And that, he realized, described his relationship with his daughter. Something he couldn't see hung between them, but he could feel the connection. He wanted to teach her about life—the cost of freedom, when to fight and when to turn the other cheek. Those lessons came not with words but with action. That was the kind of bridge John could build.

He turned back to Abbie. "I want to do something special for Susanna. Does she know how to ride?"

"She steeplechased in Middleburg last spring."

John thought of the stream behind the parsonage. It ran high into the mountains and carried trout. "Has she ever gone fishing?"

Abbie chuckled. "We live six blocks from the Potomac. She baits her own hooks."

John had run out of ideas when it occurred to him to teach her what he did best. "Would you mind if I taught her how to shoot?"

Abbie's eyes flashed with an intensity John didn't understand. "I'd be grateful. It's a dangerous world for a woman. Would you teach Robbie, too?"

"Sure. I'll teach him like I taught—" *You.*

Their eyes locked as they traveled together back in time. John remembered wrapping his arm around her waist and snuggling her bottom against his hips. Holding her that way had made him hard and he'd let her know it. Rebel that she'd been, she had wiggled closer.

Looking at her now, tense and dressed in gray, he wondered what had happened to that girl. She had turned into a fine mother, but John suspected the rebel had died a slow death. Looking at her now, he wanted to take off that prim hat and loosen her hair with his fingers. The urge had nothing to do with sex, or at least not much. Mostly he wanted to give her back the boldness that had been squeezed out of her.

With their conversation dangling unfinished, John

focused on the needs of the day—a wedding without a kiss, a marriage without a bed. No flowers. No rings. No future. He was doing the right thing...so why did he feel like a selfish prig?

The answer hit him hard and low. He felt like a prig because he'd been acting like one. He'd been so bothered by his own worries that he hadn't considered Abbie's feelings. Getting married again had to be hard for her, too. For both their sakes, he needed to loosen up. This marriage couldn't be consummated, but he could still help her make a new start.

He did it for widows all the time. When he saw a woman at a social wearing blue or gray for the first time in months, he would ask her to dance. He'd pick something lively, a reel or a polka. He'd smile and compliment her. He'd make her feel brave for dancing with a reformed scoundrel when he was really the safest man in Midas. That dance always broke the ice. Whatever man had been eyeing Widow So-and-so would glare at John, march over and cut in. Pleased with her courage, the woman always said yes.

Looking at Abbie with the book in her lap, John realized that her circumstances were even harder than the ones faced by a woman who had lost a man she loved. Abbie had never been properly courted. That was his fault, too. But today he could charm her and make her smile.

As the train picked up speed, he stared out the window at the thinning pines. Raton was just minutes away, so Abbie tucked the book into her bag and laced her fingers in her lap. The whistle blew a warning and the train slowed to a crawl. As soon as it squealed to a stop, she stood and walked ahead of him.

John touched her elbow and escorted her down the steps, ready to catch her if her heel caught on the grate. As soon as they stepped onto the platform, the sun hit him in the face. It was a beautiful day, he thought. A perfect day for a wedding.

The courthouse was just two blocks away, so they walked with the crowd to the brick building. When they reached the steps, John saw a Hispanic boy selling a mix of flowers ranging from lupine to roses. While holding three bunches in one hand, the kid offered a bouquet of daisies with the other.

"Flowers for your bride, mister?"

John couldn't remember the last time he'd given flowers to a woman. Maybe not ever. But then he recalled walking with Abbie in Kansas. He'd plucked a dandelion out of the grass and handed it to her.

If your grandmother grew roses, I'd give you pink ones to match your cheeks.

Lord, what godawful sweet-talk. He'd do better than that today. Reaching into his pocket, he said, "I'll take all of them. How much?"

The kid's eyes popped wide. "A dollar."

Judging by the boy's mended shirt, the family needed the money. As John slid a coin out of his pocket, the kid handed the giant bouquet to Abbie. Alone, each bunch would have been pitiful, but together they made a rainbow. Abbie's eyes shone with delight.

John wanted to think the flowers had brought her pleasure, but he knew her too well. It was the boy's excitement that had touched her. Playing the game, she looked up at John and smiled. "These are the most beautiful flowers I've ever had."

Sadly, John suspected it was true. The boy dropped the coin into his pocket and looked at John. "I have rings, too. They're pretty. Would you like to see 'em?"

Abbie touched his sleeve. "I'd love a ring."

Knowing he could buy the ring or watch Abbie buy it for herself just to help the boy, John said, "Let's see what you have."

He reached into his other pocket and took out three silver bands, each one set with a mix of turquoise and pink amethyst. "My pa's a blacksmith, but he makes silver bells and rings on the side. My ma decorates them."

"They're lovely." Abbie examined each one and then selected a band with a pink quartz and four chips of turquoise. "I like this one. It has the most stones."

"How much?" John didn't care, but bargaining was part of the game.

The boy looked him in the eye. "Five dollars."

Which meant the boy would be thrilled with four and happy with three. John paused, glanced at Abbie who knew exactly what he was up to. She touched his sleeve. "It's absolutely beautiful."

John huffed to let the kid know he'd driven a hard bargain and handed over the money. "Here you go."

The boy held the ring out to John, but Abbie took it and slipped it on her finger, making it clear she considered it a souvenir and nothing more.

"Thanks, mister!" The boy scampered off, then stopped and looked over his shoulder. "I forgot to tell you. My ma says her rings are magic. Each stone counts for a baby, so you're going to have a girl and four boys."

With that bit of cheerful news, the boy took off down the street, leaving John with his mouth gaping and Abbie trying to pull the ring off her finger. Only the darn thing wouldn't budge. There they stood— two adults acting like children who had just run into the bogeyman. John wanted to howl with misery, but Abbie chuckled.

"We're pitiful," she said. "You'd think we actually believed that silliness. It's just a ring."

Or was it? John didn't believe in magic, but he *did*

trust in a God who liked to show off. Glaring at the silver band, he frowned. "Try a little spit."

Abbie sighed with impatience. "Don't tell me you're superstitious."

"Hell, no." But the ring scared him to death. Mostly because he didn't want her to take it off. Pictures flooded through his mind—Abbie sharing his bed… Abbie big with his child…a houseful of toy trains and bugs in jars…a family…a future.

All the things he couldn't have, barring a miracle.

Chapter Eleven

Twenty minutes later they had filed for a marriage license and were standing in the foyer outside the judge's chambers. A male clerk opened the door and motioned for them to enter. "Mr. Leaf? The judge is ready for you and your bride."

John put his hand on the small of Abbie's back and guided her into the office. A white-haired man wearing a black robe stood up from his desk and extended his hand to John. "I'm Judge Connor. So you two are tying the knot."

"Yes, sir," John replied.

The judge shifted his gaze to Abbie, taking in the flowers and the ring. "Looks like Julio's on the job."

Abbie smiled. "He's a nice boy."

"And quite a salesman." As Connor rocked back on his heels, his gaze narrowed to John and darted back to Abbie. John understood he was sizing them up and deciding what to say. He took his job seriously, just as John did.

He addressed Abbie first. "Where are you from, miss?"

"Back East."

The old man eyed John. "And you, Mr. Leaf?"

"I've been here awhile."

As the judge weighed the evidence at hand, John realized he and Abbie were woefully unprepared to answer questions. In spite of Julio's flowers, they looked like what they were—two people marrying for less than ideal reasons.

"So how did you two meet?" the judge asked.

Abbie looked up at John who thought of the telegram that had led to this moment. "We've been corresponding."

Frowning, Connor said, "So this is one of those mail-order marriages. Since you two don't know each other very well, I'm duty-bound to point out a few things."

John wanted to tell the old goat to hurry up. They were here to make things legal, not to hear a lecture. But Connor was already glaring at him.

"We're going to start with you, Mr. Leaf. This woman isn't a plow horse you can whip or a slave you can boss around. If she burns your dinner, eat it anyway. If your shirts are wrinkled, shut up and wear 'em. And one more thing—I don't tolerate wife-beating. Is that clear?"

John didn't care for the assault on his character. "I certainly do. I intend to treat Miss Windsor with the utmost respect."

The judge shifted his gaze to Abbie. "Life is hard here, miss. Whatever you do, don't start whining. Men hate it when women fuss about nothing. It makes them ornery, and that's when the fighting starts. Do you understand?"

"I certainly do." Abbie's snappish tone caught John's attention. Her jaw had tightened and she was clenching the flowers hard enough to make them shake.

The judge gave a nod. "You two are making a trade. With a little luck, you'll fall in love. If you don't, look for the good and tolerate the worst."

John fumed in silence. Where was the talk of love and honor? Even with the limits of this commitment, he wanted to make Abbie happy. The day called for something more. A kiss would have smoothed the rough edges of the judge's lecture, but John had promised at the creek that he'd never touch her that way again. All he could do now was look at her, hoping his feelings showed in his eyes as the judge recited the vows.

"Do you, Abigail Moore Windsor, take this man to be your lawful husband, in sickness and in health, for richer or for poorer, for better and for worse, as long as you both shall live?"

"I do."

"And do you John Horatio Leaf take this woman to be your lawful wife..."

John knew the vows by heart, so he focused on Abbie. Her eyes were burning with an anger he understood. For all their good intentions, Judge Connor seemed to be sentencing them to a loveless marriage. Abbie was mad about it and so was John. In fact, it couldn't be tolerated. He couldn't kiss her the way a bride deserved to be kissed, but surely she'd welcome a brush on the cheek.

"Mr. Leaf?"

John had missed his cue, but it didn't matter. As he wrapped his hands around Abbie's, the flowers stilled and he spoke from his heart. "I, John Horatio Leaf, take this woman to be my lawfully wedded wife, for better or for worse, for richer or for poorer, in sickness and in health until death us do part."

The judge wrinkled his brow. "I guess you *were* paying attention. All right, then. You may kiss the bride."

Gazing into his wife's eyes, John raised his hand and touched her cheek, gently tipping her face to his. He hoped she saw the good intentions in his eyes— the love he felt for her, the promise to keep her safe. Bending to her, he closed his eyes. But instead of feeling the silk of her cheek against his lips, he got whapped in the nose by her hat. As he opened his eyes, John saw Abbie glaring at the judge. "Are we done?"

"Yes, ma'am," Connor replied. "It's official. You two are man and wife."

Clutching the flowers, she spun on her heels and raced out of the room.

Abbie had been Mrs. John Leaf for all of thirty seconds and she already wanted to murder him. He had tried to kiss her. He had sworn that he'd never touch her again, but she had seen the look in his eyes. She'd also smelled smoke on him. That had been the last straw in a stack of ugly memories.

Wife beating! Dear God, did it show? Did the judge know that Robert had blackened her eyes and cracked her ribs? Could he see that her husband had raped her and burned her with his damned cigarettes? Memories had exploded in her mind as the judge spoke, and she'd come close to telling him to shut up.

That's when John had steadied her hands and spoken his vows, meaning every word. She had wanted so badly to believe in those promises. She had curled her fingers around the bouquet and imagined the pretty flowers in a vase on John's kitchen table. They were a testament to hope and new beginnings.

With tremors of longing rippling through her, she had looked into John's brown eyes and ached to be seventeen again.

If only...maybe...

But icy fingers had squeezed her heart. She was dead inside. Barren. Damaged. The old panic had welled from the depths of the past. She knew how to fight it, so she had gotten hopping mad and stormed out of the judge's office, down the hall and into the street. Julio was nowhere in sight, so she tossed the flowers in the hedge and tried again to pull off the ring.

John strode up behind her. "I'm sorry that wasn't easier. The judge jumped to conclusions."

"The judge!" Abbie clawed harder at the ring. "You're the one I'm mad at. We've been married two minutes and you've already broken a promise."

John's sympathetic gaze hardened to irritation. "Which one? You look mad enough to hang me, but it's not till death us do part—at least not yet."

"You know what you did." She tightened her jaw. "You promised you wouldn't kiss me again."

John's face turned to stone. "A kiss is expected."

"I don't care if it's expected or not." She tugged harder on the ring. Why, oh, why wouldn't it come off? After heaving a sigh, she lowered her hand to her side and clutched at the reticule hanging from her shoulder. Only the weight of *Huckleberry Finn* stopped her from turning her back on John completely.

"If we hurry, we can catch an earlier train." Turning abruptly, she paced down the boardwalk.

Stay angry...stay strong...

But tears were pressing behind her eyes. Even now she wanted to believe in the vows they had just taken. She had so much to give and John had so many needs. Abbie swallowed back an ache. If she lost control, she'd slide into a crying fit that would last for hours. She couldn't let that happen. She had to remember that John was just like any other man— arrogant, bossy and hardheaded. He snored and left dirty clothes on the floor. Plus he smoked cigarettes. She smelled them all the time.

The human chimney caught up to her with four strides. "Abbie, have a heart. My side's killing me."

She didn't want to slow down for him, but how could she not? The wound had healed, but she was practically running. She eased her pace, only to have John step right in front of her, forcing her to come to a halt.

"We have to talk *now.*" He motioned to a narrow alley between two storefronts. "This way."

Abbie turned the corner. Walking in front of John, she paced by woodpiles and trash until she found a private nook behind a staircase. With her back against the siding, she said, "So talk. I'm listening."

As he planted his hands on either side of her head, the scent of bay rum filled her nose, mixing with the smokiness of his hair and clothes. His eyes burned into hers. "I had no intention of kissing you like a bride should be kissed."

She could see the early shadow of his beard and the black slash of his brow. His jaw had tensed but his lips were slightly parted, as if he wanted to kiss her as he had at the creek. Her belly quivered with awareness.

"You're lying," she insisted. "I saw it in your eyes."

The starch in his shirt had mixed with the heat of his skin. The scent was uniquely his...and alluring. He leaned an inch closer. "I never said I didn't want to kiss you. I said I wouldn't do it."

But the wanting was enough. Desire kept a person up at night and caused a pain that tore a woman's heart in two. She knew that for a fact, because she wanted to kiss him right now. Here in the alley with fury racing through her blood and the train whistle blasting through the air. With wagons clattering down the street and the sun beating down on them. Her breath caught in her throat.

Stay angry. Stay strong...

He brought his head an inch closer, then closer still. If he kissed her now, she could kiss him back. She was mad enough to fight fire with fire. His eyes were burning into hers and she could see the pulse in his throat. He parted his lips and closed his eyes. She waited and hoped...but instead of plundering her mouth with his, he turned his head and heaved a sigh.

Abbie saw three shades of red, but then her temper faded to a washed-out pink that matched her wrapper. To her shame, she wanted to cry. Needing to hide her weakness, she ducked from under his arms and smoothed her skirt. "I'd say that proves my point."

John muttered a mild oath. "I don't know what the hell just happened."

But Abbie did. The burned-out pine of a man still had a fire burning in his belly. So did she, but she couldn't stand the heat when he poked at the coals. Taking pity on him, she said, "I'll think about going home sooner than I planned. In the meantime, I need to move out first thing in the morning."

John looked her in the eye. "If I can't find a place for you, I'll stay at the hotel."

"That would be fine."

In silence they walked out of the alley and headed for the train depot, each lost in private thoughts that were very much the same.

After three hours of silence on the train and the strained conversation at the supper table, John had escaped to the porch. Lounging in his chair, he snuffed out his fifth cigarette and considered lighting another one. The sun had set hours ago, and he'd been staring at the stars trying to figure out what the devil was wrong with him. In spite of telling Judas to settle down, John had finished kissing Abbie in that alley a dozen times, with each daydream more intense than the last.

Annoyed, he looked at the butts in the tin of sand. Smoking was a poor substitute for where he really wanted to put his lips. He hadn't been this lustful since he'd been a kid in his first whorehouse. Sure, he noticed women. But noticing and imagining were two different kinds of fire. The first was a match he could snuff with his thumb. The second was an out-of-control blaze. God help him, John had a forest of thoughts ready to go up in flames. Every time he blinked, he was back in that filthy alley, kissing Abbie, wanting to mold his body to hers, wanting to do more than kiss her. But not everything, he consoled himself. For *that* he wanted the privacy of his bed.

John stifled a low moan. He'd always imagined temptation as a snarling beast he could fight, but his attraction to Abbie was more like a boulder he couldn't move. Just a blink brought a picture of her body so vivid he ached to make love to her. He had tried going over the boulder by thinking about Sunday's sermon, but "love thy neighbor" had turned into "husbands love your wives." He'd tried tunneling under the rock by smoking himself half to death, but he'd just gotten a headache.

The stars offered no comfort at all. Twinkling and bright, they matched the ring Abbie had finally coaxed off her finger with soap. Nor did the full moon ease his restlessness. The silver glow reminded him of the shimmer in her eyes, and the shape of it matched the curve of her breasts. Wincing, John pinched the bridge of his nose. Left to his instincts, he would have asked her to walk with him to the stream. They needed to talk about the fiasco in Raton, but mostly he wanted her company.

So ask her...kiss her again...

John told Judas to shut up and looked at the stars. Where was God when a man needed a cold rain to settle him down? John knew the answer. The boulder of temptation had to go, so he bowed his head and blasted it with prayer. He prayed that Abbie would find peace and joy in a new life. For himself he prayed for the wisdom to know what she needed and for the strength to resist his own desires.

After a final glance at the moon, John pushed to his feet and walked into the kitchen. As he poured himself a glass of water, the grandfather clock chimed twice. He was about to head to his room when he saw a dim glow under the door to the bathing room. It was too late for anyone to be in there, but he still paused to listen for sloshing. Hearing only silence, he tapped on the door, waited a few seconds and then opened it. A cloud of steam swirled around him, dampening his face and making him look at the claw-footed tub that wasn't empty after all.

There, in all her Eve-like glory, was his wife. Eyes closed and relaxed with sleep, she lay with her hair spilling over the edge of the tub and her arms resting on the porcelain sides. With her neck arched and her lips parted, she could have been in the throes of making love.

She'd be angry if she caught him looking, but John didn't much care at that moment. His gaze traveled from her hair to her flushed cheeks, down the column of her throat to her breasts. He remembered them from Kansas, perfect white mounds that had shaped themselves to his hands. He was lost in that memory when his gaze honed to a line of ugly red welts— each as round as the tip of a burning cigarette.

That goddamned son of a bitch! Robert Windsor had branded his wife like livestock. He'd taken the greatest gift God could give a man—a loving wife— and he'd hurt her, both inside and out. John wanted to kill him.

A gasp jerked his eyes from the welts to Abbie's face. With her eyes blazing, she crossed her arms over her breasts and slid into the soapy water to hide herself.

"Get out!" she cried.

She could have been holding a gun to his head and John wouldn't have budged. He hated bullies, brutes and bastards with his whole heart. He'd been beaten, too. He had felt the pain, the helplessness, even the degradation of peeing himself. He'd been nine years old when Isaac Leaf had come at him swinging a pickax like a sword. Trapped against a wall, John had lost all dignity. But even so, his humiliation seemed small compared to what Abbie had endured. Married or not, when a man forced sex on a woman, John called it rape.

He'd seen it once. A member of the Too Tall gang had taken a girl out into the darkness beyond their camp. John had heard her cries for help and stopped the jackass with a kick to his ribs. The girl had wanted to stay with John, but he'd said no. Her hair had been reddish and loose across her shoulders, like Abbie's was now.

John held her gaze. "If Windsor weren't dead, I'd kill him for you."

"I would have done it myself if I could have."

Her voice shook with a thirst for vengeance that John understood. The rebellious girl in Kansas was still alive. He wanted to say how much he admired her, but first she had to get out of the tub. For that maneuver she needed privacy. Keeping his eyes on her face, he said, "I'll wait for you in the kitchen."

"No, don't."

He was about to say they had to talk, when she

pushed up from the water. Streams glistened down her breasts, dragging his gaze to her waist, her womanly hips, the apex of her thighs, the swatch of hair that protected her most private place. He stared with both wonder and male appreciation. This lovely creature was his wife, a woman to treasure and enjoy, but loving her meant denying himself that privilege.

Holding back an oath, John turned his head to the side and stared at the wall, praying for the strength to do the right thing.

"Go ahead and look," she said sarcastically. "You might as well see everything."

John's whole body clenched. He wanted to see and smell and taste every inch of her. He wanted to hear her cry out with pleasure and sigh when it was over.

But by "everything" Abbie had meant her flaws. That misconception had to be laid to rest right now. In John's eyes she was perfect, so he turned his head and looked. He let his eyes linger over the length of her legs, the slope of her belly, the mole below her breast, her nipples, the scars. When he reached her face, he said, "You're a beautiful woman from top to bottom."

She looked down and focused on the scars. "You've already seen these," she said, tracing the welts with her finger. "I have to wear high collars even in the summer. Evening gowns used to be a problem. The other wives would be wearing all sorts of pretty things to fancy dinners, and I'd be dressed like a governess."

She had uttered the last word with disgust, reminding him of the ash-gray dress she'd worn on the train. No matter what else happened between them, Abbie would leave Midas with a trunkful of pretty clothes.

"I also have a bad shoulder. It got dislocated when Robert slammed me against a wall. He was mad because I had to feed Robbie." She pointed at a fan of silver marks on her belly. "He said these were my fault because I got so fat with Susanna."

John wanted to stop the lies, but Abbie had to finish. Looking bleak, she held up her right hand. The lamp caught the shadow and exaggerated her fingers against the wall, turning them into a claw. "My fingers are crooked from being broken. That's why the ring wouldn't come off this morning."

She lowered her hand and looked straight at him. "I was trying to lock my bedroom door when he pushed his way inside. I fought him, but he was so much bigger. He pushed me against the wall and hit my face. He broke my ribs and then he—he raped me."

"Abbie—"

"I have other scars that don't show." Her voice

started to wobble. "I don't see well out of my left eye. It's full of spots. And I can't—" She clamped her lips tight against the sobs, but she couldn't stop the tears from spilling down her cheeks.

John put iron in his voice. "Let me tell you what I see."

She shook her head no, but he wasn't about to let her stand there feeling flawed.

"Those marks on your belly tell me you're a mother. They make you more beautiful than you were in Kansas. You could have walked away from the pain on those glorious legs of yours, but you stayed because of your children. And those scars on your chest—they're badges of honor." A horrible possibility pierced John's thoughts. Robert had tormented her for a reason, and he was afraid he knew what it was. "You were protecting Susanna, weren't you?"

She looked at him with stark anguish. "He wanted to know your name. I told him you didn't care—that you didn't even know about her—but he kept hurting me until I told him everything."

John didn't think he could feel more despicable than he had after shooting Ben Gantry's sons, but he did. Nor could he imagine lighting another cigarette as long as he lived. They were all going in the trash. "Can you ever forgive me?"

"It's not your fault."

But it was…he'd planted his seed and left Abbie to tend it alone. Somehow he'd make it up to her—starting right now. He lifted her robe off the hook and held it open for her. "It's over, Abbie. No one will ever hurt you again. I swear it."

Looking down, she touched the empty sleeve and burst into tears. "No one has ever done this for me, covered me up, I mean." Sobbing, she stepped out of the tub, slipped into the robe and pulled the sash tight. She was murmuring she was sorry and embarrassed, explaining that once she started to cry, she couldn't stop.

Wanting to soothe her, John put his arm around her shoulders. "Let's get you out of here."

"I don't want anyone to see me like this."

"No one is going to." John knew all about licking wounds in private. "We're going to my room."

Abbie recoiled with terror. As much as he wanted to hold her close, he stepped back and held his hand palm up in a gesture of submission. "You're completely safe with me. You know that, don't you?"

Her eyes widened. "I do."

"Good," he said. "Because I have a sure cure for the shakes."

He snuffed the lamp and guided her from the bathing room. In the kitchen he took a pint of whiskey out of the pantry and led her to his room where he set the bottle on his desk and lit the lamp. The sudden glow revealed jumbled sheets and his navy-blue comforter.

John glanced at Abbie who was hugging herself as if her stomach hurt. The sobs had eased, but her breath was still shallow.

"Get in," he said. "I'm going to tuck you in, pour you a shot of whiskey and sit here until you fall asleep."

She shook her head. "I can't. Beth gets up at dawn. What if she sees me leaving your room like this?"

"She won't," he replied. "I can move without making a sound. Once you're settled, I'll get a dress from your room. With the curtains open, the sun will wake you at first light."

She looked at the bed with longing and then perched on the edge, huddling forward as she hugged her waist. John poured a shot of whiskey in a glass and handed it to her. After turning the desk chair, he sat across from her and watched as she downed the amber liquid. As if the will had gone out of her, she handed him the glass, scooted to the middle of the bed and let him tug the comforter up to her chin. A kiss to her forehead would have been fitting, but he didn't want to crowd her so he sat back down.

She laced her fingers together, making a shelter of sorts across her middle. "You don't have to stay. I'll be all right in a while. I've had this happen before."

"Me, too," he said. "You need to talk it out."

"I have." Her voice sounded steadier. "I have wonderful friends in Washington. We listen to each other, cry together. We've all been down the same road. I've told them pretty much everything."

Just as John had told Silas "pretty much" everything. No one on earth knew John had murdered his own father. Did Abbie have any buried secrets? If so, he knew what it was. "Did you tell them about me?"

When she pressed both hands to her lips, John's gut clenched. If she started to cry again, he'd feel like dirt. But a closer look revealed a twinkle in her eye. The woman was holding in a bad case of the giggles.

"What's so funny?" he asked.

"I told Maggie about my first time."

John tried not to groan, but he knew this joke was on him. "This can't be good."

Abbie chuckled softly. "Maggie called you a two-legged goat."

"Now that's a picture," he said dryly. Judas wanted to make a better defense, but John refused to think about it.

Abbie smiled at him. "She said worse things about Robert. Those were true, but you were good to me, Johnny. First times aren't always nice."

"But they should be." Needing to console them both, he reached across the bed and took her hand.

"Lord knows, if I could live that night again, I'd make things right. I'd change everything, especially how it ended."

"But we can't," she said. "Besides, marriage just isn't for me. Why bother with the misery if I can't conceive?"

Can't conceive...can't conceive...

Her words echoed in John's mind like a shout from heaven. More than anything, he feared passing on his bad habits to an innocent child. If Abbie couldn't have more children, that would never happen. He could make love to her without the fear of planting his seed in her womb. He could kiss the scars on her body and heal the wounds on her heart.

"Are you sure?" he asked.

Her green eyes filled with sorrow. "After years of hoping, I'm positive. Something happened during Robbie's birth. I figure I have scars inside as well as out."

"I'm sorry," he said softly.

"Me, too." She shrugged off the sadness the same way she ignored the pain in her shoulder and the spots in her eye. "At least it simplifies my choices. If it weren't for the arrangement between us, I wouldn't have married again."

John suspected why. "Don't tell me you think those scars matter? You're a beautiful woman, Abbie, and so brave it shames me."

"I'm not brave at all. I can't even think about bed-room things without crying." She pulled her knees to her chest, then turned her head to hide her quivering lip. "Do you know how it is when you smell bread and instantly think of home?"

"Not really." His mother had rarely baked. "But I know how it feels to see a shovel and remember being whacked with it."

Her pupils narrowed in the lamplight, making her irises even greener. "Then you understand. That's why I panicked after that kiss at the stream. I can't forget."

John had walked that bitter road with Silas, talk-ing late into the night. The old man had been both tough and kind, but mostly tough. *You gotta face the ghosts…*

John made his voice firm. "If I can stop sweating at the sight of a shovel, you can get over Robert."

Abbie shook her head. "It's not a choice. I just react to things."

"That reminds me." John stood and opened the drawer that held his cigarettes. He scooped up the two packs, set them in the washbowl and poured water on them. "You won't smell smoke on me ever again. It's a bad habit anyhow."

Abbie sighed. "It's a nice gesture, but it won't fix me."

John looked down as Abbie settled into his pillows

and yawned. Earlier he'd prayed to be delivered from the temptation to take her to bed. Now he wondered if the good Lord was sending him a message of a different kind. She needed to be touched with sure and gentle hands. She needed healing and love. They were married…he could give her those things with a clear conscience, but then how could he let her leave?

He couldn't. And neither could he ask her to share his life knowing that his past was a threat to them all.

Abbie snuggled into the feather mattress with a contented sigh. "Thank you, Johnny. You've been so kind."

Bending low, he kissed her forehead, watching as her eyelids fluttered shut like tired butterflies. He couldn't give her the things she needed most, but he could see to it that she spread her wings a bit. He could provide for her needs and make her feel pretty again. He could buy her those new dresses… underthings with a bit of lace…a nightgown that held no memories.

Without making a sound, he closed his door and went to her room where he opened the wardrobe in search of the gray dress. He found it hanging neatly on a hook and checked the tag. Just as he thought, the garment had been made by a dressmaker named

Jayne Trent. Along with the dress, he gathered fresh underthings, her shoes, a hairbrush and handful of hairpins.

Walking with his old stealth, he slipped back into his bedroom where he laid her things on a chair and opened the drapes as he promised. After putting on his black coat, he strode to the stable where he saddled his mare for a ride out to the Trent ranch.

Chapter Twelve

The Trent place had changed in the time since John had married Ethan and Jayne on a nearby knoll. The cabin had been replaced by a frame house, and the barn held four fine quarterhorses. As he rode through the meadow, he noticed the lupine just beginning to open in the morning sun. The stalks reminded him of Abbie's wedding flowers.

Damn, but he was aching again—for himself, for Abbie, for the things that couldn't be. He had to focus on the needs he *could* meet, not the ones that pulled at his groin as well as his heart. Forcing his gaze away from the flowers and the new grass that matched Abbie's eyes, John rode across the yard and dismounted.

As he swung out of the saddle, Ethan stepped onto the porch. The man who had once resembled an angry grizzly was already shaved and sipping coffee. He hadn't lost his instincts, though. When he saw John, his eyes narrowed with suspicion. "What's wrong?"

Ethan's dire tone matched John's mood perfectly. Looking just as grim, he said, "I need a dress."

Ethan arched an eyebrow. "Should I be worried about you?"

Realizing how peculiar he'd sounded, John chuckled. He'd made a similar remark to Ethan when the rancher had hijacked a trunk full of Jayne's clothes during their courtship. "You've waited a whole year to get back at me for that crack, haven't you?"

"I sure have." Ethan held out his hand and the two men shook. "Come inside, Reverend. Have some breakfast and tell us what's got you in a twist."

As John followed Ethan into the house, the aroma of biscuits tickled his nose. He was close to relaxing when a baby's delighted squeal reached his ears. He'd dedicated Louisa Margaret Trent last winter. She was six months old and blond like her mother.

John's heart squeezed. His daughter had made baby sounds he would never hear. She had nursed at Abbie's breast and he hadn't seen that flow of milk and the love in her mother's eyes.

Before he could collect his thoughts, Jayne came around the corner holding Louisa on her hip. Yesterday he would have reached for the little girl and plopped down in the rocker. Today he couldn't make his arms move.

"Hello, Reverend." Jayne's eyes filled with worry. "Are you all right?"

That's when he realized he hadn't shaved for two days and his eyes were red-rimmed and bleary. The work shirt under the black coat wasn't exactly fresh, and the blue chambray didn't match his usual attire. Not wanting to explain himself, he focused on the task at hand. "Do you remember a gray dress you had for sale at the Emporium?"

"Sure," she answered. "A suit with pearl buttons and a high collar."

"I need you to make about five more in the same size, but in pretty colors with buttons and what-not." His voice picked up speed. "She needs underthings, too—just as pretty as you can make them. And night-gowns and a wrapper. Any color but pink... How long will it take?"

"I finished two dresses yesterday that are just her size. Have a seat and I'll get them."

John shook his head. "I'd rather stand. I'm in a hurry."

Judging by her expression, John had stirred up her imagination as well as her curiosity. Jiggling the baby, she said, "This wouldn't be for your houseguest by any chance?"

John hated gossip. "What have you heard?"

"Only that she's young for a widow...and very pretty."

When Jayne smiled, John scowled. "She's had rough go of it. It's time she made a fresh start."

Ethan and Jayne both nodded, somewhat solemnly. Because their own love had come after a brutal heartbreak, they understood the cost of new beginnings. Jayne broke the silence. "Mrs. Windsor is lucky to have you for a friend."

Jayne had said the right words, but Cupid had put a twinkle in her eye. John put his hands on his hips. "Don't get the wrong idea. I'm just helping her a bit."

Ethan raised one eyebrow. "And what *wrong* idea is that? Seems to me it might be the *right* idea."

John felt as if the walls of the cozy home were falling on top of him. The fool rancher probably made love to his wife three times a day. She'd rub his back and kiss his neck. He'd return the favor... they would snuggle and talk. And then... Ah, hell. John was so jealous that all he could do was growl. "You know darn well what wrong idea. That is *not* why I'm here today."

Ethan snorted. "Of course not."

Jayne looked even less convinced, but she had the decency to be professional. "I'll get the dresses."

Turning, she handed Louisa to Ethan who propped the baby on his shoulder. When she kicked like a rambunctious lamb, the rancher grew six inches in front of John's eyes. Swaying to rock the baby, he looked at John. "Have you heard the news?"

"I hear all sorts of things—both good and bad."

Ethan grinned. "This is good. Louisa's going to have a little brother or sister sometime in the spring."

John blinked and imagined Abbie growing round with his child. It was a foolish thought, but he felt an ache deep in his chest. At the sight of Ethan's smile, John's usual request for a cigar turned into a lump of envy in the pit of his stomach. He had just managed to say congratulations when Jayne walked back into the room with two dresses draped over her arm. She set them on a chair and lifted the first one for his inspection.

"What do you think?" she asked.

John's mouth went dry. The dress matched the color of Abbie's hair, a reddish brown with tinges of gold. It had black brocade on the front, two rows of fancy frog-ties and the high collar she needed to cover the scars. It made him think of smoke and flame. "It's perfect."

Pleased, Jayne held up the second dress, turning it to show off a column of dainty buttons running down the red linen. "Not all women can wear bright colors. Do you think—"

He thought, all right—about undoing the buttons one at a time. "I'll take them both."

Jayne nodded. "I have a full set of underthings I can send with you now."

John managed a crisp nod, but unmentionables were the last thing he wanted to be thinking about.

His intentions were to make Abbie feel womanly so she'd be ready for love when a good man came into her life. As for the temptation to be a real husband to her, he had to stop thinking about undoing her buttons.

Jayne interrupted his thoughts. "I'll wrap everything up. Would you like to stay for breakfast?"

"You're more than welcome," Ethan said, chuckling. "But be warned. Louisa might put cereal in your hair."

As if she understood, the baby made a "bah" sound and then kicked her legs. *"Bah!"*

Ethan clicked his tongue to soothe her. "She's hungry. Two more minutes and she's going to be screaming."

John wanted to run from the cozy house, but he had to pay Jayne for the dresses. With Louisa kicking and shouting "bah, bah, bah" like a Gatling gun, he felt like a man under full attack. Sure enough, before Jayne returned with his packages, the little girl was screaming her lungs out…all because she was afraid she'd go hungry. And there was John, ready to wail with her because he was hungry, too. Only instead of food for an empty belly, he wanted Abbie.

When the baby let out an ear-piercing shriek, Ethan headed for the kitchen. "Jayne's in charge of the cereal, but I can manage some applesauce. How about you? Want some coffee?"

"No, thanks," John answered.

Coffee didn't appeal to him right now, but apples did. He flashed to Abbie wearing the red dress. The next thing he knew he was back in her grandmother's orchard picking fruit. Only instead of the sweet wine saps she had made into a pie, he was plucking rotten apples off the tree in his mind. Worry. Fear. Doubt. The certainty that he was doomed to starve…just like Louisa.

And that's when it struck him. The temptation he had to fight had nothing to do with wanting Abbie in his bed. That yearning had a purpose like a baby's hunger. His mistake was thinking he knew what the future held. Pure and simple, it showed a lack of trust in the same God who had healed Bones and kept John off the gallows.

When Ethan upended a spoonful of applesauce into his daughter's mouth, she took it like a baby bird and opened for more. John wanted more, too. He wanted to know the same contentment that had changed Louisa from a banshee to a blond angel.

His problems were more serious than hers. Ben Gantry posed a real threat, but what did John really know about the future? Gantry could be playing horseshoes with his boys in heaven, or he could have left Bitterroot and made a new start. John had always trusted his crazy intuition. It had been necessary for his survival, but now it was in the way of other things, like hope.

As for his cursed blood, Abbie's confession put that concern to rest. He was sorry for her but relieved for himself. While Gantry remained an unknown, John's family legacy of violence and bad tempers was certain. His heart was picking up speed when Louisa sputtered a mouthful of applesauce straight at her daddy. Chuckling, Ethan wiped his cheek. "Tell the truth, John. Wouldn't you like to have a little darling of your own?"

I already do... But that confession would have to wait. He needed to get home to Abbie. He had a proposal to make—one that had nothing to do with business and everything to do with love.

When he didn't reply to Ethan's question about children, the rancher raised an eyebrow. "I'm not hearing your usual 'hell no, there's not a woman in the world who could put up with me.'"

John glowered at his friend. "That's because I'm not saying it."

The rancher had the good sense to shut his gaping mouth, but Jayne wasn't nearly as circumspect when she emerged from the back room carrying three wrapped packages. They were decorated with fancy gold ribbons that turned them into courtship gifts.

"I added something special. It's kind of fancy, but she'll love it." Her eyes said, *So will you.*

John was on the verge of making another denial, but his friends had already seen right through him. Reaching for his billfold, he said, "How much to do I owe you?"

She named a price for the three packages and another one for the clothing she still had to make. "Mrs. Wingate placed a big order for the Emporium last month, so most of it's nearly finished. Ethan can drop it off on Friday."

In time for a week from Sunday. An idea lit John's imagination on fire. He'd have to work quickly, but why not? He had already waited too long. Besides, the opportunity to shock Ethan down to his socks was more than John could resist. Keeping his face blank, he said, "Could you do me another favor?"

"I'll try," Jayne replied. "What do you need?"

"Make one of those new gowns a wedding dress."

The next thing John knew, Jayne was hugging him and squealing in his ear, Ethan was slapping him on the back, and Louisa had nailed him smack on the nose with a handful of applesauce.

Shortly before noon Abbie opened the front door to the parsonage and nearly passed out from shock. Her father was standing on the steps with a valise at his side and a hang-'em-high look on his face. "Good afternoon, Abigail."

"Father!"

He glowered at her with a coldness she remembered all too well from her childhood. "You seem to have forgotten your manners. May I come in?"

"Of course." She stepped back and ushered him into the front room. As always, he was wearing a black suit and standing straight to take full advantage of his height. As a lawman and a judge, her father had developed the habit of studying his surroundings with more than average interest. He was doubtlessly noticing the dated furniture and worn rug. John rarely used this room and Abbie didn't care for it, either. She motioned at a Queen Anne chair with a lump in the seat. "Make yourself comfortable."

As her father sat, she positioned herself on the divan. There was no point in making small talk with the judge, so she took the offensive. "Why are you here?"

"My grandson sent me a telegram, and I've come to take him to Kansas like he asked."

So that explained how Robbie had spent his money from the café. Abbie held in a sigh. She'd have to talk to him about honesty, but first she had to deal with her father. "Robbie is twelve years old. He's not in charge of where he lives."

The judge huffed. "Abigail, I'm shocked. You

traveled two thousand miles with a girl who should be in finishing school and a boy who's grieving his father."

"Not quite," she said. "Susanna is staying with friends."

Her father ignored the reference to his granddaughter. "Nor did you advise me of the trip. The question isn't why am *I* here, but rather, why are *you?*"

If he thought she'd be cowed by his tone, he was mistaken. Abbie wanted to order him to leave, but she couldn't risk offending him until she had control of Robert's estate. If her father discovered she and John had formed an alliance for financial reasons, he'd make her life miserable. The best strategy was to be as cool as he was.

Never mind that the temperature in the room had risen twenty degrees and she'd been awake most of the night. At least she was dressed for battle in her gray dress. Squaring her shoulders like a Confederate general, she decided to take the advice John had given Robbie about deception. She couldn't reveal their marriage. John didn't care what people thought, but Abbie was keenly aware of his reputation as a minister. If word of their wedding got out, he'd be trapped into explaining the annulment when she left. But if she mixed fact with fiction, she could fend off her father and protect John.

"Father," she said, taking a breath. "I have some surprising news."

"Don't play games with me, young lady. The last time you had a surprise for me it was humiliating. Exactly why the *hell* are you here?"

Her father never swore in front of women. It was the most blatant disrespect he could have shown. As for the snide reference to Susanna, Abbie wanted to tell him to shut his mouth. Instead she laced her hands in her lap. "I think you'll be pleased. I'm engaged to be married—to a minister."

The judge glowered at her. "Am I supposed to be impressed? I'm not. I'm sure Robert left you well-to-do. How do you know this man isn't after your money?"

Abbie could have laughed at the irony. She'd never known anyone less concerned with money than John. Rich or poor, he would be the same man.

"John is comfortable in his own right."

The judge scoffed. "From Sunday offerings? I doubt that very much. How did you meet this fellow?"

He's Susanna's father. But that information was dangerous. All those years ago, when her father had forbade her to utter John's name, she'd been resentful. Now she was grateful. If the judge learned she was visiting the man who had "ruined" her, he'd fight for custody of Robbie. Abbie couldn't take that chance. Sitting primly, she began a tale she hoped her father would believe.

"Robert and the Reverend had some business dealings. When John learned of Robert's passing, he wrote a letter of condolence. We've been corresponding since March."

Sort of. Abbie figured Susanna had sent her letter in late spring.

The judge sat tall, as if he were holding court. "Go on."

"It became apparent we were in similar circumstances. He needed a wife and I needed a husband, so he invited me to visit. We decided to get married just yesterday. Robbie doesn't know yet. I'd appreciate it if you wouldn't say anything to him."

The judge wrinkled his brow. "I certainly won't. If I have anything to say about it, this marriage isn't going to take place."

It already has... Holding in the retort, she replied, "I have deep feelings for John. I believe he has honorable intentions."

The judge snorted, taking her back to the night he'd forced her to choose between marrying Robert and giving up her baby.

I won't have that bastard child in my house.

But Father...she's mine.

Abbie knotted her hands. Her father had never laid a hand on her, but he'd been cruel in other ways. She had grown up starved for affection, which explained why she hugged her kids every day—and why she wanted John to be a father to their daughter.

The judge pursed his lips. "Suppose this man *is* sincere. A courtship should last at least a year. Nor is it proper for you to be living under his roof."

Heat rushed to Abbie's face as she relived waking up in John's bed with morning sun in her eyes. The sheets had smelled like him, and she had imagined his head denting the pillow next to hers, his hands stroking her breasts, her belly, the curves of her bottom. Fire had licked through her veins, spreading from her neck to her toes until she'd curled herself into a ball. Clutching her middle, she'd let the sensations build until she wondered if she could manage to be a real wife to him. But then her bad shoulder had started to ache and the spots in her left eye had eclipsed the sun. Instead of imagining John's touch, she had wept for what she had lost to Robert.

She felt those tears now, but she couldn't afford them. Blinking, she focused on her father. She knew from experience that he respected facts and not feelings.

"John has separate quarters," she explained. "Robbie and I live upstairs along with another houseguest. It's quite proper."

"You're not even out of mourning."

The judge knew darn well she hadn't loved Robert.

Annoyed, she said nothing, letting the silence make her point. Her father stared back, drumming his fingers in a rhythm that was too slow to be unconscious. He was trying to goad her into a fight, but Abbie ignored the manipulation, forcing him to break the stalemate.

"You're gullible, Abigail, just like your mother." When he pushed to his feet, she steeled herself for the shout she knew was coming. "What the *devil* makes you think you can trust this man?"

Because he saw me naked and covered me up. Because he tucked me into his bed and brought me clothes.

Abbie battled the urge to jerk down the collar of her dress and show her father the burns on her chest. How dare he call her gullible! He'd forced her to marry a cruel man whom he had treated like a son. She had survived fourteen years of abuse and raised two children—one of whom he had criticized and the other whom he wanted to steal.

Abbie was close to exploding when the front door opened wide, revealing John looking disheveled and holding three packages wrapped with gold ribbon. She needed to speak to him before her father revealed her deception, but the judge had already turned to him.

"Mr. Leaf, I'm Judge Lawton Moore. I expect a full accounting of your interest in my daughter."

Her father had deliberately withheld John's title of "Reverend" as a sign of disrespect. Abbie tensed. If the judge sensed weakness, he'd go for the kill.

After assessing her father with a stare of his own, John set the packages on the table by the door and hung up his hat. He looked at the judge and then at Abbie. She gave a small shake of her head to signal…she didn't know what. If she said too much, her father would see through the deception. But if she said nothing, John could stumble into a trap.

She had decided to stall by offering refreshments when John squared himself in front of the judge.

"Mr. Moore, your daughter and I are getting married the Sunday after next. If you don't like it, that's too damn bad. On the other hand, I'd be pleased to get to know you. Robbie tells me you're a retired U.S. marshal. He speaks well of you."

"I see," said the judge, not giving an inch. "You're a confident man, Mr. Leaf."

"And I love your daughter," John replied. "I intend to see to her every need. That includes raising her children as my own."

At the reference to Susanna, Abbie stopped breathing. Her father paid no attention to his granddaughter, but it was possible he'd see the resemblance to John. She waited and prayed God would strike him blind, at least for now. When he grunted, Abbie sensed her prayer had been answered.

Still staring at the judge, John said, "Abbie, your father must be thirsty after that train ride. Could you make some iced tea?"

Her mind followed his to the block of ice in the cellar. "I'd be glad to. Would you bring up some ice?"

"Sure," John replied. "Mr. Moore, if you want to keep an eye on us, you're welcome to tag along."

Abbie hid a smile. By asking her father to "tag along," John had ensured that he'd stay put.

Leaning back, the judge rested his polished shoe on the opposite knee. "I'll wait right here. So will Abigail. I want to speak to my daughter in private."

"And you'll have that chance," John said. "But not until you and I get a few things straight. Right now, she's going to pour us all something pleasant to drink, and I'm going to bring up some ice. Are you coming or not?"

When the two men locked eyes, Abbie threw herself into the middle of the conversation. "Father, stay here and be comfortable. I'll be back in just a minute."

Before he could argue, Abbie hurried down the hall. John came up behind her and rested his hand on her back. As soon as they reached the kitchen, he whispered into her ear. "What does he know?" he asked.

She turned and put her hands on his chest. The beat of his heart belied his calm exterior and matched her racing pulse. "Robbie sent him a telegram. I'm terrified the lie about being engaged is going to cause trouble for you. How did you know that's what I'd told him?"

His eyes turned brooding. She could feel the tension in his muscles and smell the morning air clinging to him. His lips parted and then came together again. She'd asked a simple question. Why hadn't he answered it?

Like steam on a mirror, her thoughts coalesced into a rivulet of understanding. John hadn't heard a word of the conversation with her father. He had meant what he'd said about getting married in church. Feeling as trapped as she'd been in the alley, she pulled back. But this time he tightened his grip on her hands. "I mean it, Abbie. I want this marriage to be real. I want the world to know you're my wife, but only if you can put up with the hell that comes with me. If you say no, I'll understand."

Of all the confounded proposals…she couldn't say no without John assuming it was because of his past, but neither could she say yes. She had to take away his hope, so she raised her chin and moved her lips, but she couldn't speak. Saying no was a bigger lie than their incomplete marriage. She wanted to be his wife more than she could say. She ached to give him every comfort, every joy, the best things life had to offer. She yearned to share his vision and his dreams, to be a partner to him. Apart, they were two lonely souls. Together they were…better. She wanted that wholeness, but how could she have it? She was a shattered woman.

Choking with frustration, she whispered, "I don't know what to say."

His eyes flared with confidence. "Come to the oak tree at midnight. We'll talk."

Telling John that she couldn't marry him would be awful, but that's what she had to do. "I'll be there," she said. "But you aren't going to like what I have to say."

Needing to break his gaze, she turned away, opened a cupboard and reached for a glass. John came up behind her and clasped her shoulders. His lips grazed her ear. "You can fight, but I'm going to change your mind."

He released her shoulders and stepped out the door, leaving her to cope as she busied herself with the jar of sun-tea. Why were they talking about marriage when her father was just ten feet away? They needed to plan for the next five minutes, not five years. John came back to the kitchen carrying the ice in a leather strap. As he set it in the sink, Abbie opened the drawer holding the ice pick, making the utensils rattle so the judge would hear them.

"We need a plan for dealing with my father," she whispered.

"Leave him to me." John drove the ice pick into the block. Chards clattered against the metal sink. "If he wants to butt heads, that's what we'll do."

But Abbie didn't want them to argue. She wanted her father to leave her alone. She wanted the comfort of her Washington home, her friends, her garden, her backyard full of birds. She shook her head as she filled the glasses. "We have to appease him. He's threatening to take Robbie away from me, and he always gets what he wants."

"Not this time," John replied. "But I'm a fair man. We'll give him a chance to adjust to the situation."

Abbie's blood drained to her toes. "What are you going to do?"

"I'm going to treat him to lunch at Mary's so he can see his grandson. After that, I'll tell him who I am—and who I was."

"You can't!"

John looked at her with careful eyes, then he touched her cheek. His fingers were cold from the ice and his words were just as hard. "Are you ashamed to know me?"

"Don't be ridiculous!" she hissed. "This isn't about

you. It's about my children. If my father finds out about you and Susanna, he'll fight to take Robbie away from me. Please, John. Don't do that to me."

At the creak of the hall floor, Abbie jerked back and composed herself. Her father stepped into the kitchen, eyed the jar of tea and then glared at John. "Must have been a stubborn block of ice."

"Not at all," John replied. "Your daughter's the stubborn one. She thinks you're here to steal her son. I told her you weren't that despicable."

The accusation hung in the air like a bad smell until her father narrowed his eyes. "You're a tough man, Leaf. I respect that." He jerked his head toward the door. "Let's take a walk."

"That suits me fine. We'll go to the hotel. You can book a room and see Robbie. He works in the café."

At the mention of his grandson, the judge almost smiled. "Lead the way, Reverend."

John opened the door, then waited for her father to pass through. It was an act of respect, a reward for the old man's compromise. As the door swung shut, Abbie heard John's voice through the window.

"Robbie tells me you have some wild stories about your days as a marshal."

"I've got a few."

"Me, too," replied John.

Abbie stared down at the ice-filled glasses, watching as the condensation dripped down the sides. She could only pray John wouldn't tell a particular story about a night in Kansas.

Chapter Thirteen

Judges in general made John clench his teeth. A good one would have sent him to the gallows. A bad one had let him off with a slap of a prison sentence. They were still God's children, but that didn't lessen his aversion to men of the bench. To soften his irritation, he tried to put himself in Moore's shoes. His grandson had sent an alarming telegram, and his daughter had taken off for New Mexico. John would have stormed after Abbie, too. And neither would he have been pleased with a hurried marriage.

That bit of understanding made it easier to set aside his irritation. They would all be better off if Judge Moore accepted the engagement as real. Later John would work on convincing Abbie to marry him in church, but for now he could help her most by appeasing the judge. And by giving her wayward son a few things to think about—such as the consequences of going behind his mother's back.

The men stayed on neutral topics until they reached

the café where John directed the judge to a table by the window. After a quick word with Mary, he went to the kitchen and found Robbie washing dishes.

The kid looked up at John. "I hate syrup. I'm never going to eat it again."

Robbie had grimaced, but his words were mild. John gave him an even stare. "Someone wants to see you."

"Is Susanna here?"

He seemed pleased, a reaction that John took for a good sign. Considering the judge worshiped his grandson, Robbie would be either a persuasive ally or an effective enemy. If he was still a betting man, John would have given the outcome even odds. "It's not your sister. It seems you sent a telegram to—"

"My grandfather?"

"That's right."

John watched Robbie for signs and they were all there—pleasure, guilt and the realization that he'd started a chain of events he couldn't control. John knew that feeling, so he gave Robbie a pat on the back. "Mary says you can take a break. Come have lunch with us."

Grinning, Robbie took off his apron and sped out the door. John followed, watching as Lawton Moore sprung to his feet and hugged his grandson. After Robbie squirmed away and sat, John returned to the table. Moore had already signaled Mary and was ordering ice cream for Robbie and fried chicken for himself. To keep things on an equal footing, John ordered a meal even though he wasn't hungry.

Moore got down to business. "Son, I've come to take you home with me. As you'd expect, your mother isn't pleased with the idea, but she's not thinking clearly. It's what your father would want."

Using guilt from the grave struck John as a low blow, but he refused to turn Robbie into the rope in a game of tug-of-war. Instead he watched as the boy's brows came together in a frown. "To Kansas?"

"For now. Later we'll move to Chicago so you can attend the Billings Academy. It's an excellent school. Your father had plans for you, and I intend to see them fulfilled."

"But I don't like school."

John almost felt sorry for the kid. He'd dug himself into a hole with that telegram. He could put up with his mother's discipline, or he could let his grandfather run his life. John had to give Lawton credit. He'd dangled a luscious carrot in front of Abbie—and John, too. He wouldn't have traded his tried-by-fire education for anything, but he would have enjoyed studying the Bible with real scholars. Later he'd share that thought with Robbie, but right now the boy needed support of another kind. He was looking across the table at John. "Is my mother mad about the telegram?"

Another good sign. John saw a chance to add some timber to the bridge he'd been building between himself and Abbie's son. "We'll talk to her together," he said mildly. "I suspect you had a good reason to do what you did. I'm also sure your grandfather is glad to see you."

"I'd be even happier to see him on the train to Kansas," Moore added. "I don't want him raised in this pitiful town."

Robbie looked confused. "Does that mean we're staying here? Is it because of Susanna?"

"What about her?" growled the judge. "I thought she was staying with friends."

Moore was eyeballing John when Mary approached. "The ice cream's here!"

As she set the plates on the table, John stared back, daring the judge to see a resemblance between himself and Susanna. When the old man didn't speak, John took it as a reprieve and turned to Robbie. "This isn't how your mother and I planned to tell you, but I've asked her to marry me and she said yes." At least he hoped she would, but Robbie didn't need that detail.

The boy's face reflected a mix of surprise and the superior knowledge that only a twelve year old could have. "She likes you."

"I like her, too."

Robbie gave a shrug and dipped into his ice cream.

"I guess that's okay. Things have changed since I sent that telegram. I wouldn't mind staying here. Tim's my best friend and I like Mary."

Lawton Moore slammed his fist on the table. "Over my dead body!"

Robbie's eyes popped wide. "Grandfather, don't say that! Do you know who the Reverend is? He could shoot you dead. Tim told me all about it. He was in the Too Tall gang. They robbed trains and—"

"I see." The judge stared at John. "I should have put it together. You're Johnny Leaf. You murdered those boys in Bitterroot. If I'd been sitting in that court, I would have hung you three times, once for each of them."

"But, Grandpa—"

Moore pushed to his feet. "Robbie, come with me. I won't have you associating with a child-killer."

Being called that name never got easier, but John had learned to hold his head up. God's forgiveness demanded it, so he stood and looked the judge in the eye. "Sir, I wish you'd been that judge. You'd have spared me the hell of prison and a guilt I'll never put down. I should have hanged, but the good Lord had other plans. Whether you like it or not, those plans include your daughter."

"Take her," said the judge. "And her bastard daughter, too."

John itched to claim Susanna, but Abbie's pleas

were echoing in his ear. Nor did Robbie need to learn the truth in this manner. The boy had stayed seated across from John, oblivious to the dot of ice cream on his chin.

"I know all about Susanna," John said to Moore. "It's a story for another time."

"It's a shame that should be buried." Moore looked at his grandson. "Robbie, come along now."

"No, Grandpa. You're wrong about the Reverend. He's nice now. We're making a train out of wood. He knows all about engines. And you should have seen it when he saved my ma from that man with a knife."

"A knife!" Moore turned red enough for apoplexy. "What the devil is going on here?"

"My ma was being brave."

In lurid detail, Robbie described the incident at the boardinghouse. He hadn't witnessed the fight, but he'd heard talk in town and the story had grown legs. He made John sound more righteous than Wyatt Earp and Christ combined. By the time Robbie finished, Moore's eyes were bulging and John was speechless as well.

"So, Grandfather," Robbie said, "I've changed my mind. I'd like to stay here after all. Since my ma's getting married, maybe you could, too."

John glanced at the judge whose scowl was melting faster than the ice cream. When Moore sat, so did John. Their gazes met in the middle of the table. "Mr. Leaf, what else do you have to say to me?"

Knowing the judge had made a huge concession, John decided to make one of his own. "We'd be honored if you'd perform the ceremony."

Robbie nodded. "My ma would like that."

John had his doubts about Abbie's appreciation, but they would all be happier if Moore accepted the changes in his daughter's life.

After a long pause, Moore turned to John. "If it will make Robbie happy, I'll do it. But we're not done with the discussion about my grandson's future."

"I understand," John replied. In the judge's world, one good turn deserved another, but what mattered most was Robbie. When the time came for a decision, they'd have to talk it out. Until then, John had other priorities, namely convincing Abbie to marry him again—this time for keeps.

Abbie leaned against the oak tree with her hands behind her back, trying to steady her nerves as she waited for John. The evening with her father had been awful. John had steered the conversation to the judge's glory days as a lawman, but she'd been a bundle of nerves.

She'd also been mildly furious—at her father for not asking about Susanna and at John for buying the two prettiest dresses she had ever owned. When she'd tugged the gold bow off the first package and seen the red linen, she'd almost wept. The fabric had smelled new and freshly pressed. She had held it to her chest and looked down at the skirt, imagining herself as truly alluring for the first time in years.

But what was the point of a courtship? Being a wife to him wasn't a matter of willingness. Every time she looked at him, she felt a deepening of her love. She also knew that she had kissed him twice and panicked both times. The pretty dresses were a kind of lie. They covered her scars, but they couldn't heal the hurt.

Needing to play the part of his wife-to-be, she had worn the red one and still had it on. She had wanted to change into something old, but she couldn't risk a conversation with Beth by going upstairs. Nor had she wanted to deal with Robbie, though his apology had done much to soothe her irritation.

I'm sorry, Ma. I was mad when we first came here.

Like mother, like son. Abbie was a tad bit mad herself, and she intended to stay that way until she convinced John to set a fake wedding date in December. With a little luck, her father would tire of Midas and head home. She and John would finish their business with Hodge and be done with their foolish marriage.

Abbie was thinking about her backyard in Washington when she heard John walking down the path. When he reached the oak, he parted the low branches and stepped beneath the canopy. Moonlight streamed through the leaves, striping him with silver light. The shadows hid his expression, but his posture belonged to a confident man—hands loose at his sides, chin raised, boots planted a foot apart.

The darkness concealed Abbie against the trunk of the tree, so he hadn't seen her. As rude as it was, she stayed hidden. Just looking at him gave her a spark of pleasure that shot from her heart to her toes. She wanted to enjoy it, because it was all she could have.

Peering into the dark, he said, "Abbie? Is that you?"

His voice washed over her as she pushed away from the oak. It would have been easy to step into his arms, but she had no hope of tolerating more than a kiss. Needing to be direct, she stepped into a patch of light and faced him. "I appreciate what you've done for me, but we can't take this marriage charade any further."

"Why not?"

His whiskey voice took her back to his bed where she'd downed the alcohol to soothe her nerves. She could have used a shot right now to slow her pulse. Surely it was sinful for a preacher to sound so... desirable. At the very least, it was a trick of the devil, giving her good feelings that would turn bitter if she acted on them.

He had asked a direct question, so Abbie decided to give him a direct answer. "I meant what I said about having scars you can't see. I can't give you the affection a man needs from his wife."

"You're talking about sex."

"That's right." She fought to steady her voice. "You saw what happened in the bathing room. That same panic comes over me every time we kiss."

As John closed the space between them, Abbie pulled the shawl around her shoulders and turned away. A branch brushed her hair, almost like a hand. Her heart jumped into her throat.

John stood right behind her. "What I saw last night was courage."

But she wasn't the least bit brave. Last night she had been a trapped animal defending herself because she'd had no choice. Needing to put space between them, she stepped to the edge of the stream. It had rained that afternoon, turning the trickle into a rush that matched her pulse.

John moved with her, positioning himself so that his breath grazed the nape of her neck. "I love you, Abbie. I want to make this marriage real."

Like a man testing ice to see if it would hold his weight, he put his hands on her upper arms and stroked. She could smell his clean shirt, traces of soap, the heat of his skin. Overwhelmed, she looked down at the skirt of her dress. In the dim light it looked black, reminding her of the mourning attire she'd worn on the train. Squaring her shoulders, she stepped back and faced him. "You should be having this conversation with Emma Dray."

His eyes glimmered. "I don't love Emma Dray."

When he took a step forward, she took a step back. She was scared that he'd kiss her. But instead he bent at the waist, dipped his hand into the stream and lifted a smooth stone the size of her palm. Moonlight glistened on the granite as John pressed it into her palm and wrapped her fingers around the weight of it.

"What's this for?" she asked.

"It's a promise. At one time that rock was nothing but broken edges. It probably got knocked loose in a rockslide caused by a storm. More rain dragged it down the mountain. Over and over, that stone got bashed against other rocks until the rough edges were gone. Now it's smooth to the touch and big enough to be useful."

Tears pressed into Abbie's eyes. That stone could have been her heart.

"That's how God changes us," John said quietly. "I'm not afraid of rough edges, Abbie. Time and Mother Nature will take care of what's worrying you."

Abbie weighed the stone in her hand. A smart woman would have dropped it into the stream, but she couldn't do it. Instead she put it in her pocket—another souvenir to go with Julio's ring. She gave John a wry smile. "It's a nice story, but I doubt you have as much patience as God."

"I don't, but I have the faith to believe I won't need it."

He raised his hand to her cheek and traced a line from her ear to her chin. Then he stared at her lips. Just stared. No movement. Not a whisper. Just his eyes on her lips, forcing her to remember the silk of his mouth on hers. She inhaled sharply, dragging in air so that her lips felt parched. To relieve the chapping, she touched the bottom one with her tongue and hoped he wouldn't notice.

A half smile lifted the corners of his mouth. "You have the loveliest lips I've ever seen. Did you know they're bow-shaped? It's like there's hope inside of you trying to get out."

Abbie shook her head. "You're being silly."

"I'm a man who loves his wife."

He lowered his head to hers, slowly, until she closed her eyes. She felt his mouth just a breath away and then the touch of his lips. He was kissing her as if she were delicate, testing her reactions, daring her to open her lips and her heart.

How could a man express all those feelings with just his lips? Abbie didn't know, but she could feel her body yearning for his. Holding back from him was nearly impossible. It was also a bald-faced lie. She wanted to be his wife, but allowing herself to melt into his arms would have been cruel. A kiss by its very design shadowed the intimacies to come, and she couldn't make that commitment.

She kept her lips sealed until he lifted his head and went back to staring at her mouth. His gaze alone made her tremble, but he was touching her, too. She felt his fingers following the nerves running down her neck, her shoulder, her wrist. Clasping her hand, he pressed his lips against her palm and feathered the flesh with kisses. She needed to pull back, but she didn't want to break the spell. The stirring in her belly gave her hope. But the desire in her heart would shrivel if John did more than kiss her. She was like the dogwood blossoms in her backyard. They thrived in the mild Washington spring but wilted in the summer heat. Sad beyond reason, she took back her hand. She had to focus on her problems, not a dream that wouldn't come true.

She made her voice firm. "What will you do if I say no? Will you tell my father we're not engaged? I could lose everything, even Robbie."

John looked up like a man lost in the fog. She saw the confusion clear in layers, revealing first irritation and then conviction. "Did you just ask me if I'd blackmail you into marrying me?"

"No!"

"Good, because that thought is repulsive. No matter what you say tonight, I'll keep the promise I already made. If you want to fake an engagement—fine. But I don't think that's what you want."

"You have no idea what I want." But she was afraid that he did. As the weight of the promise rock pulled at her dress, she lifted it out of her pocket. She wanted to believe her broken parts could be made smooth, but doubts were tumbling through her mind. *Toss it in the water... Heave it across the meadow...*

As she gripped the stone, she looked up at John and saw a challenge in his eyes. "Go ahead and throw it," he said. "I'll just hand you another one."

To make his point, he gathered a handful of smaller rocks. Stepping back for leverage, he hurled the first one so far across the meadow that she didn't hear it land. "That was for your father," he said. "In some misguided way, he loves you. But the man gives me a headache."

"Me, too."

He hurled another one into the night. "That was for Robert, who should have been horsewhipped."

"And this one—" he tossed it farthest of all "—is for that fool kid in Kansas who left you pregnant and alone. If he had to do it again, he'd buy you a ring, find a preacher and whisk you off to Oregon."

Abbie tightened her grip on the promise rock. She'd spent the past fourteen years wondering what her life would have been like if she'd gone with Johnny Leaf to Oregon. The thought of spending another fourteen years wishing she'd taken a chance on a real marriage made her miserable, and that was unacceptable. After putting John's rock in her pocket, she bent low, picked up a rock of her own and threw it as hard as she could.

Facing him, she said, "That was for regrets. I don't want any more of them. I'm scared to death, but I love you."

"I love you, too," he said in a throaty voice. "I always have." He took her hands in his—nothing more—and then tenderly kissed her forehead. He meant well, but the caress made her feel like a child. Her insides started to churn. John was expecting a church wedding. How could she make this marriage public without being sure of herself? She knew the feelings she had to fight. They lived low in her belly, swimming in murky water and sucking at her courage.

Until now, Abbie had fought the fear by becoming angry. Rage at Robert's cruelty had given her the courage to start a new life. Without those strong feelings, she felt vulnerable and afraid. But they had no place in a future with John. Hoping that love would be enough, she clasped his shoulders, pushed up on her toes and gave him a bold kiss.

Just as she expected, he took full advantage and so

did she. She liked the glide of his lips, the spreading wetness, the coarse texture of his tongue. As he bent her head over his arm, he caressed her back with a rhythm that pulled her up, up, up. Kissing him without the taste of tobacco was pure joy! Instead she tasted the sweetness from tonight's dessert and realized that she and her husband tasted exactly alike.

A long time ago, they had made love. Was the taste of herself on his lips a sign that their marriage was meant to be? Full of hope, Abbie pressed so hard that John had to step back to brace himself. When their teeth clinked, he broke the kiss and chuckled softly.

"We don't have to rush," he said, cuddling her close. "It's going to take time, just like that rock."

But she *wanted* to rush. She had to be sure she could be a wife to him. The thought of being trapped in an unhappy marriage made her shudder, but even more horrifying was the picture of John locked behind the same iron gate.

Deliberately calming her voice, she said, "What if I can't get over the past?"

His gaze stayed on her face. "What happens when *my* past shows up? Are *you* going to leave *me?*"

"No!" Abbie's throat tightened as she pulled out of his arms. "I'd never walk out on you, but neither will I hold you to a marriage that can't be consummated."

"Isn't that my decision?"

"Not if we're equal partners."

John crossed his arms over his chest. "You bet we're equal. God made Eve from Adam's rib because he knew Adam needed a partner. That's what I want for us."

But Abbie knew better than to listen to sweet talk. Patient or not, John would want sex, and he deserved that passion. Tears pressed behind her eyes. A long time ago, she had been young and full of hope, and she had let a drifter take her to bed. She had loved him. She still did. She wanted to be his wife—truly, she did—but not at the risk of trapping them both in a failed marriage.

Still wary of his promises, she looked at John who was standing with his feet planted in the dirt and his arms loose at his sides. He seemed content to wait for her answer, but a twitch of his jaw betrayed the tension.

Abbie squared her shoulders. "It's easy to make promises, but it's harder to keep them."

"With a lot of love and little faith, we can have a marriage made in heaven. Say yes, Abbie."

Say yes...say yes...

But the panic was rising in her and she felt as if she were drowning. She needed a gulp of air, a plan that would let her breathe if she couldn't overcome her fear. Looking up at the stars, she thought of the vows they had taken in Raton. Those words had been spoken for practical reasons, but they gave her the escape she needed now. They were already married. Surely he wouldn't object to taking his wife to bed before they renewed those vows in church.

With her heart pounding, Abbie made a snap decision. If they failed to consummate the marriage before the church ceremony, she would call off their "engagement." If the problem with Hodge wasn't resolved, she'd take her chances with her father. She hated the thought, but at least she wouldn't leave Midas feeling like a chicken. She intended to seduce her husband. It was the bravest thing she could possibly do.

Glancing over her shoulder, she saw John waiting for her answer. The twitch in his jaw had turned to a full clench. She enjoyed having that power over him. Hiding a smile, Abbie decided to drive him a little bit crazier. Staring at the stars, she counted them in silence as the stream rippled past her toes.

When she got to twenty-five, John spoke with a low growl. "You haven't answered my question."

Abbie tipped her face in his direction. "Do you remember wading in the stream in Kansas?"

His eyes glimmered with the memory. "As I recall, we ended up just shy of buck naked."

Abbie had never learned how to entice a man. She felt funny doing it now, but the circumstances called for boldness. Still looking at John, she sat on a flat rock, pointed one foot at him and raised her skirt to her knees so she could take off her shoes. "I'm going wading. Would you care to join me?"

"It would be my pleasure."

Taking his cues from her, he took off his boots and rolled up his pants while Abbie peeled off her stockings. Her stomach was hopping like a jar full of frogs, but she wasn't about to stop. She pushed to her feet, turned her back to John and looked over her shoulder with a glint in her eyes.

"Would you help me with the buttons?"

A chuckle rumbled in his chest as he came up behind her and grazed her skin with his fingers. "I thought about doing this all night."

With each pop of a button, Abbie felt the dress loosen until it slid off her shoulders. Her chemise covered almost as much of her as the dress had, but it was far more delicate. As she tugged a sleeve down her arm, she felt John's lips on the nape of her neck. At the same time, the dress fell to the ground in a puddle of red linen, leaving her upper chest and shoulders bare to the night. Abbie choked back a cry of panic. She felt naked and exposed. She had gone too far, too fast, and she didn't know how to stop the momentum.

Still kissing her neck, John trailed his hands down her bare arms, then he took one of her hands and gently turned her around. "Let's get our feet wet."

Abbie nodded, somewhat stiffly. He was telling

her he'd felt her trembling and would protect her. She liked that reassurance, but she also wanted to scream that she didn't need to be treated like glass. But all those thoughts fled when she dipped her foot into the stream. "It's freezing!"

"Let's go to the middle where it's sandy."

With the water rushing at her ankles, Abbie followed him to a spot where the strong current reached her knees. It pushed her against John who wrapped his arms around her. For a long time, they stood chest to chest beneath the stars.

All the forces of nature were at work tonight—the swollen current pushing her against him, their bodies cleaving together for warmth, the age-old rise of a man's hardness looking for home. Abbie ached to shelter him in that way, but she was also relieved that he had tucked her head against his throat and was merely stroking her back. When her toes were numb with cold, she looked into his eyes.

"We should go inside," she said.

"Not yet." His voice rumbled in his throat. "One more kiss...something to fill your dreams."

Instead of seeking her mouth as she expected, he brought his lips to the shell of her ear and whispered, "I love you." His breath echoed through her head, making her shiver with sensations she'd long ago forgotten. His words were soothing, but the touch of his lips made her cling to him. As she buried her face against the hot skin of his neck, she couldn't decide if the shivering felt good or made her more afraid.

When he smiled against her cheek, she knew that John felt victorious even if she didn't. Confusion pulsed with each beat of her heart. At best, she was a fragile seedling. One false move and she would be crushed beyond hope. As if he sensed her feelings, he kissed her tenderly on the mouth, leaving her more afraid than ever.

Holding in tears, Abbie prayed silently for God to smooth her rough edges more quickly than he'd made the promise rock.

Chapter Fourteen

John stood on the deck listening for the midnight chime of the grandfather clock. With a little luck, he'd go inside and find Abbie in his bedroom just as he had the past three nights. Much to his pleasure, his wife was dead-set on seducing him before the church ceremony. He was just as determined to take his time.

Every instinct told him she was trying too hard, and he worried about the pressure she was putting on herself. He knew from experience ghosts could spring to life without warning. He didn't want that to happen, so he had decided to take his time. He also wanted to get her as hot and bothered as he was. Hunger gave a frightened child the boldness to steal food, and a starving man could kill with his bare hands. With a little luck, a woman full of desire would be just as ready to put aside her fears.

That's why John had insisted on taking her for walks in the moonlight and smooching like kids. A smile curled his lips as he listened for the clock to chime. He intended to take things a step at a time, just as they had in Kansas. But instead of rushing to bed the minute she blinked, he'd insist they wait some more, giving that fire time to turn them into red-hot coals.

He wanted their lovemaking to melt their bones the way a blacksmith's forge softened metal so that it could be reshaped. He wanted Abbie's body to mold itself to his, and he wanted his to be a column of strength for her. He wasn't at all worried the fire would burn itself out. Judas had taken to whining, but John didn't care. Judas wanted sex, but John wanted to make love to his wife.

He was lost in that thought when the clock chimed twelve times. John sauntered to the back door of his bedroom and went inside where, just as he had expected, Abbie was waiting for him. Only instead of being dressed for a walk beneath the stars, she had on her robe and was reading the notes on his desk.

He wasn't sure how he felt about her reading his sermon-in-progress. His own jagged edges showed in that scribbling. Sometimes it took awhile to figure out what God wanted him to say. It also took soul-deep honesty. As he closed the door, Abbie looked at him with pity.

Frowning, he said, "That's not finished."

"I know, but it's so sad. How can you think you

don't know what love is. It's what you did for me at Sally's. It's the way you've given Robbie pride. But you don't understand that, because no one has ever loved you back."

The night had taken a strange turn indeed. He'd come in here ready to be studly and noble and had ended up feeling like the kicked puppy he'd been as a child. He didn't want to answer her questions, so he shrugged. "I've had my share of misery."

Abbie ran her fingers over the pages on the desk, as if she were touching his cheek, and then looked into his eyes. "Who was Isaac?"

The last person John wanted to think about right now was Isaac Leaf. The ugly memories, his guilt, the hatefulness—he didn't want to share those things with anyone. But the glimmer in Abbie's eyes had shifted from pity to a silent plea. *Share with me... let me help you. Show me I'm not alone...*

John's pulse sped up with understanding. As things stood, he appeared to be a whole man, while she felt like a glued-together mirror. They weren't on equal footing now, but John hadn't always been content. He loathed the thought of smelling Isaac's blood again, but he'd do it for Abbie. He'd be building a bridge of sorts, a trestle across a canyon of pain, linking two people who had endured similar trials. With a little luck, Abbie would walk across that bridge and straight into his arms.

If he had to relive that awful day, he wanted to be comfortable, so he sat on the edge of the bed, took off his boots and leaned against the headboard. "Isaac Leaf is the man who fathered me," he said to Abbie. "He was the meanest man that ever walked this earth. I don't like to talk about him, but there are things you should hear."

She sat on the mattress, facing him with her hands folded in her lap. "I want to know all about you."

"There's no easy way to say this," he said. "The first man I killed was my own father."

Instead of backing away, Abbie reached for his hand. "He beat you, didn't he?"

John nodded. "He'd use whatever was handy, mostly an old shovel. He'd hit me in the back, the knees, the head—it didn't matter. I used to get awful headaches. They stopped in prison, but for a long time I thought Isaac had done permanent damage."

"I'm glad they stopped."

"Yeah, me too."

The love in her eyes washed over him as he slipped back in time to that rancid cabin in South Dakota. John saw it all—the November snow, the deer's blood, the bare aspens. From the front yard he'd walked into the cabin with its cracked windows. Along with the smoky fire, he'd smelled homebrew and his father's sweat.

"It was bitter cold that day," he said to Abbie. "I

was fifteen years old, and my ma had been gone for some time."

"How did she die?"

John shook his head. "For all I know, she's still alive. One morning she packed her clothes and walked to town. I never saw her again. I'm pretty sure she went crazy. She talked to herself and saw things no else could see. Some madness runs in the blood. It's one of the reasons I don't want more children."

Abbie gripped his hand with confidence. "You're not crazy and neither is Susanna. The poor woman lost her mind living alone in the middle of nowhere. Women need friends, though I don't see how she could have left her own son."

An old sadness made John's belly feel empty. "Half the time she didn't even know I was there."

The look of pity in Abbie's eyes made him wish he'd never gone down this path. "Don't waste your time getting misty-eyed. I'm over it."

"No one gets over that kind of neglect," she insisted. "From this day onward, I won't let a day go by without telling you how much I love you or doing something nice like scratching your back."

"I like the way that sounds." And he did—though he could think of another itch that needed scratching even more, especially with Abbie so close he could see the lines on her lips. He thought about kissing her, but he needed to finish building the bridge. "Are you sure you want to hear the rest?"

"I think you need to tell it."

"Probably so, but it's still horrible. I'd gone riding just to get away from the place and came home to see that Isaac had skinned a deer. The carcass was on the ground, and the meat was hanging from the eaves. Butchering's gruesome, and he hadn't cleaned up a thing."

"And you walked into that?"

John nodded. "Farm kids understand the need to kill an animal for food, but this was different. Isaac wanted me to see the slaughter. When I walked into the cabin, he was drunk and holding the bloody knife."

Where the hell have you been, boy?

Riding.

What the hell are you doing riding when there's work to do!

John's voice thickened. "He was mad as hell when he came at me. I don't know if he would have used the knife or not, but I didn't give a damn. I grabbed the rifle by the door and shot him in the head."

Abbie gripped his hand. "Don't you dare feel guilty! It was self-defense."

John hated being that close to Isaac Leaf and he hated himself, too. But not for the reason she thought.

"I don't feel guilty for killing him, Abbie. I feel bad that I enjoyed it."

Her eyes burned into his. "I dreamed of doing worse to Robert."

"But you didn't and I did. Killing turned easy after that. I sold my gun to anyone who wanted to pay for it. At first I found honest work. I guarded gold shipments for a few years. I liked the danger, but then greed set in and I started to steal a bit here and there."

"Just like you told Robbie."

"Being two-faced pays off," he said. "I stole a tidy sum and headed to Wyoming. That's where I hooked up with the Too Tall gang."

"They robbed banks."

"And trains. We wore masks, so know one could identify us. It was sheer luck I wasn't on the job that put the rest of them in jail."

"Where were you?"

John wanted to dodge the question, but he didn't want this bridge to have any missing planks. "I was shacked up with a whore in Cheyenne. I did that sometimes. I'd leave the gang and disappear for a week. I'd stay drunk and… well, you can figure out what I did."

Abbie's eyes brimmed with emotion. "You'd get lonely."

"Randy as a bull is more like it."

"I don't think so," she insisted. "You were looking for love."

"Don't fool yourself, Abbie. I didn't give a damn about anyone but myself."

She gripped his hand even harder, leaned close and kissed the scar below his ear. Talk of the past had made his blood churn. He wanted to bury himself inside of her and forget, but he'd sworn to leave that hunger unfed. Except Abbie needed to give her love as much as he wanted to take it. A small compromise seemed in order. "Lie next to me," he said, sliding down the mattress.

Suddenly shy, she turned down the lamp, pressed tight against his chest and thighs, and laid her head on his shoulder. He could feel her warmth seeping into him, melting away the November snow and ugly memories. More relaxed than he'd been in years, he felt his lids growing heavy. Sleeping with Abbie in his arms felt like a bit of heaven. But Abbie didn't have sleep on her mind. With her breath coming in puffs, she kissed his mouth and whispered, "I want to make love to you."

John liked the idea just fine, but her voice had a quiver and she'd knotted her fingers in his shirt. Going slow was the wise thing to do, so he decided to test the waters with a bit of talk. If talk led to touching, he'd be a happy man. If it led to buck-naked lovemaking, so much the better.

Smiling, he kissed the crown of Abbie's head. "So what exactly do you have in mind?"

"I don't really know," she replied. "I figured you'd... you know—take over."

John made his voice grim. "In that case, we have a serious problem. I can't remember where the parts go."

Abbie huffed. "I seriously doubt that."

"I don't know," he drawled. "The whole idea is pretty strange. You have to wonder what God was thinking when he made Adam and gave him that thingamajig to contend with."

Abbie's cheeks flushed pink. "I think he was practicing on Adam so he'd do better with Eve."

"It sure paid off." John pulled Abbie into his arms and nuzzled her ear. This was the kind of married banter he wanted, the easy laughter, the closeness. Stroking her hair, he said, "You're a lot nicer to look at than I am."

"That's a matter of opinion." Abbie's voice had gotten righteous and John smiled. He liked the idea of being bossed around in bed... *Touch me here, touch me there...* He was enjoying that thought when she snuggled closer. "Apart from Kansas, I got an eyeful of you during the fever. You're quite magnificent."

John puffed up like a rooster. Things were going well indeed, but he wanted the fire to be fully stoked before nature took its course. "Can I ask you something?" he said.

"Sure."

"I know what Adam thought when he saw Eve for the first time. He took one look and thought she was the most beautiful creature on earth. But what did Eve think when she caught a glimpse of Adam—without the fig leaf?"

Stretching fully against him, Abbie stroked his chest. "I know exactly how she felt. She was shocked to her bones at the thought of feeling him inside her."

John was hanging on to Abbie's every word. "And after the shock wore off?"

"Well," Abbie said, dragging out the word. "Once she got used to the idea, she wanted to touch."

And that's what Abbie did next. Through the fabric of his trousers, John felt the bend of her knuckles tracing the length of him. He needed to keep his hands to himself a little longer, but Abbie could touch him wherever she wanted. More aroused than he'd been in his life, he laced his fingers behind his neck and blew out a breath. "Hellfire," he muttered.

Abbie's smile tickled his chest. She had all the control and was taking full advantage. He liked it that way, at least for now. Someday he'd tumble her to her back and rub his face between her breasts. He'd kiss and stroke her most private places. He'd make her laugh and weep with the intensity of their love. Over the years, he'd learned more than a single man had a right to know about the female body. He intended to put every bit of that sinful knowledge to use for his wife's pleasure.

But first she needed to get used to him. John figured seducing Abbie was like filling a bathtub. He'd put the cold water in first and then warm it up with kettle after steaming kettle. Right now, he was doing the boiling, but it had to be that way. If he wasn't careful, she'd end up in a panic and they'd lose ground. As it stood, she was forging ahead by tugging his shirttail out of his waistband and rubbing his belly with her hand.

When she undid the top button of his trousers, John closed his eyes and wondered what she had in mind. Using her index finger, she drew an upward curve to the left and made a downward sweep. Then she made a curve to the right and another soft trail. John chuckled softly. She'd just drawn a heart around his belly button.

"I love you, too," he said.

When Abbie pushed up on her elbow, he reached down and pulled her into his lap. She wiggled so that her bottom was on the mattress, leaving her thighs loose over his hips and curled against his belly. Turning, she undid the buttons on his shirt one at a time. After parting the sides, she put her hand over his heart and kissed him full on the mouth.

Of all the kisses they'd shared, this one held the most knowledge of the journey to come. She knew what to expect from him—a gentle passion, caresses to her throat and neck, even her eyes and ears. And he knew what to expect from his wife. She was kissing him with something close to a vengeance.

The tangle of their tongues reminded John of pirates dueling on the deck of a ship. Back and forth. In and out. Up, down and all around. At this rate, he wasn't going to wait for the church's ceremony to make love to his wife. He wasn't going to wait five more minutes. With his arms strong around her shoulders, he slid their bodies downward so that they were lying hip to hip and still kissing. Lost in the taste of her, he caressed the side of her breast.

He'd just dragged his thumb over the sensitive tip when he heard a hitch in her breathing. Instantly, John stopped touching her. "Are you all right?"

She nodded in small jerks. "I'm fine."

But her voice had a shake in it and she had hunched her shoulders. Nor was "fine" the way he wanted her to feel when they made love for the first time as man and wife. John slid his hand back to her upper chest and then down her arm, tugging her close so that his hips spooned her backside. "Sleep with me," he whispered.

When he felt her body relax, he knew he had made the right call. Sure, he wanted to finish the dance they'd just started, but not tonight. Not until he was sure his wife wouldn't run crying from the room.

John soon discovered that living without sex completely was easier than living with the hope of it. Every night for the past week, Abbie had come to his room, and every night she had seemed a little more desperate. John had assured her that time and tenderness would solve the problem and that he wasn't at all concerned, but her frown only deepened.

With the wedding set for tomorrow, he was worried about her, which was why he was sitting on the porch watching the sunset. In another hour he'd be in the dark, a fitting end to a week that had left him confused and frustrated. A cigarette would have been nice. Ah, hell. Who was he fooling? He wanted a whole pack. Instead he hunched forward in the chair and replayed the details of last night. The midnight picnic under the oak had been Abbie's idea and he'd liked it just fine—until she'd pulled the whiskey bottle out of the picnic hamper. He didn't want his wife drinking for courage before they made love.

"Reverend?"

Judge Moore's voice came from the front of the house. John stifled a groan. If the old goat decided to lecture him about the duties of marriage, John didn't think he could endure it. Nor did he want to hear the judge extolling the virtues of a good education for Robbie, while taking potshots at Susanna's character. John's heart had changed completely since visiting the Trents. He could hardly wait to claim Susanna as his own. He knew they'd all need time to adjust, but he hoped that someday she'd call him Pa.

He was imagining hearing that word for the first time when Moore came around the corner. Shaking off his irritation, John pushed to his feet and motioned at the chair that now belonged to Abbie. "Hello, Judge. Would you care to join me?"

"Sure."

After they both sat, Lawton pulled a pair of cigars from his coat pocket. "Care for a smoke?"

If it hadn't been for his promise to Abbie, John would have taken the cigar with pleasure. For one thing, it was an eight-inch Cuban, but even more important, the cigar was a peace offering. John considered making the compromise, but a single whiff of smoke would do awful things to his wife, so he shook his head. "I wish I could, but your daughter's not fond of tobacco."

The old man waved the cigar right under John's nose. With each pass, the darn thing got longer and more fragrant. John could almost taste the spicy tobacco, feel the smoke calming his restless thoughts.

But he liked the taste of his wife a lot more than he liked cigars.

"Are you sure you don't want it?" said Moore.

"I'm positive. Smoke it for me later."

The judge gave a dry laugh. "So you're henpecked already."

For the hundredth time, John wondered if he had made the right call when he'd asked Lawton to perform the ceremony. Abbie had gone along with the plan in the spirit of keeping the peace, but John wished he'd been more careful.

The judge lit the cigar and puffed a cloud of smoke. "I want to talk to you about Robbie—man to man."

The judge could talk all he wanted, but John had an ace in the hole. This afternoon he had received a letter from Jefferson Hodge advising that the transfer of Robert's estate was final. As John had requested, he and Abbie were joint executors. He planned to tell her tomorrow as a kind of wedding present.

With the papers in order, they no longer had to appease the judge, but neither did John want to offend him more than necessary. "So what's on your mind?"

"I'd like to enroll Robbie in the Billings Academy for the fall term. It's run by one of my Harvard classmates."

"I see."

The judge blew another cloud of smoke. "Raising another man's son is a burden I wouldn't expect you to take on. I'll pay his expenses, of course. I'd also expect him to visit his mother every summer."

Between the smoke in his face and the judge's slight to Susanna, John had gotten a snootful of his arrogance. Wise or not, he decided to take a jab of his own. "What about your granddaughter?"

"She's a bad seed." Moore tapped the cigar with his finger, crumbling the ash. "You *do* realize she's illegitimate?"

John was itching to shout the truth—that Susanna was his and he was proud of her—but provoking the judge would serve no purpose. Instead he made his voice firm. "I know everything—including the fact she's bright and wants to go to college."

"That's none of my concern. I'm here to look after Robbie, which means I won't be leaving town until my daughter agrees to do what's best for my grandson."

John kept his voice even. "We can discuss it after the wedding."

Grunting, the judge pushed up from his chair. "I feel strongly, Reverend. I intend to take Robbie with me when I leave."

"Like I said, we'll talk later."

For the second time, Moore held out the cigar. "Take it. You can enjoy it behind Abigail's back."

Or, John thought, he could shove it up the judge's… never mind. By the grace of God, he waved off the Cuban and managed to sound pleasant when he said good night.

After watching Moore saunter back to town, John thought about finding Abbie. The old coot had made him irritable and he needed to blow off a little steam, but she was upstairs with Beth, trying on her wedding dress. Tomorrow at this time they'd be alone in the house. Beth had already rented a room for herself, and Robbie would be with his grandfather at the hotel.

With the stars flickering, John breathed a prayer for Abbie. Soon they'd make love. She'd open her arms and welcome him home. Certain of the joys to come, he lingered on the porch, watching as the moon rose above Broken Heart Ridge. The silver glow paled compared to the shaft of light streaming from Abbie's open window. At the ripple of female laughter, John smiled. He would have liked to have been a fly on the wall, but he contented himself with listening to whispers until the window went dark and he knew Abbie had gone to bed.

He sat for another hour, listening to the hum of the night and thinking about his wife. She claimed she could live with the threats from his past, but John wondered if she understood what he was asking. Guilt for killing Gantry's sons followed John like a shadow, and tonight that awareness made him peer down the path to town. Gantry would always be a train ride away. Even now he could be in Midas and who would know? John's dirty bones hadn't rattled in some time, but they were jangling tonight. Hoping he could sleep in spite of his rushing blood, he walked around the porch to his bedroom.

Even before he turned the knob, he felt his neck hairs prickle. He told himself he was overreacting and stepped inside, but why was the lamp burning? And who had closed the drapes he'd left open? It couldn't have been Abbie. Just this afternoon, they had joked about the groom not seeing the bride and he'd told her he'd miss her visit.

If Abbie hadn't opened the drapes, who the hell had? Had Gantry found them? Was this a sick game? John wanted his Colt but he'd left it in the front room. The shotgun was under the bed.

Tense and wary, he finally spotted Abbie standing in the corner by the open window, dressed in her pink robe and inhaling the night air. When she turned, he saw her glimmering eyes and lips that were moist and slightly parted. John wasn't at all in the mood for talk and touching. He wanted the kind of feverish joining that would chase away every thought, every fear. He wanted to lose himself in her. But he doubted Abbie had that kind of tussle in mind. Feeling surly, he said, "Aren't we supposed to wait for the wedding night?"

"We're already married," she reminded him.

Common sense told John to walk out of the room, but he didn't want to do it. Maybe he'd hold her for a while—that was all. Just a touch to know she was safe. Just a kiss to help him settle down. With a low-pitched chord thrumming through him, he closed the door with a hard click.

Chapter Fifteen

Abbie felt like a fool standing in front of John, but time had run out. Tomorrow at noon, everyone in Midas expected her to become Mrs. John Leaf, a full partner in her husband's work and someone they could count on. Abbie loved the idea. She wanted to teach a special class for adolescent girls and to hold a fund-raiser for a scholarship fund. She had dozens of ideas for the town, but first she had to succeed in the bedroom.

She'd come close to making love to John the other night, but her traitorous nerves had twitched when he'd touched her breast. She'd figured out that her throat was her breaking point. Anything north of her collarbone felt good. Anything south made her wary. As for her sensitive nipples, she wondered how she had managed to nurse two babies without falling apart. She had even enjoyed it, especially the rhythm of rocking in time to the baby's need.

She *had* to get past that barrier, but how? This

afternoon she'd found the answer tucked inside the box holding her wedding gown. Jayne Trent had enclosed a lacy nightgown and a note inviting her to have lunch next week.

That note had taken Abbie straight to her kitchen in Washington where she had sipped coffee with her friends. She didn't doubt for a minute that Maggie would have told her to be brave. So tonight, after Beth had hugged her good night and Robbie had fallen asleep, she had put on the nightgown, covered it with her familiar pink robe and snuck into John's room.

Judging by his expression, she had shocked the daylights out of him but he'd recovered quickly. Leaning against the door, he said, "I'm glad you're here."

Abbie's nerves prickled. What in the world was she supposed to do now? John was standing still, watching her too carefully. She hated that control in his eyes. What gave *him* the right to hold back from *her?*

Raising her chin, she loosened the belt on her wrapper. Keeping her gaze on her husband's face, she let the sides drift apart to reveal the sheer lace she wore beneath.

A whoosh of air hissed through his lips, then his gaze traveled downward, not missing a curve. Her skin burned inside the gown. Keeping her eyes locked on John's face, she slid the robe down her shoulders, praying her fears would go with it. But the butterflies in her belly only fluttered more. Even so, she let the robe fall to the floor. The heat of the lamp pushed through the glass chimney and seared her spine. As she took a step forward, she saw a double shadow on the mattress—the solid one of her body and the winglike one of the lace.

When she had stood naked in the bath, she had been defiant, daring him to look at her scars. Expecting a rejection, she simply hadn't cared. But tonight she felt every flick of his eyes, the twitch of his jaw as he perused her hips, her middle, her breasts and finally her face.

"Are you sure?" he asked.

The rumble of his voice, dark and hungry, gave her courage. "I am."

She stayed in front of the lamp, watching as he turned the lock. As the metal clicked, a memory of Robert locking the door to their bedroom surfaced like a bubble rising in boiling oil. She swallowed hard to make it go away, but she couldn't stop herself from raising her hand to the scars. She *would not* panic. She'd go numb before she'd break down. She had to remember that John loved her. He'd be gentle and careful. If she focused on his eyes, she'd be fine.

As he crossed the room, his gaze felt heavy on her

body just as it had in Kansas. Only tonight his features revealed the expectations of a mature man. In his eyes she saw everything—his need for love, hope for their future and, God help them both, worry for her. She hated that hesitancy. If he asked her again if she was sure, she'd fall apart.

Stay brave...stay strong...

When he was three steps away, Abbie lowered her hand from the scars. The lace of the gown dragged across her nipple, causing the tip to throb. She didn't like how it made her feel—needy and small—but she couldn't stop now. John stood in front of her with his back to the bed. The desk and lamp were behind her. Already she felt trapped and he hadn't even touched her.

To hide her eyes, she dipped her chin. "I want to turn out the lamp." Fear had made her voice husky, a sound she hoped he'd mistake for passion.

"I like the dark, too."

Leaning forward, he reached around her waist to turn down the wick. As his chest brushed the lace, the nightgown abraded her skin with even more intensity. Just as she winced, the room went dark. Relieved that John hadn't seen her expression, she breathed evenly until she realized he was pulling back the drapes. As air wafted through the open window, a beam of moonlight fell across the bed, turning the sheets even whiter. John stepped in front of her and rested his hands on her shoulders. Saying nothing, he caressed the muscles in her back.

"If I do something you don't like, just say stop," he said quietly. "No matter what, that's what I'll do."

But she didn't want that temptation. If she failed to make love to her husband tonight, she wouldn't take vows tomorrow. But neither would she surrender without a fight.

Making her voice seductive, she said, "I appreciate the concern, but I won't say it."

To make her point, she put her arms around his shoulders and kissed him, warm and openmouthed. Groaning, he kissed her back with an urgency she recognized as a lifetime of loneliness.

She wanted to reach across that void in his life, to span the gap between Kansas and now, but the gown was scraping more fiercely, bringing with it memories that made her hate the lace. Why did women wear such frilly things? But she knew why—it gave them power. John had lost all resolve at the sight of her in the blasted thing.

That power gave her courage. Breaking the kiss, she raised her hands to the top button of his shirt. She undid it quickly and worked downward until his torso was bare. As she slid her fingers around his waist, she felt the satin of his skin stretched tight from his hips to his ribs. Where Robert had been flabby, John was hard. It gave her courage. So did the ridge of scar tissue on his side.

Dear God, she loved this man. She wanted to give him everything—her heart, her body, her future. Wanting with her whole heart to be brave, she pushed his shirt off his shoulders.

With his eyes burning, he turned his hands wrist up. "Don't forget the cuffs," he said, smiling.

She felt embarrassed. "I've never done this before."

"I'm glad. I like first times."

It was awkward, but she undid the buttons and tugged the sleeves down his arms. As the shirt fell to the floor, his chest came into full view. She could almost count the strands of his chest hair, silky and straight. From his firm muscles, her gaze traveled down his arms. The tight skin on his biceps looked satiny and she touched it, trailing her hands up to his shoulders.

Looking at her with pure longing, John untied all seven of the ribbons on the negligee. Moving as deliberately as she had, he spread the gown wide to reveal her breasts. She felt the lace on her nipples again, but the irritation stopped when he pushed the gown off her shoulders and sent it fluttering to the floor.

"It's pretty," he said. "But you're even prettier without it."

Abbie shivered with dread. She knew John was

watching her face, gauging her reactions in the dim light. When she stayed steady, he put one arm around her waist, pulling her close so that her neck arched and her mouth tipped upward. In a single motion, his lips met hers and his hand cupped the white mound of her breast. She'd been expecting the caress, so she managed to stop herself from stiffening. Instead she pressed herself into his hand, hoping he wouldn't feel her trembling. At the same time, she felt his erection brushing against the apex of her thighs, asking questions, telling her that he loved her, desired her. But she also felt his hesitation—that damnable worry that made her weak.

She forced herself to touch him in that place that belonged only to her. She stroked him twice but then pulled back. With his jaw tense, he turned them with a step so that the backs of her knees bumped against the bed frame. Her feet got tangled in the nightgown and she lost her balance. As she clutched at John's shoulders, a gasp of fear slipped from her throat.

He stopped kissing her instantly. "Are you all right?"

"I'm fine," she lied. Go numb, she thought. Feel nothing.

But that wasn't possible with John. She was feeling everything—love and loathing, fear and hope. She wanted to relish the pleasure, to give herself to him, to be a good wife. But along with that yearning came a response so primitive she could hardly stifle it. What woman didn't cry out when she tripped on a rug and started to fall?

John was pressing closer, still caressing her breast, still kissing her so that her head was tilted back. Too far, too far... Her knees buckled and she fell to her back. The downy mattress cushioned her fall and grabbed her at the same time. A panicked cry rose to her lips, but John had stayed with her, inhaling her breath so that the cry sounded like a moan of pleasure.

Tears pressed into Abbie's eyes. Desperate to put a bit of space between them, she planted her hands on his chest, spreading her fingers wide.

Don't push. Don't push.

But then he put his knee on the bed. The wool of his trousers scraped at her bare thigh, reminding her that she was naked and he wasn't. Robert had played that game. The first time he'd raped her, he'd been fully clothed.

Go numb. Stay still.

But she was falling...she couldn't breathe or see. She could only sense danger as the rocky ground loomed below her. A cry ripped from her throat as she pushed John away with all her might.

"I can't—I can't—" Hot tears ran down her cheeks as she struggled to sit up. She hated being on her back. She hated the moonlight, the mattress, her nakedness. Rolling off the bed, she pawed the floor for her robe, but she couldn't see through her tears. "Where the hell is my robe? I want my damn robe!"

She saw John's feet move, then he bent to pick up the cotton. He stood two feet away, holding it out to her as if she were a wild animal that needed to be calmed. "It's right here," he said gently.

She couldn't stand his kindness. He had to be miserable and it was all her fault. She snatched the robe and shot to her feet, covering herself in a blur of cotton. "I made a terrible mistake. I'm sorry—I can't—" She couldn't stop the words spewing from her throat.

"Abbie, look at me."

"No." She yanked the tie on the robe until it cut into her waist. Then she looked straight at him. The love in his eyes nearly dropped her to her knees, but she had to stay strong. "The wedding's off."

Without a hint of anger, John shook his head. "We're already married—till death us do part, in good times and bad."

"But what good are vows if I can't be a real wife to you?" Sobs shook her entire body. She couldn't stand being in this room another minute. If he talked, she might believe that things would be better next time. But she didn't want a next time.

Abbie sped around the foot of the bed, heading for

the door. As soon as she reached it, she turned the knob, but the lock only rattled in the frame. "Let me out," she whimpered. "Please let me go."

Somehow through the panic she heard John's voice, but she couldn't make out the words. Had he put the key in his pocket as Robert had done? Would he make her stand here and beg like a child? She wanted to be angry, but she didn't have the strength to do anything but sob. Finally his voice cut through the fog.

"Abbie, look at me."

When she turned her head, she saw him standing on the other side of the bed, holding out the key. If she stretched her arm, she could reach it without taking a step. She understood he was being kind, but not even his best intentions could take away the terror of standing behind a locked door while wearing her pink robe. Avoiding his gaze, she snatched the key from his fingers and put it in the lock.

"You're safe," he said gently. "Stay with me, Abbie. I need you."

But she had nothing more to give. She turned the key, opened the door wide and ran down the hall.

John charged after his wife, but his foot caught on the nightgown. The lace slid across the wood floor, throwing him off balance. He grabbed the bedpost to keep from falling, but the stumble had given Abbie the edge. She was already halfway up the stairs when he reached the hallway.

Her sobs rasped through him like a saw taking a man's limb. He wished to God he'd kept his wits about him tonight. Every instinct had told him she wasn't ready, but that see-through lace had been his undoing. He was a man, and he wanted to make love to his wife—if not tonight, then tomorrow or next month. Hell, even next year if that's what it took.

Abbie needed to hear that promise. Buttoning his shirt as he strode down the hall, John climbed the stairs to her bedroom. He didn't want to wake Beth or Robbie, so he settled for three soft taps on her door.

No answer, but he knew she was there. As he reached for the knob, a key turned in the lock. John understood why she'd run out of his bedroom, but that click insulted him. What did she think? That he'd hurt her? Not in a million years. He had a good mind to kick down the door, but force wouldn't help his cause and neither would waking up Robbie and Beth. Instead he stood at her door and knocked. When she didn't answer, he knocked again…and again. Every two minutes or so, he tapped lightly. And waited…and waited. Until Abbie cracked open the door.

"Stop that!"

He wedged his bare foot against the oak. "Let me in."

"No! I already told you, the wedding's off."

She tried to shut the door, but he shouldered his way inside and leaned against it so she couldn't run off. Abbie fled to the opposite wall, but she was still just a few feet away in the tiny room. With his arms crossed over his chest, John took in the sight of her tear-stained cheeks and swollen eyes. It nearly broke him in two, but self-pity wasn't going to fix their problem. Besides, as did most men, he preferred a good rant to tears and he was in a bit of a snit himself.

He glared at her. "What's this *crap* about not going through with the ceremony?"

"Don't you dare cuss at me!"

"I'll cuss if I want to," he said. "There are times when an ugly word fits. This is one of them. Running out on me like that was understandable. Locking the door was just plain mean."

To his utter horror, she buried her face in her hands and wept. "Please, just go. I'll talk to my father in the morning. I can't marry you."

The wobble in her voice made John both angry and ashamed of himself. Adam had been a fool for listening to Eve, and John had been an idiot for letting Abbie seduce him tonight. The pieces started to come together—the nightly visits, the picnic, the negligee. Looking at her now, he realized she had made a deal with the devil. "It seems to me you decided we'd either sink or swim tonight."

She nodded. "I had to be sure I could be a wife to you. I can't, so I want an annulment like we planned."

"Let's see if I understand." John put iron in his voice. "I botched things in the bedroom, and now you're leaving me."

"Don't twist things around!"

"I'm not. Every instinct except one told me to keep my hands off you tonight, but I didn't pay attention." He let his voice go deep. "I love you, Abbie. And I'll be damned if I let a mistake ruin our future."

"I feel the same way. We just have different notions of what counts as a mistake." She gripped the lapels of her robe and glared at him. "I'm sorry to hurt your feelings, but I don't love you as much as I thought."

"I don't believe that for a minute."

If she hadn't been so upset, he would have laughed at the stupidity. Love had made her put that nightgown on, and love had given her the courage to take it off. The woman had just put herself through hell—for him. Staring at her, he willed her to admit that she had lied. At the same time, he saw stripes of moonlight on the floor. No matter what else happened tonight, he didn't want her to feel trapped.

"I was going to tell you tomorrow, but you should know I heard from Hodge. It's a done deal. You and I have control of your finances."

Abbie sagged with relief. "So I'm free to go home."

John made his voice gentle. "You're also free to stay."

The tears in her eyes gave him hope, but then she shook her head. "It's best if I leave."

"Best for who?" John insisted. "You just spent two weeks convincing me to be a father to my daughter, and now you're leaving the minute she gets here? You better think again."

"Don't shout," she said.

John *hadn't* been shouting. He'd barely raised his voice. But with the realization that Abbie intended to leave him, he no longer cared about waking anyone up. "You're my wife. You can't pack up just because we got naked and had a fiasco."

She clutched the robe at the base of her throat. "You didn't get naked—I did."

John had heard enough. "I don't care who I wake up," he said in his full voice. "I want the world to know that you're my wife. I'll be damned if I'll let you leave like this."

The look he saw in her eyes made him think of grass withering in the sun. Maybe he was coming on too strong. Maybe the fire in him was more heat than she could stand. Still, she needed to know how he felt.

But then her eyes flared with a heat of their own. She looked ready to chew him up and spit him out.

Fine, he thought. He'd be glad to tell her more—how she made him weak in the knees just by breathing. How he admired her courage, her spirit. The way she made him feel like a hungry boy and a giant of a man, both at the same time.

When she raised her chin, just as she had when she'd threatened to shoot out his kneecaps, John felt the friction of an age-old battle. Men wanted to control women, and women didn't like it. He decided it was wise to back down a little. Letting his eyes twinkle, he gave her a sheepish smile. "I guess we're having our first fight."

He expected her to smile back, but she turned to the window. "It's also our last. I'll explain to my father and ask Beth to tell people the wedding is off."

"You're serious, aren't you?" he said, incredulous.

"Yes, I am."

John had learned early in life to be the one who did the leaving, and he didn't take kindly to being left. That's what happened when a boy saw his mother walk down a dirt path with a satchel in her hand. She hadn't even said goodbye. She had just disappeared. John refused to let Abbie to do the same thing. "Look at me."

She turned away from the window and raised her chin like Joan of Arc. John lowered his face and stared back. "I'm going to be standing in that church tomorrow—waiting for you."

"I won't be there."

"That's your choice, but I'm not going to let you slip away like I did in Kansas. This time, our future is in your hands. The question is, do you have the guts to fight for us?"

With the challenge hanging between them, John walked out of the room and closed the door behind him. Heaving a sigh, he decided to go throw some rocks.

Chapter Sixteen

Abbie awoke the next morning to the sound of knocking on her door. Sure that it was John, she said nothing. She had no intention of talking to him before she took care of business with her father.

"Abbie? Are you all right?"

Beth's voice brought a wave of relief. Abbie needed to ask her to spread the bad news, so she pushed out of bed and opened the door. "Come in, sweetie. I have to talk to you."

The younger woman shook her head. "No, you come downstairs. John's not here, so he won't see his bride."

Before she could protest, Beth stepped into the stairwell. Abbie had no desire to rush to the kitchen, but neither could she hide in her room. Surrendering to the inevitable, she put on an old dress and pinned up her hair in a haphazard tangle. She was thinking about how to break the news when she stepped into the kitchen and saw a crowd of women. Almost on cue, they broke into a chorus of "Here Comes the Bride."

Abbie stood with her mouth gaping as she surveyed the faces. She saw Emma Dray, Emma's mother and several women from John's congregation. She guessed the blonde in a trim blue suit was Jayne Trent, and the woman leading the singing was Hildy Reynolds, the church pianist. As the chorus collapsed into laughter, the women crowded around Abbie, hugging her and wishing her well.

"You're good for him," said a woman wearing green.

"We can see how much he loves you," said another.

And from Emma, "It's good to see John happy."

Over and over, Abbie said the same thing. "I can't believe this is happening."

She needed to announce the engagement was off, but Beth was already ushering the crowd into the front room where Abbie saw a wedding brunch laid on the sideboard and a stack of gifts on the table in front of the divan.

She had to stop the celebration now, but Beth was chattering at her like a magpie. "Isn't this wonderful? In case you're curious, I didn't plan it. Mrs. Dray came to me last week."

Smiling at Abbie, Mrs. Dray lowered herself to the divan with a slowness that came from arthritic knees.

She didn't look a thing like Abbie's own mother, but she had the same silver hair and curved spine. Even without hearing the details, Abbie knew the old woman had endured her share of heartache. So had Jayne Trent, sitting next to her with a baby in her lap. And what about Beth?

Abbie's heart started to pound. Every woman in the room had cried herself to sleep at least once. And yet they had all survived and even triumphed. As her gaze moved from woman to woman, Abbie knew that if she talked about her fears, they'd share their own. If she started to cry, they would hug her and offer handkerchiefs.

She was sorting her thoughts when Beth maneuvered her into a chair in front of the presents and handed her a flat box. "Open mine first. I had to stick my nose where it didn't belong, but I think you'll like it."

The room turned silent as the women waited, each one expectant as Abbie felt the weight of the box in her hands. If she opened it, she'd be as good as married to John. As her eyes filled with tears, she said, "This is so hard, but John and I had words last night. I think...I think the wedding's off."

A hush settled over the room as the women looked at her, waiting for more and wanting to help. In Jayne Trent's eyes, she saw compassion. In Emma Dray's expression, she saw envy and a trace of hope. In

Beth, she found understanding. But it was old Mrs. Dray who seemed to look right through her.

"You're wise to be careful," she said. "I've had thirty-six years with my husband. Most of them have been good, but some were awful. You'll have hard times, Abigail, especially with John. He's a difficult man."

"Oh, but he's not!" Abbie insisted.

Beth touched Abbie's shoulder. "Open the present and then decide."

Swallowing hard, Abbie loosened the ribbon and lifted the lid to the box where she saw a double picture frame. The right side held a photograph of John wearing his preacher's coat and looking roguish. On the left Beth had inserted Abbie's favorite picture of Susanna.

Abbie didn't know whether to laugh or cry. They were so much alike and she loved them with an intensity that left her breathless. How could she not stay with John? She loved his courage and humor, the passion that made him both human and invincible. Her heart swelled as she held the frame in both hands. "Beth, it's beautiful."

Her friend squeezed her hand. "You two belong together—and not just because of Susanna."

Abbie touched her daughter through the glass. She had come to Midas because of Susanna, but the decision to stay was hers alone. Fight or flight—that was her choice. But what did a bird do when it couldn't fly? Blinking, Abbie flashed on a baby sparrow she had nursed when it fell from its nest. Just as John had said about the promise rock, love and time had healed that broken bird.

When Abbie looked up from the photograph, she saw Mrs. Dray raise her chin. "Be brave, Abigail. Life doesn't offer many second chances."

Abbie would have given the same advice to Susanna. Blinking back tears, she said, "I'm going to put this on the mantel for everyone to see. One look is going to tell you what brought me here. John is Susanna's father."

After two beats of shocked silence, Mrs. Dray broke the tension with a huff. "It's about time that man did right by you! Let me see that photograph."

Abbie passed the frame down the line of women who each admired Susanna and teased her about having a past as wild as John's. Before she knew it, she had told them about Kansas and her years in Washington. She had also opened a pile of lovely gifts—everything from a recipe book to a bottle of exotic perfume to a calendar with the Women's Auxiliary meetings marked on Thursdays.

When the gifts had been opened and brunch consumed, Beth pushed to her feet. "We need to get Abbie dressed. The ceremony starts in half an hour."

Abbie gasped. She'd been having such a good time

that she had forgotten to check the clock. Leaping to her feet, she said, "I haven't done my hair! And someone needs to tell John the wedding's on. I don't want him to worry."

A knock interrupted the chatter. Beth opened the door to reveal Justin Norris holding a bouquet of roses.

"These are from the Reverend for Mrs. Windsor," he said, looking embarrassed. "He said he'll see you at noon."

"I'd say that settles it," Beth replied. "Come upstairs so we can get you dressed. You don't want to keep the groom waiting."

Definitely not, Abbie thought. John had said he'd be waiting at the altar and she believed him. But neither did she want to keep him waiting even a minute.

John opened his pocket watch and saw that the hands had moved two minutes since the last time he'd looked. The ceremony had been set for noon and it was close to a quarter-past. In the entire time she had been in Midas, Abbie hadn't been late to anything.

Sitting with Ethan in the front row, John was doing his best not to worry. His congregation had packed the church, and Lawton had taken his place in front of the altar at exactly noon. John was sure Abbie hadn't talked to him, but neither had she sent John a word of reassurance.

He had intended to talk to her this morning, but Ethan had dragged him out of bed with a fib about trouble at the hotel. John had been ready to mop up bloody noses when he'd walked into a celebration in his honor. He was itching to look at his watch again, but he settled for glancing at Lawton who had opened his timepiece and was scowling.

Ethan stretched one leg and yawned. "Why do women always run late? I must spend three hours of every day waiting for Jayne."

But Abbie wasn't Jayne.

Ethan stretched his other leg. "They're probably fiddling with the dress some more. You know how women are—they want everything to be perfect for a wedding."

"Maybe so," John replied. But it seemed more likely that Abbie was locked in her room. He glanced back at Lawton who was tapping his toe. If John had been in the man's place, he would have sent someone to check on the bride. But Lawton had better things to do—such as inspect his fingernails.

In another minute John would have to say something to the crowd. Lord, he dreaded that thought. What did a jilted groom say to a church full of well-wishers? When Lawton looked at his watch again, John decided to face facts. Pushing to his feet, he took a final glance out the window. It faced the west side of the parsonage where last night he'd watched light spilling from Abbie's window like a tunnel through the darkness. He wanted to speed through that tunnel now, straight to her room where he'd—

A blur of ivory exploded through the parsonage door. Holding her skirt, Abbie came charging down the steps, hatless and clutching the roses he'd sent. Right behind her came Beth and then Jayne who was holding the hat that should have been on the bride's head.

"Forget the blasted hat!" Abbie cried. "There isn't time!"

Joy filled John's heart as he watched Abbie race down the path to the church. Ethan poked him in the ribs. "Don't you know it's bad luck to see the bride before the wedding."

"Not this time."

A buzz took over the room and people whispered, "She's here, she's here." Jayne slipped into the church and took a seat in the back where a friend set Louisa in her lap.

Deepening his scowl, the judge muttered, "It's about time." Then he signaled Hildy who struck the opening chord of the bridal march. As the music rang in the church, Beth came down the aisle and took her place across from Ethan.

With all eyes on the back door, the congregation

stood as Abbie emerged on Robbie's arm, holding the roses and wearing the hat Jayne had managed to pin on her head. The lace veil covered Abbie's eyes, but it left her mouth and flushed cheeks in view. How she'd moved so fast in her new button shoes and fancy gown was beyond John. Without a doubt, it was the most beautiful wedding dress he'd ever seen. The high collar was alluring without being prim. The straight sleeves gave Abbie's arms a delicate strength, while the lace top hugged her curves and flared at the waist.

In her gloved hands she held the bridal bouquet so that the roses seemed even redder against the ivory of her satin skirt. Silently he vowed that he'd never let this woman down. This was the ceremony that would matter, the one where he'd speak his heart. When Abbie reached the front of the church, Hildy played the last bar of the chorus with a flourish. The judge cleared his throat, pausing until the congregation quieted to a hush.

With his back to the crowd and his eyes on Lawton, John gained a new perspective on weddings. His stomach knotted just as it did before a gunfight. This moment would change his life—far more than the commitment in Raton because now he wanted a future.

The silent crowd turned somber. If John had been doing the ceremony, he would have told a funny story to put the bride and groom at ease. But Lawton hadn't even cracked a smile. Instead he glowered as he shifted his gaze to the congregation. "Ladies and gentlemen, we are here today to witness the union of this man and my daughter in the sight of Almighty Gaw-awd."

John had to grit his teeth. The judge's booming voice didn't have a speck of warmth in it, nor did his stained-glass tone suit John's more personal style of preaching. Glancing down, he saw Abbie press her lips into a line as if she knew what was coming.

Moore puffed out his chest and scowled some more. "I want to remind us all of Gaw-awd's purpose for marriage. Eve was created from Adam's rib to serve his needs. Women are delicate creatures. They are fragile and weak..."

Sweet God in Heaven, John thought. Women as servants? Fragile? *Weak?* He'd like to see Lawton—or any man—carry a baby for nine months, pop it out and be willing to do it again. John knew what he was talking about. Since coming to Midas, he'd been called to three worrisome births. He'd heard the suffering, seen the joy when things worked out and shared the sorrow when they hadn't. Whoever decided women were the weaker sex was a few bricks shy of a load—and so was Lawton.

John considered taking over the ceremony, but he couldn't do it without infuriating his father-in-law, so he settled for frowning as the judge aimed his gaze at the bride. "Abigail, you are to *obey* your husband."

Ah, hell. John *had* to speak up. "She damn well better not."

"I beg your pardon?" said the judge.

John refused to let Abbie make that kind of promise. It went against everything he believed about marriage—that men and women were partners, that a man was to love his wife with sacrifice and passion, and a woman was to give her all to a man who would put her needs above his own. He was gearing up for barn-burner of a sermon when he saw Abbie push back the veil on the hat. After thrusting the flowers at Beth, she put her hands on her hips and glared at the judge.

"Father, I've had a lifetime of your prejudice. I won't tolerate another minute of it. Eve was human and she made a mistake. I've made a few, too. Who hasn't? But Adam was the fool who listened to her. Why doesn't anyone ever point that out?"

John couldn't have agreed more. He'd preached on the Garden of Eden a few times, including his opinion that Adam had mush for brains. So did John, and he'd proven it last night. Glad for the chance for a fresh start with Abbie, he made his voice firm. "Your Honor, Abbie and I'll finish on our own."

"How dare you insult me!" The judge's eyes bugged as he pushed between John and Abbie and spoke to Robbie in the front row. "Young man, come with me."

When Robbie glanced at his mother, John could only imagine the ache in Abbie's chest. All he could do was pray as the boy looked back at Lawton. "I want to stay, Grandfather—for my mother's sake."

Some of the starch went out of the judge. "You're a good son, Robbie. I can respect your decision."

As Abbie reached for John's hand, Moore turned back to them. "Abigail, you have always been—and continue to be—an embarrassment. Your mother would be ashamed of you."

John wanted to tear the man's head off, but Abbie was already talking. "Father, I feel sorry for you. Mother loved you, but you didn't know her at all. Right now she's happy for me, and she wants you to enjoy your grandchildren and be part of our family. If you'd like to stay for the ceremony, you're welcome."

The judge ignored the olive branch and glared at John. "Leaf, you're a disgrace. I've never been shown such a lack of respect in my life."

"Maybe not. But you've treated both your daughter and granddaughter with a lack of love."

Grumbling, Moore strode out the door. It had been propped open, so John had a clear view of the judge's back against the blue Midas sky. When he was out of sight, John turned to his congregation. The preacher in him rather liked the stunned silence.

Quirking a smile, he said, "Anyone want to go with the judge?"

Nervous laughter filled the church, but no one moved.

"Good. I have something to say to my wife, and I'd like you all to listen."

After sharing a private smile with Abbie, he took her hand and they faced the congregation together. "First off, I need to set the record straight. What Judge Moore said about women being the weaker sex is just plain wrong. The woman at my side is the bravest creature God ever put on earth. Fifteen years ago, she aimed a gun at me. If that didn't take courage, I don't know what does…"

As he told the story of their first meeting, John felt his chest swell with love for his wife. It spilled over to Robbie who had made them both proud today, and to Susanna whose courage had made this moment happen. Still holding Abbie's hand, John squeezed gently and finished the tale. "A child came from that time in Kansas. Her name is Susanna and she's my daughter. She'll be here any day now, and I hope you'll all welcome her to Midas."

Old Mrs. Dray pushed to her feet. "Your wife beat you to the punch, Reverend. We heard all about it this morning. It's about time to you married this woman!"

"Actually, I already have," John replied. "We got married in Raton last week."

"Well, sort of." Abbie challenged him with a smile. "You never did kiss the bride."

John didn't need to be asked twice. With the crowd whooping, he wrapped his arms around his wife and bent his face to hers. Their lips were just an inch a part when Ethan tapped his shoulder. "Hold up, Reverend. You forgot the ring."

John didn't know whether to growl at Ethan for cutting off the kiss or to thank him keeping things on track. Without turning from Abbie, he held out his hand for the gold band. He had made promises to Abbie in Raton, but today he wanted to make vows of a different kind. Taking her hand in his, he slid the ring on her finger and looked into her eyes. "I'm not a perfect man, but my love for you *is* perfect. It's as strong and endless as this circle."

He'd planned to say more, but he was too choked up so he simply kissed the gold on her finger. The town of Midas had been named for a king who had lost everything because he'd wanted too much. John had nearly suffered the same fate because he'd been afraid to want anything at all. He could almost hear Silas's laughter. But with that sense of his friend came a punch to his gut. He was no longer a maverick preacher with nothing to lose. If something happened to him, Abbie and the children would grieve.

As if she sensed his burden, she lifted his hand

and slid a matching band on his finger. "I promise to be the best wife I can—now and always. I love you and believe in you. Nothing will ever separate us again."

It was long past time to kiss the bride. Years and days had been wasted. As if she felt the same urgency, Abbie put her arms around his shoulders and kissed him first.

Never again would John look down the barrel of a gun with the indifference of a lonely man. As he and Abbie sealed their vows, he saw the past connect to the future. As if looking through smoky glass, he saw pictures from the past few weeks. He remembered Abbie finding her courage and hurling the rock she'd called "regret" as far as she could. He prayed she wouldn't come to rue this day for the price that came with marrying him. He imagined Susanna coming home and making their family complete.

But he could also see Ben Gantry's gaunt face, storm clouds on the horizon and the Colt Lightning cocked and ready to fire. John pulled his wife closer, deepening the kiss, not wanting to let her go. He needed her courage, her hope, the defiance that made her love him.

Not until he heard whoops and applause from the congregation did he gentle the kiss. Even then, it was a battle to pull away from her. The end of their embrace meant the beginning of new risks, new fears.

Most grooms spent their wedding night making love to the bride. Not John. He'd be cleaning his guns and praying he wouldn't need them.

As the train sped across the border between Colorado and New Mexico, Susanna felt her pulse race with it. In Cheyenne they'd boarded the Union Pacific, traveling third-class and sitting in the back to avoid attention. From there, the train had clacked to Denver where they had switched to the Denver & Rio Grande. In Raton, they would board the Santa Fe and her journey would be almost over.

She and Silas had been traveling for over two weeks. She was tired of sleeping on the seats, feeling dirty and being hungry for her mother's cooking. She looked as ragged as she felt. Her hair had grown past her collar, and her boy's clothes needed a good scrubbing.

As the train swayed around a curve, Susanna imagined hugging her mother and saying she was sorry she had run away. As angry as she had been about being deceived, she had come to understand that the circumstances weren't as simple as she'd wanted to believe. Silas had helped her to see the facts by asking questions about herself. Somewhere near Leadville, she realized she had a good life. It wasn't perfect, but she had grown up with plenty to eat, a warm bed and believing her dreams could come true.

Just as her mother had hoped, Susanna was free to choose her future. But what choices had her mother been given? And what about John Leaf? The Pinkerton reports said nothing about where he had grown up or who his parents were. Susanna glanced at Silas. He'd closed his eyes, but she knew he wasn't sleeping. "Silas?"

The old man sat up. "What is it, child?"

"Do you know why he left home?" She didn't have to explain who *he* was. She still hadn't figured out what to call John Leaf, though Silas had no such trouble.

"That's a good question for your daddy," he replied. "I'm sure he has stories to tell. We all do."

One more day, Susanna thought. Tomorrow she'd meet the man whose blood she carried and she'd have answers. Looking out the window, she thought about the reports in her satchel and how incomplete they were. Did it really matter what he'd done, or was it more important to know the man he had become?

Susanna wasn't sure and she was too worn out to think about it. It felt much nicer to close her eyes and to let the train rock her as if she were a child. But as she slept, she dreamed of Robert Windsor and Ben Gantry's threat about the pharaohs. The memory jarred her awake just as the train sped into a canyon and the whistle gave a shrill blast.

Shivering, she realized that she wanted this journey to be over. She needed to meet John Leaf, but more than anything, she wanted to go home.

Chapter Seventeen

John put his hand on Abbie's back and escorted her from the church to the parsonage. Amid a shower of flowers and well wishes, he relived the afternoon—everything from eating cake to the moment Jed Kennedy struck up a waltz on his fiddle. The crowd had pulled back, leaving John and Abbie alone in a circle of friends. It was the first time they had danced together. Now, with the sun dipping below the ridge, John thought about the way their bodies had swayed together. It should have been a preview of another dance to come, but he cut off that thought.

He'd already made up his mind to keep his distance tonight. He and Abbie didn't need another fiasco, nor was John in the mood for romantic talk. He couldn't shake the feeling that Ben Gantry was lurking in the shadows. That worry made him edgy and short-tempered—the last kind of man Abbie needed tonight.

The celebration had kept that tension at bay, but

now those distractions were gone. Everywhere he looked he saw shadows and heard warnings. Even opening the door to the parsonage unnerved him. The rooms were too quiet, the air too still. All he could hear was the tick of the grandfather clock and the tap of Abbie's shoes as she stepped into a beam of twilight sun streaming into the room. The glare lit up the ivory of her dress, including the tiny buttons that ran from her nape to the flare of her hips. Before John could avert his gaze, she turned to him.

"I need help with my dress." Her eyes dipped to the floor. "I can't reach some of the buttons."

John almost offered to fetch her button hook, but what harm could there be in a favor? Husbands did it all the time. "Turn around," he said, his voice gruff.

"Here?"

"Why not? We're alone. I'll give you a hand and then I'm going outside."

Abbie's expression turned quizzical, but she didn't speak as she flexed her shoulders to ease the tension on the silk. As he raised his hands to the top button, he saw strands of coppery hair curling at her nape and a tiny mole behind her ear. Human as he was, he wanted to kiss that spot. Instead he focused on the buttons and worked them in rapid succession. The gown gaped, giving him a glimpse of her camisole.

"Go on and change," he said, stepping back. "I've got things to do."

"But—" *We need to talk.*

"Later." His throat tightened with irritation. He just didn't have it in him to be soothing tonight. On the contrary, he felt like breaking things. When he was in this volatile frame of mind, he wasn't fit company for anybody—especially Abbie. Leaving her with her dress gaping, he walked out the door to his favorite chair, dropped his coat over the arm and yanked at his collar. The air felt good on his throat, but the softness of Abbie's dress lingered on his fingertips.

Desire burned in his gut along with a bone-deep unease that left him spoiling for a fight. He needed to throw rocks by the stream, but he couldn't leave Abbie. He tried sucking in air as if he had a cigarette, but his mouth felt dry and he wanted whiskey. Fed up with himself, John decided to go to the stable to clean his guns. But as he stood straight, he heard the squeak of the front door and saw Abbie walking in his direction, wearing a new dressing gown and looking worried.

John forced himself to look away. All through the wedding he'd been aware of the perfume she had dabbed at her throat. The scent was spicy-hot and like nothing he'd ever smelled on a woman's skin. His need for her ran so deep it softened his heart—but not his resolve to keep away from her until he could be civil. Except she was getting closer with every step, and he couldn't leave without hurting her feelings. John managed a curt nod. "It's a nice night."

Abbie laid her hand on his bicep. "Are you all right?"

Hell, no. "I'm fine."

"You don't look fine."

Her hair was down and cascading over her shoulders in reddish waves. Each time she stroked his arm, the strands brushed against his sleeve. John had to knot his hands to stop himself from touching the curls. He wanted to feel them falling through his fingers, to lift her hair with his hands and spread it on his pillow...to make love to her so he could forget Ben Gantry and the fear in his gut.

Instead he looked up at the sky just as the first star emerged. A second one popped out, then a third. John took it as a sign. He'd get through the night one star at a time. Except those heavenly bodies were a million miles away and Abbie wasn't.

Her fingers tightened on his sleeve. "I just want to say that I'm sorry for running out on you last night. I'll never do that again."

John knew they needed to talk, but he wasn't feeling reasonable. He wanted to cuss and howl at the moon. How could he be so blessed and cursed at the same time? The future was shining like gold, but the past was a stinking mess that could hurt them all. Compared to his worries about Gantry, last night's problems seemed small. "It's in the past," he said. "Why don't you go inside?"

Looking sad, she put her arm around his waist and rested her cheek against his arm. When he didn't move, she wrapped her other arm around his belly and hugged him. That caress was like giving a starving man a crust of bread and expecting him to be satisfied. Like that needy soul, John wanted the whole loaf. He wanted to bury himself in his wife. Here. Now. But he wouldn't do it. She needed a tenderness he couldn't manage tonight, so he said nothing.

Never mind that she was drawing lazy circles on his belly and searing a hole in his skin. The motion reminded him of the heart she'd drawn in that same spot. He had wanted to get her naked and do the dance. He still did, even more than last night. But instead of a hunger for the slow lovemaking she needed, he wanted the kind of hard sex that made a man forget. Annoyed, he put his hand on hers and pressed to hold her still. "Don't."

Abbie pulled back. "I'm just trying to be nice."

"Well, I'm not in the mood for *nice*."

"Maybe I'm not, either." Her voice had turned shrill. "I'm just as tense and irritable as you are."

"I doubt that," he said dryly.

"Then talk to me."

But he wasn't in the mood to talk—not with her eyes burning into his and her breast brushing his arm. Couldn't she see? She was fanning a flame he was trying to put out. Every brush of her body made him more ornery—and more determined to keep his hands to himself. Frowning, he replied with a grunt and stared pointedly at the sky.

Abbie grabbed his sleeve. "Don't you dear clam up on me! If it's because of last night—"

"Damn it, Abbie!" John couldn't remember the last time he'd been this angry. "This has nothing to do with last night. That stuff's *easy* compared to the weight I've got around my neck. For all I know, Ben Gantry is hiding in some canyon, just waiting for Susanna so he can hurt you both. He's coming, Abbie. I feel it in my bones."

"So what? I'm scared, too! But we're partners, John. You *have* to let me help you!"

"Oh, yeah?"

"Yeah."

When she crossed her arms over her chest, John put his hands on his hips. She shot him a look that sent him back to his first night out of prison. Like a fool, he'd picked a fight with Silas over a can of peas. It had been pure craziness, but the two men had ended up brawling and then laughing their butts off.

Staring into Abbie's eyes, John saw a kindred

spirit. His wife was a fighter, someone who needed to wrestle with her fears. Looking at her blazing eyes, he realized he'd been going about their lovemaking all wrong. The choice to do battle was Abbie's, but if she needed someone to fight, he'd be glad to oblige. He gave her his most irksome smile. "You want to kiss me right now, don't you?"

"Absolutely not!"

But her eyes flared even brighter and her breath quickened. John's gaze stayed on her mouth, then traveled to her eyes where he saw the girl from Kansas. He reached up and touched her cheek. "You're lying. I can feel it."

Abbie's eyes flared. "What I want is…is…to kick you where it counts!"

John hoped she wasn't being literal, but it was a chance he was willing to take. He gave her another wicked smirk. "So what's stopping you?"

As her eyes caught fire with understanding, she grabbed a fistful of his shirt, pulling so hard that his mouth came within an inch of hers. He ached to take over but he stood still, barely breathing as her pupils dilated into fierce black circles.

Do it, Abbie. Kiss me… He was willing her to fight him like she had wanted to fight Robert—for herself, for their future—but her eyes were flickering with confusion. As a man who'd once been a prisoner, John understood the strange taste of freedom.

It stirred a man's blood and scared him to death at the same time.

Knowing Abbie needed someone who would urge her up and over that hill, he tangled his fingers in her hair. The scent of perfume filled his nose as he lifted the curls and let them fall in a fiery wave. All the while, he peered into her eyes, taunting her, willing the rebel to come out and play. When his touch alone didn't put more fire in her eyes, John grazed her ear with his lips. "If you weren't such a chicken, you'd—"

Before he could blink, Abbie had him against the wall with her knee wedged between his thighs and her hands pressed against his chest. He could feel the tension in her leg as she pressed against him—hard enough to arouse him even more, but not so hard that he'd be singing soprano. The rub of her thigh was hellishly arousing, and the fire burned even hotter when she pressed her mouth against his.

But John wasn't about to lose control—not this time. He wanted to be aware of every nuance of her hands and lips in case the fire proved too much. But right now that fire was an inferno. Abbie was kissing the daylights out of him and he tasted it all— tangling tongues, swollen lips, the belligerence of a woman who'd once been a victim and the hope of a man who wanted to be her champion. It was the most honest kiss they had ever shared.

Knowing the tide of battle could turn, John took only as much from Abbie as she was taking from him. When she gripped his biceps, he clasped her upper arms with an equal strength. When she nibbled his bottom lip, he teased hers with a tiny nip of his own. As her body grew more feverish, so did his—until they were like one creature with a single heart. No longer was she a helpless girl being forced to marry or an imprisoned wife. She was a woman staking her claim on a new life and a new man. She wanted the best of everything and so did John.

He was urging her on with his lips when she broke the kiss and stared at his face. It worried him until she cupped his cheeks and stroked his skin. Her eyes filled with light and she kissed him again—tenderly—as if the need to fight had dissolved into a thirst for innocence. Feeling that same hunger, he curled his arm around her waist and took the weight of her breast in his palm. He watched as her eyes filled with desire. Following his heart, he stroked the tip once, twice, a third time—and then stopped. With an insistent gleam in her eyes, Abbie put her hand on top of his and worked his fingers for him.

He let her play...for about five seconds. Then he tugged the tie off her robe and parted the sides, revealing a white cotton gown with a row of ribbons. He untied each one until the cotton gaped to her waist and bared her breasts. As he clasped her hips to pull her forward, she swayed against him so that her breasts pushed up. John took the swollen tip between his teeth and suckled like a babe. With a soft cry, she ran her fingers through his hair, held him to her breast and whispered, "This feels so right."

That was all he needed to hear. He hooked his arms around her shoulders and knees, scooped her off her feet and strode toward their bedroom. Bending one knee, he twisted the knob with his wrist and kicked the door open with his foot. As it flew wide, he plopped his wife onto their bed and fell next to her. In a blink they were wrestling for the top. Rolling, teasing, taunting...unbuttoning, looking, tasting... claiming possession of each other until he couldn't a wait another minute.

With the moonlight streaming across the bed and the sheets in a tangle, John straddled his naked wife and gave her a wicked grin. "This is your last chance to say stop."

"Don't you dare!"

Clutching at his back, she invited him home with tears of joy. At the same time, the bedroom took on the fragrance of a humid Kansas night. An owl hooted outside the window as he matched the angle of their hips, and the mattress cradled them both as they became one body. They were at the beginning...again. Only this time they were locked together for eternity, planting a garden that belonged only to them.

Stroke for stroke, Abbie was matching him, driving him crazy with little squeaks from her throat and the prick of her fingernails digging into his back. She was battling for release, pushing and pulling against him. Feeling her need as his own, John drove deep and held still, giving her all the control.

She took it...and his, too. That was a first for John. He'd always been able to last as long as he wanted but not tonight. Not with Abbie. With his body shuddering and hers tightening around him with spasms of her own, he discovered how it felt to be fully owned by a woman. He didn't know where she ended and he began. All he knew was that they were thinking the same thoughts and melting in the same places. Poignant tears had pushed into her eyes. Spent and empty except for her love, he felt that same welling in his own as he collapsed on top of her.

It was a profound moment for John, but it was also something far simpler. Sex was just plain fun and he wanted to do it again. Softer now but still eager, he figured he'd rest inside his wife for about five minutes. Or maybe less... Maybe he didn't need to rest at all....

Abbie wiggled against her nearly unconscious husband and laughed. "That was remarkable!"

His chest rumbled with a chuckle of his own. They were still entwined, soft and melting together. Abbie had never felt anything like the last few minutes. A radiance had filled her belly and it was still there. It wasn't the same feeling as the clenching that had pushed her beyond reason. It was more like a hot-water bottle, gentle and lasting...even healing.

Tears pressed behind her eyes. Her heart had been set free by love. Was it too much to ask that her body be healed as well? Already her husband was grow-ing hard inside of her, rocking gently and kissing her mouth. Wanting more of everything, Abbie cradled him in her hips and rocked with him. This time their lovemaking was a slow climb and she didn't miss a thing—not the taste of his mouth, not the flex of his arms as he pushed up to look into her eyes, not the passion on his face as he took her up, up up... and over the hill.

Just as before, her body clenched and she found release. So did her husband—with a mind-numbing slowness that pushed her over the edge for a third time and left her limp and weeping. Not because of the physical release, but because she hadn't ex-perienced the same warmth spreading through her womb.

Abbie thought of Julio's ring and the promise of a daughter and four sons. She knew how John felt about more children, but she had seen him holding the Trent baby after the wedding, and his eyes had brimmed with love when he'd told the world about

Susanna. Surely the past few days had changed his mind. A baby...their love alive in her womb...kicks to her belly and John's hand on her tummy. He was lying next to her now, sleepy and relaxed as Abbie stroked his hair. "Do you believe in miracles?" she asked.

"Absolutely."

"I think we just had one."

With a crooked smile, he shifted so that he was spooning her backside and stroking her belly. "You're going to have a lot of miracles."

"I expect so, but I'm talking about something else. The first time felt different. It was more than just us. Do you know what I mean?"

John cuddled her closer. "We did pretty good for newlyweds."

"That's the understatement of the year. We did great. I wonder if maybe Julio's ring was a kind of promise." Abbie took a small breath. "Would you mind terribly if we had a baby together?"

John lifted his hand from her belly and slid back. The mattress dipped as he sat up and dangled his legs over the side of the bed. "Do you really think it's possible?"

His icy tone stunned her, but then she realized that his only experience with fatherhood had been awful. Abbie made her voice gentle. "I'll never forget how it felt to hold Susanna for the first time. She was so small and alive, and I felt nothing but love flowing through me."

"You're a good mother," John said quietly. "I envy you that joy, but you know I don't want more children. If there's any doubt, I'll use a French letter."

Not if Abbie had anything to say about it, but she didn't want to argue with him tonight. Stroking his hand, she said, "That's a decision we'll make together."

"Or we can keep track of your monthly and be careful."

But Abbie had no desire to be careful in bed—not after the risk she'd taken tonight. But neither did she want to push John. Some problems couldn't be solved by talk, so she decided to let the subject drop.

"You know me," she said. "It's just a nice thought."

John blew out a breath and settled back into bed. As he stretched next to her, she rested her cheek on his shoulder, but his arms didn't feel as tight. When she snuggled closer, he stayed still. And when she tipped her head and kissed his jaw, he gave her a peck, snuggled just once and pretended to be asleep.

Robbie came home the next morning wearing a new hat and carrying five bags of penny candy. Abbie didn't mind a little spoiling. It was a grandparent's duty, but she worried that her father was trying to lure Robbie to Kansas with bribes. She also wanted to tell her son she was proud of him for staying at the church yesterday. As he sat at the kitchen table, Abbie cut a slice of leftover cake and opened the icebox for a pitcher of milk. "How was your night with your grandfather?"

Robbie's mouth drooped into a frown. "It wasn't fun like it used to be. He says John's a bad person. I don't think he is."

Abbie nearly dropped the pitcher. "I don't think so, either."

"They're out front right now." Her son looked at her with the eyes he'd inherited from his father. But instead of seeing Robert Windsor, Abbie saw a young man with a mind of his own.

"I hate shouting," he said. "I didn't like it when Father yelled at you. I never said that before."

A lump rose in Abbie's throat. She wanted to hug him, but she knew that young men had their pride. Instead she set the milk in front of him and ruffled his hair. "You made me very proud yesterday. You're growing up."

"Yeah, I guess." As he lifted the fork, he wrinkled his brow. "Grandfather wants me to go to a fancy school."

Abbie stifled a sigh. She wanted the best education for her son, but she was just as concerned about his character. Between studying the law and living with love, she put more weight on the love. Since love came with respect, she decided Robbie had earned a say in the matter. "What would you like to do?"

As he swallowed a bite of cake, he looked up. "I want to stay here. Do you think John will teach me how to shoot?"

Abbie didn't hesitate. "I already asked him and he said yes. But you have to do exactly what he says. It's dangerous."

"Thanks, Ma." He smiled wide, then in that awkward way of boys, he said, "I love you."

"I love you, too." She wanted this moment to be tender and honest, so she said, "I'm sorry I didn't tell you about John and your sister before the wedding. It had to be a shock."

Robbie turned even redder. "Ma, I'm almost thirteen. I know about...stuff. I figured it out myself."

When her son looked shocked at himself for mentioning "stuff" to his mother, Abbie hid a smile. "Just so you know the truth."

As she pushed to her feet, the front door opened and closed with a thud. John paced into the kitchen, saw Robbie and paused. Abbie knew he wouldn't grumble about Lawton in front of the boy, but Robbie's curiosity had already been piqued. "What happened?" her son asked.

John glanced at Abbie, silently asking her if she wanted to include Robbie in the conversation. She had questions of her own, so she said, "We all need to understand the circumstances."

John grimaced. "I'm not sorry I interrupted the ceremony yesterday, but I shouldn't have asked your father to marry us in the first place. Anyhow, I apologized for the upset, but he didn't want to hear it."

"It's water under the bridge," Abbie replied.

Robbie looked up at John. "He's pretty mad, but I'm glad you spoke up for my ma. She's smart. You should listen to her."

John looked at Robbie with a hint of male conspiracy. "Let me tell you a secret. Your ma is the smartest woman I know. We should *both* listen to her, except about eating creamed turnips."

"And grits—I hate grits," Robbie added.

All three of them laughed, then John turned serious as he faced Robbie. "Now I have a question for you. Do you remember saying you wanted to be called Robert instead of Robbie?"

The boy nodded. "I like Bert even better."

"Then Bert it is. You stood up for your mother and me. It meant a lot to both of us."

Robbie beamed a smile. "I like Bert, but Robbie's okay, too. Since we're staying here, my ma says you can teach me how to shoot. Can we start right now?"

John looked at Abbie who nodded her permission. "It's okay with me, but be careful—both of you."

"Yes, ma'am," John replied. After sharing a look with Robbie—one she suspected included some eye-rolling—her husband kissed her cheek. "You can watch if you'd like."

But Abbie shook her head. She had to make up her old room for Susanna. Any day now their daughter would arrive.

Chapter Eighteen

Robbie had the worst aim John had ever seen. They had gone to a field on the far side of the parsonage and were shooting at cans on a stump. Robbie was having a heck of a time aiming the gun. After a half hour of bullets straying in the dirt, John was convinced the boy needed spectacles.

"Remember to use two hands," he said. "Point at the middle of the first can and pull the trigger gently." The bullet missed the target by a mile. So did the next five shots.

"Rats!" declared Robbie.

"It'll get easier," John said. "Want to see how it's done?"

Robbie's eyes popped wide. "Sure."

"You know what to do."

John supervised as the boy turned the cylinder and pushed the ejector rod to remove each of the spent casings. After they had all plinked to the ground, Robbie handed him the weapon. John filled the six chambers with bullets from his gunbelt, took aim and blasted the cans to kingdom come. Showing off for Robbie, he twirled the gun and holstered it.

A familiar voice boomed across the yard. "Not bad for a preacher," called Silas.

John's gaze locked on the girl walking at his friend's side. Dressed in trousers and a denim shirt, she could have been John at the same age. She had a coltish build that matched his lanky frame and the same brown eyes he saw in the mirror when he shaved. Even her eyebrows were like his. The dark slashes had a winglike flare that made her look bold enough to take on the world. At the sight of her cropped hair, John stifled a smile. She'd tucked it behind her ears, emphasizing the stubborn chin she'd inherited from her mother. He had thought about this moment for days and had rehearsed what he planned to say.

Hello, Susanna. I understand we have a lot in common.

But looking at her now, he couldn't find his voice. He remembered what Abbie had said about holding her baby girl for the first time. That same awe filled John now. That Susanna was nearly an adult only made his love deeper because so much had been lost.

He unbuckled his gunbelt and handed it to Robbie. "Put this on the workbench and get your ma."

The boy called a greeting to his sister and ran off. John approached Susanna more slowly, giving her time to look at him. He wanted to do more than nod at her, but he hadn't earned the privilege, so he greeted Silas with a back-slapping hug. "It's good to see you, old man."

"I imagine it is." Stepping back, Silas nodded at Susanna. "I brought someone who wants to meet you."

John held out his hand. "Hello, Susanna. I'm glad you're here."

She glared at his fingers and then at his face. John held the pose for five seconds and then lowered his hand. The rejection stung no less because he understood it. Knowing she wanted honesty, he said, "You're going to hear the truth—every last word. Most of it's pretty ugly."

As her eyebrows lifted with surprise, the front door burst open and Abbie came running down the steps. "Thank God...thank God..."

At the echo of her mother's voice, Susanna's face crumpled into a sob. Turning, she ran and flung herself into Abbie's arms. Hugging and weeping, the two females blurred into one as moisture pushed into John's eyes. He could almost feel Abbie's desire for another child, but Silas's presence was a grim reminder of John's past. He was about to ask about Ben Gantry when Robbie scuffed his boot in the dirt for attention. John motioned for him to come closer. "Women cry when they're happy," he said. "It's something men have to get used to."

When Robbie smiled, John gave him a manly slap on the back. At the same moment, Susanna turned and saw the affection. When her eyes narrowed with anger, John understood why. She'd played second fiddle to Robbie for years, and she was feeling the same way now. He'd have to change that impression as soon as he could.

With Abbie focused on Susanna, John turned to Silas. "'Thank you' isn't enough for what you've done."

The old man pursed his lips and tried to look tough. "She's a fine young woman, John. You take care of her and her ma, or you'll be answering to me."

John smiled at the bluster. "You don't have to worry. Abbie and I got married yesterday."

Chuckling, Silas replied, "She must be a remarkable woman to put up with the likes of you."

"She is, but I'm worried. What's Gantry up to these days?"

Silas shook his head. "This isn't the time. You and I need to talk in private."

But John didn't want to wait. Ever since the wedding, he'd been sensing hell on the horizon. "Tell me now."

Silas had just started to reply when John spotted

Judge Moore charging down the path from town. The man looked like a steam engine about to blow, and he was headed straight for Abbie and Susanna. John strode across the yard, but Lawton reached the women first.

"What the devil is going on?" he demanded. "I'm at the café, and I see my granddaughter dressed like a *boy* and walking around with a *negro!*"

John had no patience with that kind of talk. He was about to tell Lawton to take a hike when Susanna pushed away from Abbie and stood tall in front of her grandfather.

"His name is Silas. He's good and kind, and you're a hateful old man."

Lawton twisted his mouth into a sneer. "You're shameless, young lady! You should never have been born."

If the judge hadn't been Robbie's grandfather, John would have slammed his fist into his jaw and repented later. Instead he settled for poking him in the chest. "Listen up, Lawton. You will *apologize* to *my* daughter right now. And while you're at it, you can *politely* thank Mr. Jones for bringing her home."

The judge's gaze darted from John to Susanna and back to John. "You son of a bitch! You're the bastard who knocked up my Abigail!"

Knowing it would gall the judge, John quirked a smile. "Yes, sir. I'm Susanna's father and proud to claim her. But I take exception to your crude language. You owe my *wife* an apology, too."

John didn't expect to hear one. But neither was he prepared for the slam of Lawton's fist against his jaw. Pain shot to his ear, but he didn't fight back. As long as Abbie and Susanna were out of harm's way, he preferred to turn the other cheek. Rubbing his jaw, he said, "I think that settles it."

But Lawton hauled back and took another swing. This time, John sidestepped. "There's no point to this, Judge. I won't fight you."

Sputtering with rage, Lawton shouted, "You're despicable! How dare you call yourself a man of Gaw-awd!"

John felt a sermon coming on about Christ loving the lowest of the low, but he decided to save it for Sunday. Lecturing the judge wouldn't help anyone, but neither could he bring himself to love this particular neighbor as himself. Knowing he might regret it, he goaded the old man with a smirk.

"I'm not a perfect man, Judge. And neither are you. Your breath can stink as bad as anyone's."

When Lawton's eyes bulged, John realized the judge had taken that last comment personally—not as the general observation of human failing that John had intended. There wasn't a person on earth who didn't fall short, including John. But Lawton had missed that point. All he'd heard was an insult.

"I'm going have you barred from the pulpit!" raged the older man.

If it would have done any good, John would have explained himself, but Lawton really did have bad breath and a possible friendship was a lost cause. "Go ahead and try," he said with a shrug.

Lawton strode back to town, leaving them all stunned and silent. John steered his gaze first to Abbie, who looked like a fan at a prize fight, and then to Susanna who resembled a frightened deer. Robbie had taken a protective position by his mother, while Silas was standing behind John and chuckling softly. "You're as ornery as ever," he said. "Maybe even worse."

John rubbed his jaw. "Only when it comes to people I love." He looked at Susanna, hoping to see camaraderie in her eyes. But instead of the tomboy who had defended Silas, he saw a child…who had just discovered that her mother had married a man she despised.

As she looked across the yard at John Leaf, Susanna's insides started to shake. He'd gone toe to toe with her horrid grandfather and she had wanted to cheer. But he'd also killed children…and married her mother. Susanna jerked out of her mother's grasp. "You *married* him?"

"Yes, sweetie. I did. We have a lot to talk about."

Susanna couldn't imagine what her mother would say. Why hadn't they waited for her? Did this mean they weren't going back to Washington? Susanna felt like a passenger on a runaway train. "I just wanted to see what he looked like," she cried. "I hate him! He killed children and he left you in Kansas."

Her mother turned pale. "It's not like that, Susanna."

"I don't believe you. You've lied to me about everything."

"Yes, I did," Abbie said. "But we're starting over—right now—with the truth. You can be angry, but we're not keeping any more secrets."

The confidence in her mother's voice threw Susanna even more off balance. In Washington, her mother would have gone limp with guilt—but not today. She had a look that left no room for discussion. Susanna almost bolted out of the yard, but she had nowhere to go. Her gaze landed on Silas who was holding the satchel she'd dropped when she'd seen her mother. Next to Silas stood the Reverend, wearing his black coat and rubbing his jaw. Her grandfather had hit him hard. It had to hurt, but Susanna didn't care.

After lowering his hand, the Reverend turned to her brother. "Robbie, take Silas for ice cream at Mary's."

"Sure."

Shocked to the core, Susanna stared at Robbie. Her brother never did what he was asked. If he liked John Leaf, she had another reason to hate him. Silas crossed the yard and handed her the satchel. His eyes were full of understanding, but they also held the same challenge to listen that she'd seen on top of the stagecoach.

As Robbie and Silas walked away, John Leaf looked at her mother. Even before he spoke, something private passed between them. She didn't like it at all.

"Go and buy whatever she needs," he said to her mother in a hushed tone.

"No!" Susanna cried. She didn't want to be alone with him. She wasn't ready to open the satchel and ask him questions. Her feelings were too confused.

Her mother glanced at her and then back to the Reverend. "Maybe I should stay."

Robert Windsor would have glowered, but John Leaf's expression was full of kindness. "We'll be fine, Abbie. Don't worry."

When her mother looked into his eyes with trust, Susanna felt betrayed. Somehow by searching for her father she'd lost mother, who was looking at her now with pity. "Sweetie, I'll be right back."

Susanna knew her mother wanted to hug her, but she kept her arms at her sides until Abbie hurried down the path to town. Susanna was staring at her mother's back when the Reverend walked to the porch and sat on the steps. He looked right at her. "You must be hating all of us right now," he said gently.

He could have been taking to a lamb, but Susanna felt trapped. If she said yes, she'd be agreeing with him. If she said no, she'd be saying she wasn't mad. She decided to say nothing. Maybe if she didn't move, he'd go in the house and leave her alone.

Instead he leaned down and plucked a weed out of the flower bed. "I know how I'd feel in your place. I'd be furious. You went looking for me because you needed answers, and now the questions have changed."

Susanna peered into his eyes and saw a strength of mind she recognized as her own. She had started the fight with her grandfather, but he'd finished it. That counted for something, but she didn't know what. She was searching for something to say when the Reverend's eyes twinkled. "Can I ask you something?"

"All right."

"Do you put a lot of pepper on your food?"

How did he know? Susanna loved black pepper. Robert Windsor used to get mad at her because he thought it wasn't ladylike. Susanna had a taste for spicy food, but she didn't want to say so. Neither did she want to lie, so she asked a question of her own. "Did my mother tell you that?"

John Leaf shook his head. "No, I was just wondering. I put pepper on everything. My old man did the same thing. It used to scare me that I liked pepper so much. I thought it meant I was just like him."

"Are you?" Susanna had blurted the question before she could think. "I mean, do you look like him?"

"Not much." The Reverend twirled the dandelion between his fingers. "You and I take after my ma. She had some Lakota blood in her. She walked off when I was nine years old."

In spite of her anger, Susanna felt sorry for him. "Was your father nice?"

He tossed the weed back into the dirt. "Isaac Leaf was the meanest man that ever walked this earth. I hated him, Susanna. That's why I understand how you feel."

Of all the stupid things, tears pushed into her eyes. She looked pointedly down the path leading to town, but she knew she had reached the end of the road. When the lump in her throat eased, she faced him again. "I have Robert Windsor's file on you. It says you killed children."

"I did."

"Silas says you've changed."

"I have."

The Reverend looked at the satchel in her hand. "Do you want to show me those reports now?"

The weight of the bag pulled at her shoulder. She longed to put it down, but she needed time to sort through her feelings. She also wanted to talk to her mother before she confronted John Leaf. To change the subject, she said, "I'm kind of hungry."

His eyes brightened. "Have you ever had a tamale? Mrs. Garcia brought a whole pan this morning. They're spicy enough to burn off your tongue."

Susanna had discovered tamales in Colorado. She loved them, but she shrugged. "They're okay."

He stood and held the door for her. As she walked into the house, she glanced at the fireplace. On the wooden mantel stood a double picture frame holding her photograph and one of John Leaf. Had she come home at last? She didn't know, but she liked tamales enough to give him a chance.

At the crackle of packages in Abbie's arms, John pushed up from the chair and opened the back door for her. He and Susanna had managed to spend an hour talking about food, Silas's milk cow and finally the weather. He'd been on edge the whole time, expecting her to accuse him with the Pinkerton reports, but she had left the satchel on the floor unopened. To John, it felt like a bag of snakes.

Abbie's arrival brought pure relief. So did her smile

when she set the packages on the table next to the empty tamale pan. "Did you eat them all?"

"Every bite," John said. "You two need some time. When Silas gets back, tell him I'm in the stable."

Susanna picked up the pan and put it on the counter as if she felt at home. John figured they had made a start, but he didn't envy Abbie the next few hours. Untangling the past would take time, and children could be unforgiving. So could adults, especially when they'd been wronged in the way John had hurt Ben Gantry.

After releasing Abbie's hand, he turned to Susanna. "See you later."

She nodded, which he took for a good end to a hard morning.

He needed to clean the Colt after Robbie's shooting lesson, so he walked into the stable and pulled a stool up to the workbench where he kept his cleaning tools. He had just disassembled the pistol when Silas walked through the door. He pulled up another stool and sat straight. Peering down at the weapon, he said, "Are you still as good as you were?"

John rammed the cleaning rod down the barrel. "Do I need to be?"

"I hope not, but Ben's headed this way."

As Silas summarized the events in Bitterroot, John wiped the lead from the rifling. With each twist of the rod, he felt a lash of guilt. His family was in danger, and it was all his fault.

When Silas finished the story, he frowned. "You've got a mess on your hands. What are you going to do about it?"

"I'm going to be ready to protect my family."

Silas motioned at the Colt. "With *that?*"

As a boy in Georgia, Silas had been whipped half to death, and at Bull Run he'd witnessed a bloodbath. John knew how his friend felt about violence.

"This is a last resort," John said. "I'm going to send Abbie and the kids to Washington. I'll face Gantry alone—and unarmed."

Silas shook his head. "That's flat-out stupid. Ben's half crazy. He wants 'an eye for eye,' but hurting you isn't going to bring his boys back. Besides, fair or not, you did your time in Laramie."

"I should have hanged."

"Well, you didn't, so get over it," Silas ordered. "Your daughter needs you, John. You can't just send her away."

"Send who away?" Abbie walked through the doorway, passing from sunshine into the shadows. "It better not be me. And if you think Susanna's ready to leave, you're wrong."

John didn't want to scare her, but they had to face the facts. Still holding the gun, he said, "Gantry's coming. I want you and the kids safe in Washington."

To make his point, he slipped the cylinder into the frame and snapped the ejector rod into place. Abbie came up behind him and touched his shoulder. "We need to make this decision together."

John's blood turned cold. "It's not safe, especially for Susanna. This is my call." He was sorry to be highhanded, but he didn't have a choice, so he added a glare to his arsenal.

Abbie let go of his arm but didn't take her eyes off his face. "There's more at stake than Susanna's safety, but I didn't come out here to argue with you. I came to see Silas."

She took the older man's hand in both of hers. "I can't thank you enough for bringing my daughter home, Mr. Jones."

"The pleasure was all mine. She's a fine young lady. And please, call me Silas."

As Abbie released his hand, he pointed to the stool he'd been occupying. "Have a seat. I'm fond of your girl. If I can help you folks at all, I'd be glad."

Abbie perched on the stool. "Right now she's sound asleep. We talked some, but she needs to get her bearings before she hears the whole story. What bothers me the most is Robert's file. She's convinced it's true."

John grunted. "It is."

"Don't be a fool," Silas said. "She knows half the story. It's up to you to finish it. Give her time."

"Damn it!" John slammed his fist on the workbench. A can of nails rattled like bones. "We don't have time! Gantry could be in town right now."

He had seen Abbie startle at the noise and he felt bad for frightening her, but he refused to apologize for the show of temper. She had to understand—his filthy past made him contagious. He wanted her to leave him alone, but instead she stroked his biceps until he looked at her. Their eyes were just inches apart, hers green and lush with life, his as brown as an open grave.

She reached up and touched his cheek. "I won't leave you—not ever."

But she was a mother, too. John tried to sound matter-of-fact. "A trip to Washington makes sense. You and the kids can pack up your things and say goodbye to your friends. As soon as I can, I'll join you and we'll come home together. It'll be fun."

Abbie shook her head. "We don't need to go back. Maggie can ship what we need. As for the house, it belongs to Robbie so we have to keep it. Maggie can still rent rooms, and we can save for Susanna's schooling."

John admired the plan, but he wasn't concerned about five years from now or even five months. The next few weeks were critical. If logic wouldn't persuade Abbie to flee, he'd have to play on her heart. Turning to Silas, he said, "Tell her what happened in Bitterroot."

Silas rocked back on his heels. "Gantry saw me with Susanna. He's hell-bent on revenge. Your husband's right to be worried."

John would have done anything to take the terror out of his wife's eyes, but what could he do? He had to be true to the man he'd become, but neither could he escape the man he'd been. With the smell of gunpowder in his nose, he looked into his wife's eyes and made his voice dangerous. "You have to leave, Abbie. It's for the best and you know it."

"What I know is that we took vows."

Abbie wandered to the door where a shaft of sunlight made a diamond on the floor. Dust motes glistened like lost stars, and she wondered if her heart would ever stop pounding. Susanna had told her about Ben Gantry's threat, but Abbie was just as concerned about the state of her daughter's mind. Every adult in her life had betrayed her trust. Unless she and John could restore Susanna's faith in the people she loved, suspicion would plague her for the rest of her life.

Blinking, Abbie flashed on the day she had arrived in Midas, full of worry for her daughter and ready to defend herself against John. Love had softened her heart, and she wanted that wholeness for her daughter.

And for John, too. If she left with the kids and

something awful happened to him, she'd never forgive herself. Nor would Susanna have the answers
she needed.

But the risk… Abbie turned back to John who was
wiping the gun with an oily rag. Fear prickled down
her spine. She knew John would do everything possible to protect them, but she was just as certain he
wouldn't defend himself against Ben Gantry. She
could see it all—Gantry raising a gun and John re-
fusing to defend himself because of his guilt.

Fury burned through Abbie's veins. Understandable
or not, Gantry's threats were pure evil. The man had
become a bully. Abbie hated bullies—and she'd fight
hard before she'd let one steal her happiness. Nor did
she want to teach her children to run from trouble. If
John wouldn't defend himself, she'd wage the battle
for him.

He was dry-firing the Colt when she faced him.
"You're not going to like my decision, but the kids
and I are staying."

John glared in silence, but Silas's eyes glinted
with admiration. "God will see you through, Mrs.
Leaf."

"I'm counting on it. And please, call me Abbie."

"I will from now on, but I like the sound of Mrs.
Leaf. I think John does, too."

Abbie doubted it, at least at the moment. Her husband had turned his back, so she finished up her

business with Silas. "I fixed a room for you at the top of the stairs. If you need anything else, just ask."

After nodding his thanks, he excused himself, leaving Abbie alone with John who was screwing the cap back on the gun oil. Without turning, he said, "You're not going to change your mind, are you?"

She walked up behind him and wrapped her arms around his waist. He turned to stone, so she held him tighter, pressing her cheek between his shoulder blades. "It's going to work out. I know it will."

She wanted him to take her in his arms, but instead he reached down and pried her fingers off his waist. "I have work to do."

She understood the need to sort his thoughts in private, but she didn't like it. What had happened to yesterday's vows? Abbie walked away in silence. He couldn't make her leave town, but he'd slammed an even heavier door in her face.

Chapter Nineteen

Two weeks had passed since Susanna's arrival, and John felt edgier than ever. Supper had just ended and he'd had another argument with Abbie. He wanted to go to the stream to throw rocks as hard as he could, but he didn't dare leave the house. Instead he paced to the side of the parsonage where he could melt into the dusk.

He wanted a cigarette in the worst way—not to mention a shot of whiskey. But those escapes were out of the question. Preparing for Gantry meant staying sharp, just as John had once gotten ready for fights that were far less noble. The problem was Abbie. Every time he tried to talk her into leaving, she gave him the same lecture about standing up to bullies. John didn't want to hear it, and he'd just told her so.

But he did want her in his bed…alone in the dark, they'd make love with needs born of fear and hunger. Some encounters were so sweet he ached inside.

Others were so naughty that she blushed. Deep down he was childishly grateful she had stayed, but then she would talk about the kids, her new friends, a future that sounded too good to be true and John would turn to stone.

Leaning on the porch railing, he stretched his neck to relieve the tension. He was about to go find Silas when he heard Robbie and Susanna in the front yard, playing with the puppy he'd brought home this morning. With its shaggy coat and soulful eyes, the mutt reminded him of Bones. John's common sense had told him not to do it, that a dog would create another heartbreak, but how could he not reach out to his daughter after yesterday's talk?

They had ridden alone to a box canyon where he taught her how to shoot. She was a crack shot and he'd been proud. Afterward they had eaten tamales and talked about everything—her schooling, why Robbie was a brat and finally about Bitterroot and Isaac Leaf. John had spared her the details of Isaac's demise but not his memories of the shovel. She hadn't said much on the way home, but he knew he had built a bridge. That's why he'd brought home the dog. When she wanted to name it Bones, he could almost believe that someday she'd call him Pa.

He was thinking about how that would feel when he heard Abbie's laughter mixing with the noise from the kids. Fool that he was, he wanted to play, too.

And why not? If he had nothing to give them except memories, he wanted to make them good.

After a glance at the fading sky, John sauntered into the yard where the kids were playing tug-of-war with the dog and a length of laundry line. Bones couldn't get a grip with his baby teeth, so John sat and took off his boots and his socks. "Here," he said, holding up the cotton. "Use one of these so Bones can hold on."

As Susanna took them, she gave a playful wrinkle of her nose and Abbie chuckled. John took his wife's hand and squeezed. While watching their kids and the puppy shred his best pair of socks, he felt the deepest fear he had ever known.

Abbie pressed tight against John's arm. She wanted the moment to last forever, but the sky had faded to lavender and shadows were stretching across the yard. "All right now," she called to the children. "It's time to clean up and go to bed. Susanna, make sure Bones is cozy in his box. And Robbie, check his water."

Robbie scrambled past them first, followed by Susanna carrying the exhausted puppy. At the same time, Abbie and John pushed to their feet and smiled. She recognized the look on her husband's face. He wanted to make love and so did she. But she also had news—her monthly was late.

Abbie hadn't forgotten his reaction when she had first mentioned the possibility of a baby, but so much had changed. Happiness stirred in her belly, as if she could already feel life, and she had a wonderful picture of telling John the news under the oak tree. She'd bring a blanket and seduce him under the stars. Relishing the thought of moonlight and bare skin, she gave him a special smile. "Let's walk down to the stream."

John shook his head. "I need to stay close to home."

But Abbie wanted the seclusion of the oak and the ripple of the current. "Silas can watch for trouble," she said lightly. "I have something to tell you."

John wrinkled his brow. "Is it Gantry? Have you heard something?"

His tone made her wish she had never opened her mouth. "It's nothing like that. It can wait."

But waiting wasn't in her husband's nature. Gripping her hand, he led her to the side of the porch. "If you've heard any kind of talk, I need to know about it."

She considered telling him about Maggie's last letter instead of her real news, but the twilight streaks of pink and turquoise matched the ring on her finger. She was still deciding what to do when John glared up at the darkest part of the sky and frowned. "I wish to God I could make you face facts about Gantry."

The bleakness of his expression made her sigh. He

had cause for concern, but they also had a reason to celebrate. Abbie touched his arm. "Maybe we should face another fact first. Do you remember what I told you on our wedding night—about a miracle?"

His gaze locked on hers. "I remember everything," he said in a toneless voice.

"Then you already know what I'm going to say… We're going to have a baby."

Full of hope, she watched as his expression changed in fragments. His eyes darkened as he lowered his chin. His lips tightened, then he spoke an oath so ugly she cringed.

"You don't mean that," she said gently.

"Are you sure? It's only been—"

"I'm positive." She clutched his hand. "I've wanted another baby for so long. Be happy, Johnny. This child is a gift."

"It's not a gift. It's a tragedy!" He jerked his hand out of hers. "With the hell that's coming this way, a baby is the last thing I want. I wish to God I'd used a French letter."

Raw fury pulsed through Abbie's veins. How dare he reject an innocent child! It was inhuman, ugly and selfish. She knew it was fear talking and not John, but his attitude couldn't be tolerated. Someone had to set him straight, so she stepped back.

"Listen up, Reverend. I've put up with your foul mood for two weeks now. You've been short-tempered with me for no good reason—except in bed, which doesn't count. It's going to stop tonight."

His eyes narrowed. "Or else what?"

She wanted to shake him out of his dread just as he'd riled her enough to kiss him hard. Only she couldn't think of a thing he'd find threatening. Still, she had to try, so she said, "Or else you'll be sorry."

He chuffed like a mule. "I already am."

"Not as sorry as you should be. You're letting Gantry destroy us and it's not right."

"Damn it, Abbie! I'm trying to protect you and you're blowing sunshine in my face. A baby is one more worry. Do you have any idea what it's like to feel trapped? Like the walls are about to come tumbling down all around you?"

"Yes!"

"Like hell," he muttered.

Abbie stood taller. "That last remark was an insult. I know all about threats and bullies, and I have the scars to prove it. I lived like a trapped animal for fourteen years. You owe me an apology."

"Fine, I'm sorry."

"You could at least *try* to sound like you mean it!"

"Maybe I don't," he said, raising his voice. "Staying here is just plain foolish, and a baby right now—"

"—is nothing but a joy!"

When John clamped his lips together, Abbie knew she'd lost this round of the battle. What could a woman say to silence? Nothing. But there were other ways to shock some sense into a man. She decided to gamble. "You win," she said bitterly. "I'm sick of your self-pity. The kids and I will be on the next train."

His shoulders sagged. "I'll meet you in Washington."

"Don't bother. I don't want this child raised by a man who doesn't want it."

She raised her gaze to his, daring him to admit that he wanted their baby, but he said nothing. Disgusted, she spun on her heels and walked away, praying with every step that he'd stop her.

"Abbie?"

Tears welled in her eyes as she halted in midstep. She was a breath away from running back to him when she heard a defeated sigh. "I'll check the train schedule tomorrow. Can you be ready by Friday?"

Saying nothing, she walked away, letting the solitary tap of her shoes send a message of their own.

John looked at the train tickets on the kitchen table and frowned. He'd bought them the day after Abbie had told him about the baby. Ever since, he'd wanted to tear them into pieces. He wouldn't, though. Ugly or not, their parting was necessary and just minutes away.

At the tap of his wife's shoes in the hallway, he

couldn't stop himself from looking up. He hadn't seen her since yesterday. He'd been sleeping in the stable because he knew himself too well. If he touched her, they'd make love and all the barriers would fall. He couldn't let that happen. Even when she had come to him in the middle of the night, he'd sent her away. God, he felt like scum. Especially now because she had given up on him.

He watched as she lifted the tickets and tucked them into her bag, keeping her eyes off his face. He could see that she'd been crying—for him, herself, Susanna, the baby he might never know.

One word and she'd be in his arms... To keep from saying it, he picked up his coffee cup.

Robbie and Susanna came down the stairs at the same time. They were both dressed for travel, Robbie in the same suit he'd been wearing when they'd arrived, and Susanna in a navy-blue dress that made her look all grown up. John had to choke back a longing so strong it made him shake. He wanted to see his daughter graduate from college. He'd dreamed of walking her down the aisle...but mostly he wanted her to call him Pa. If he heard it just once, it would be enough.

But that wasn't likely in the next few minutes. John raised the bitter coffee to his lips and forced himself to drink it all. When no one spoke as he lowered the cup, he said, "Good morning."

His voice was too hearty, and both kids shot

daggers with their eyes. He couldn't blame them—he'd made a mess and they were caught in the middle, especially Susanna. John watched as she dropped to her knees, lifted Bones out of his box and cuddled him against her chest.

When she looked at her mother, he saw tears in her eyes and hated himself anew.

"I want to take him with us," Susanna said.

Abbie put false cheer into her voice. "I'm sorry, sweetie, but we can't."

"I hate Washington," Robbie declared. "Why do we have to go anyway?"

Abbie stared at John. *Ask us to stay...tell me you love me...*

The moment called for an acknowledgment that something hard was taking place, but John didn't have it in him. He had tried to explain everything to Robbie last night, but the boy was at an age where he felt invincible. Unfortunately he thought John was invincible, too. As for Susanna, she had stayed silent.

Trying to sound normal, he said, "Did Tim Hawk pick up the baggage?"

Abbie nodded. "All of it."

"Good," he said. "You don't want to be late."

Last night he had told Abbie he'd walk with them to the depot, but she had insisted on saying goodbye here. It didn't matter to John. He planned to follow them in a few minutes, just to be sure they were safe on the train. He reached to shake Robbie's hand first. "Look after the ladies, son."

Robbie gave him a surly look. "I still don't see why we have to leave."

There was nothing more to say, so John looked at his daughter. Glaring at him, she said, "We might never see you again."

Because he'd sworn to always tell the truth, he said, "I hope that's not true, but I can't make promises. I made a mistake when I didn't settle things with Mr. Gantry in Bitterroot. Now I have to square it on my own."

Robbie looked befuddled. "Why don't you just fight him?"

"Because I did him wrong," John said quietly.

When Susanna gave Bones a last cuddle and put him back in his box, John cursed himself again. But it was the fury on Abbie's face that nearly dropped him like a bullet.

What in God's name were you thinking to give a child a dog she couldn't keep?

He wanted to plead with them to understand, but what could he say? That he loved them too much? That he'd rather die himself than see them come to harm? He had tried to explain to Abbie again last night, but his throat had closed up. He hadn't even apologized for his smart remark about French letters.

Of all the stupid things he'd said in his life, John put that at the top of the list.

He wanted to tell her the truth—that he was awed at the thought of his seed growing in her womb—but the wall around his heart had cracks in it. If she touched him, the bricks would tumble down, leaving them all unprotected from Gantry. So instead of kissing his wife and telling his kids he loved them, John looked at the squirming puppy. "If I can't take care of him, Silas will."

Abbie gasped. "Don't you dare talk like that! Can't you see what you're doing?"

"Hell, yes! I can see—it's killing me. But this is for the best."

"Who says?"

"I say." He hated the edge in his voice, but he needed to cut them out of his life, at least until Gantry wasn't a threat. He hoped she'd forgive him. Then he wondered if he could ever forgive himself for causing all this pain.

Just as John would have done, Susanna walked out the back door without a goodbye. Robbie followed his big sister, leaving John alone with his wife. So much needed to be said. *I love you... I want this child... You're my life, my hope...*

But he didn't dare open his mouth. Instead he tossed the dregs of his coffee down the sink. "Are you sure you have enough money?"

Abbie tightened her lips in a line. "More than enough and you know it."

"Wire me from somewhere along the way. I want to know you're safe." As he set the cup down with a thunk, he dared to look at her.

Her gaze raked his face. "If you're that worried, come with us."

Her voice called to him like whiskey and smoke. Like milk and bread. Like all the comforts he yearned for and couldn't have. John shook his head. "I can't, Abbie. The mess with Gantry has to end once and for all."

When she took a step toward him, John opened the back door. "Go on, now. You don't want to be late."

Without another word, she walked away.

As she took her seat on the train, Abbie wondered if it was the same car that had brought her to Midas. She could smell the oil, and grime still coated the window. She couldn't stop hoping that John would change his mind. Nor could she stop herself from peering out the window, longing for a final glimpse of him. She was craning her neck to see the boardwalk that led to the platform when the conductor came down the aisle.

"Mrs. Leaf?"

"Yes?"

"I have a message from your husband. He wants you to get off the train."

But why hadn't John come himself? Abbie wasn't a fool. "How do you know it's my husband?"

"I guess I don't, but he said to tell you that a man named Gantry just got on the train and knows where you're sitting."

The pieces snapped together. John would be pursuing Ben, and that's why he had sent the conductor. Robbie and Susanna were already pushing into the aisle as she grabbed the satchel and charged toward the door.

"Wait," she called to the kids. She wanted to be in front, but Susanna had already gone down the steps, followed by Robbie. When Abbie reached the door, she stood on the top step just as she'd done six weeks ago, scanning the crowd for her children.

"If you scream, Mrs. Leaf, I'll shoot your daughter right here."

When Abbie's gaze locked on a wiry man with glittering eyes, she knew she'd been duped by Ben Gantry. He had pulled Susanna against his side and was poking her in the ribs with a gun hidden under his coat. Abbie didn't doubt he'd pull the trigger. His eyes held the worst kind of insanity. She recognized it, because she'd felt it herself the night Robert had burned her with his cigarette. She would have done anything to escape the pain—anything at all.

With a sickening roll of her stomach, she knew why John had wanted them to leave. Forcing herself to stay calm, she walked down the steps. "Don't hurt her," she said. "Take me instead."

"I'm taking all three of you. If you make a sound, she's dead."

Clutching her satchel, Abbie weighed her options. She considered telling Robbie to run for help, but the risk was too great. She wanted to lunge at Gantry herself, but she didn't have the physical strength to tackle him, nor did she have a weapon. She thought about swinging the bag at his head, but her bad shoulder made an attack too risky.

Sick to her stomach, she realized she had been in this position with Robert many times. She'd have to fight with her wits. "Are you sure you want to do this, Ben?"

He pulled his mouth into a sneer. "Get in front of me and hold on to the boy. If he runs, she's dead."

As Abbie gripped Robbie's arm, Gantry nodded at a buckboard waiting on the street. "You and the boy climb in first."

Abbie scanned the crowd for someone she could signal, but the platform was full of strangers. Knowing Gantry had the gun in Susanna's side made her careful as she climbed into the wagon. So did the sense of his eyes on her back.

"Don't even think about running," he said.

With chills tripping down her spine, Abbie watched as Gantry shoved Susanna onto the seat. Keeping the weapon tight on her ribs, he squeezed next to them, took the reins in one hand and drove out of town.

Chapter Twenty

John stood like a sentry in the kitchen, watching the clock tick off ten minutes before he grabbed his coat and headed for the train station. If he couldn't see Abbie and the kids through the window, he'd ask a conductor to check on them. He had to know they were safe on the train. Then he could focus on Gantry.

When he reached the platform, he saw a porter lugging Abbie's trunk toward the baggage car. The sight of the scratched wood sent John back to the day she had arrived, dressed in black and furious. So much had happened in six short weeks. He was wearing his black coat as he always did, but everything else about him had changed. The loner who had nothing to lose had become a man with every reason to live.

As the porter slammed the door on the baggage car, John looked toward the passenger section of the train. All around him, couples were hugging and waving. Some folks had tears in their eyes, but they were all staying strong…for each other. Had he been wrong to ask Abbie to leave? No, he thought. It was for her own good and the safety of the children. But letting her go with anger between them had been selfish. He hadn't been protecting Abbie when he'd turned her away last night. He'd been guarding his own heart.

John felt about two feet tall. What kind of husband let his wife get on a train with harsh words hanging between them? At the very least, he had to tell her he loved her and wanted their baby. Not once had he touched his daughter—not a hug or handshake. Nor was he setting a good example for his stepson. Fool that he was, John had just burned all the bridges he'd worked so hard to build.

As the engine worked up the steam to pull out of the station, he ran alongside the train searching for Abbie's face in a window. Seeing only strangers, he charged into a passenger car and peered down the length of it. He scoured the travelers with his eyes, but Abbie and the kids were nowhere in sight. He paced through a second car, then a third. The whistle blasted and the engine started to puff more rapidly. A second blast told John that he'd barely have time to say goodbye.

He was almost running when he burst into the last car and saw nothing but empty seats. A conductor entered from the caboose and eyed him with curiosity. "Can I help you, sir?"

"I'm looking for my wife."

The old man pursed his lips. "What does the missus look like?"

John described Abbie and the kids.

"They were in the front car. I brought her a message from a man who said he was her husband. He didn't look a thing like you."

An unholy terror ripped through John's chest. "What was the message?"

"Just that she should get off the train because of some fellow named Gantry."

John bolted for the door and skidded down the steps, scanning the crowd for clues. Everywhere he looked he saw evil. Suspicion. Fear on the faces of strangers as he jostled them out of the way. Where had Gantry taken them? John didn't know, but he knew about revenge. The man would leave a note—but where? Nothing had been left at the parsonage and now Gantry had three prisoners to manage.

John figured the easiest way to send a ransom note was to drop it at the post office, so he ran down the street, elbowing past strangers and ignoring friends. As soon he entered the storefront, he asked Bill Norris for his mail.

"Sorry, Reverend. It's not up yet."

"Check the slot," John ordered.

After giving him a funny look, Bill glanced at the box under the slot in the counter and lifted a smudged envelope. "Someone must have just dropped this."

John snatched it from his hand and tore open the seal.

They're going to suffer, Leaf. And so are you. If you want to see them one last time, go to the canyon where you taught your girl how to shoot. I was watching…I've been watching. Now it's your turn. Be there at dawn.

The signature read "Benjamin Gantry," a sign the man had no shame or hope, and that he was willing to hang for the crime he planned to commit.

John refolded the letter and put it in his pocket. Instinct told him to go after Gantry with his gun, but the man had picked the spot for his hostages well. He'd probably hole up in the old mining shack at the back of the canyon. He'd see John coming, and the rock walls made it impossible to approach from any other angle. The canyon was a dead end in more ways than one.

"Something wrong, Reverend?"

John shook his head at Bill. He could send out word and have twenty men at his side, but a crowd would only add to the danger facing Abbie and the kids. He had to fight this enemy alone. Whatever it took…John didn't care.

After assuring Bill he was fine, he headed home. He had letters to write to his wife and children. If he died tomorrow, he wanted it to be with as few regrets as possible.

"Mama?"

Abbie's heart clenched at the sound of Susanna's whisper. It was past midnight, and the three of them were tied up and huddled together in a shack. Robbie had fallen asleep with his head on her shoulder, a boy again in spite of his efforts to be brave. Susanna was leaning against Abbie's other arm, but she hadn't surrendered to the exhaustion that had come from twelve hours of captivity.

As for herself, Abbie was fighting mad. She had done her best to talk sense into Ben. She had tried everything from sympathy to outrage to bargaining, but he'd refused to listen. She had also kicked and punched when he tied her up. For that effort he'd slapped her hard. She could still taste blood from the cut inside her mouth. Aside from offering them swigs of water, he had stayed outside the shack, holding a rifle and whistling "Amazing Grace."

The music gave Abbie chills as she leaned close to her daughter. "How are you doing, sweetie?"

Tears welled in Susanna's eyes. "I wish he'd stop whistling. What do you think he's going to do with us?"

Abbie wiggled her wrists in the rope, trying again to loosen them. "I don't know, but I'd guess he left a ransom note. Your father will come for us. I'm sure of it."

A whimper escaped from Susanna's throat. "I'm so sorry, Mama. I caused all of this."

"Don't be silly." Abbie was glad for the chance to sound like a mother. "If anyone is to blame, it's Mr. Gantry, though I suspect he's half crazy. If something happened to you and Robbie, I'd go crazy, too."

"I know about that day," Susanna said in a hush. "*He* told me all about it yesterday."

Abbie knew who *he* was. She and Susanna had made their amends, but her daughter hadn't figured out what to call John. Abbie hadn't pushed, but the time had come to knock on that door. "So what do you think?"

Susanna's shoulders started to shake. "He told me about feeling dead inside before he met Silas, and how sorry he was for the bad things he did. Now I know why he wanted us to leave."

"I do, too." Not being able to hug her daughter made Abbie's throat ache. "John loves us all very much."

In a whisper, Susanna said, "I want to call him Pa."

Fighting tears, Abbie kept her voice low. "You can call him Pa when this is over. He'd like that a lot."

She wished she could be as certain of John's feelings for the baby. She wiggled her hands inside the rope until her wrists stung with the chafing. Her jaw ached from where Gantry had struck her, and his whistling filled the night with hopelessness. She was aching for them all—even Ben—but she wanted that death song to be for him and no one else.

Susanna shivered against Abbie's arm. "I'll never forgive myself if something happens to any of us."

The lament in her daughter's voice sent blood pounding to Abbie's head. Ben Gantry had no right to revenge—to justice, yes. But not this cruelty. With her bloody wrists and aching jaw, Abbie figured she knew how to do two things in life—she knew how to love and she knew how to fight. No matter what happened tomorrow, she and the kids wouldn't sit here like cooped-up chickens.

She pulled again at the ropes on her wrists. If she could loosen one hand, they'd have a chance. She'd claw Ben's eyes out. She'd attack him from behind and tell the kids to kick at his knees. If she could find a weapon, so much the better. In the dim light, she scanned the cabin. It held nothing but Ben's bedroll and the satchel she had carried off the train. The bag held Abbie's treasures...including the promise rock John had given her at the stream. Just as he said, it was smooth enough to fit in her palm and big enough to be useful.

Abbie turned to Susanna. "Can you wiggle your wrists?"

"Just a little, but I'll keep trying."

"Good. If we can get free, I have a plan."

It was hours past dusk when John finished writing the letter to Abbie. He added it to the ones addressed to Susanna and Robbie and then opened his Bible where he kept the letter he'd written to Ben Gantry. The pages had yellowed with time, but the words rang truer than ever. After putting it in his coat pocket, John picked up the letters to his family and walked into the kitchen. After tracing Abbie's name with his finger, he set the envelopes on the table along with a note to Silas that explained everything.

John stepped back and blew out a breath. His friend had been badgering him all day, demanding to know why he'd let Abbie leave in a tiff. Annoyed, John had gone to his room and locked the door so he could write the letters in peace. Now that the task was done, he felt the emptiness of the house in his bones.

Silas was sleeping upstairs, but John didn't want to wake him. His friend would try to talk him out of his plan, but John had weighed the options. Asking the sheriff for help would lead to trouble, and so would rounding up a band of men. One false move and Abbie and the kids would be dead. He thought about asking Silas to help him with a midnight rescue, but two men weren't enough to guarantee his family's safety.

That left John standing alone. No, he corrected himself. He'd be taking a posse of angels and praying Ben would be satisfied with his remorse. If that wasn't enough, he knew what he had to do. He'd offer up a trade—his life for Abbie and the children.

He wasn't keen on dying tomorrow, but he'd go with a clean conscience. With the letters written, he headed for the stream with the intention of throwing rocks. He needed to empty his mind. If he thought too hard about Abbie, he'd lose the coldness he needed to face Ben. Neither could he think about Susanna or the baby he might never hold. John blocked those thoughts by counting his steps, but as soon as he heard the water rippling through the pines, he imagined Abbie's voice. When he reached the canopy of the oak, he felt her standing at his side. Twice he'd proposed to her on this spot. He'd seen his daughter's face for the first time while sitting beneath the branches. In the past two years, he had spent hours here seeking God's face and finding understanding in the stars.

Needing that peace now, he sat on a boulder at the edge of the stream and took the letter to Gantry out of his pocket. With moonlight streaming down from the heavens, he read it for the hundredth time.

I'd trade my life for theirs if I could...

John meant every word of apology, but the truth was that he couldn't change the past. Nor could he predict the future. That's why he'd written a letter full of passion to his wife. For Susanna he'd penned words of understanding. He'd told her he loved her and challenged her to live big. Robbie's letter had encouraged him to grow into a real man—one who could love and fight at the same time. He'd ended each letter with the same thought.

You'll see me in the stars at night. I'll be watching from heaven every minute of the day...

A lump pressed into his throat. If he died tomorrow, Abbie would grieve. He hated himself for causing that pain, but he took solace in knowing she'd take comfort from the letter.

I said awful things to you when you told me about the baby. Tonight, alone in our bedroom, I'm more sorry than I can say. If I had that moment to live again, I'd lift you in my arms and swing you around in a circle. Knowing you're carrying my child is a joy to me. If it's a boy, I'd like to name him after Silas. If it's a girl, let's name her after your mother. Dorothea Leaf has a nice ring to it, don't you think?

So did Susanna Leaf. Maybe someday she'd call him Pa. He could only pray it wasn't at his grave. *Please God, let this cup pass from me...*

But the die was cast. If talk failed and Ben raised a hand to Abbie or the kids, John would do what had to be done. If he could get off a shot, he'd send Ben to eternity. If not, he'd make a trade. And at last, the Leaf family curse would come to an end.

At the rustle of leaves on the path, John looked up to see Silas striding out of the pines. He came to a halt in front of John and threw the three letters on the ground. "You damned fool!" he bellowed.

John picked up the envelopes and glared at him. "Since when did you start reading other people's mail?"

"You should have told me about Gantry. You owe the man amends, but he's got no right to come after you like this. Vengeance belongs to the Lord—not to Ben, no matter how much he hurts. And not to you, no matter how guilty you feel. You have to fight for Abbie and the kids."

Seething, John pushed to his feet. "Don't you think I know that? I've done nothing but weigh the options, and it all comes out the same. I have to face Ben alone."

"You're just being prideful," Silas said, crossing his arms. "You never did like asking for help."

John gave a sad smile. "Maybe so, but right now

I'd call in the U.S. cavalry if I thought it would save them. As it is, I'm dead sure it would make things worse."

"Then you'll have to think harder. Going after Gantry alone is too risky, even for you."

"I know what I'm doing." John clenched his jaw. "All that matters is my family. Abbie's strong. No matter what happens to me, she'll be all right."

Silas gave him a look that seared his skin. "What about your daughter?"

"I've done my best."

Silas's eyes glimmered in the dark, and the pale blue of his shirt took on the hue of iron. He resembled a prophet from the days of old, threatening to call down a bolt of lightning with John as the target. His voice rumbled out of the dark. "You're a fool if you think dying is the answer. Susanna led Gantry here. If you get yourself killed, she's going to carry that guilt for the rest of her life."

"It's not her fault," John insisted.

"Maybe not, but she'll think it is. Put yourself in her place, John. How'd *you* like to walk around thinking you killed your own daddy?"

John had never told his friend about old Isaac, but in Silas's eyes he saw a truth that turned his guilt to gold. The way to end the Leaf family curse wasn't by dying, but by living well—by loving Abbie and raising four boys and the daughter they already had.

John didn't need to explain the shift in his heart to Silas. The old man had always been able to read his mind. "We need a plan."

Silas nodded. "Tell me about the canyon where they're holed up."

Crouching, John drew a diagram in the dirt, using twigs to block out the landscape. Silas tossed out an idea, but it needed three men to work. John searched for another option, but he couldn't come up with one.

Silas looked him in the eye. "You know what you have to do."

"Yeah," John said. "I have to ask Lawton for help."

Silas gave a low chuckle. "Let's hope he shoots Gantry and not you."

It didn't take more than a minute to convince the judge to strap on a gun. Together the three men walked to the parsonage where they worked out the details of the plan. The strategy called for Lawton to position himself on the rim of the canyon where he'd have a shot at Gantry, and for Silas to hide near the shack so he could rescue Abbie and the kids. It was up to John to draw Gantry into the open, hopefully alone, though he had to consider the possibility that Ben would use Abbie or Susanna as a shield.

The prospect turned John's stomach into jelly. He'd taken on Ed Davies knowing the man didn't want to die. The opposite was true with Ben. John had no bargaining power except the knowledge that Ben wanted revenge, and that he'd regret it beyond measure if he took an innocent life. Somehow John had to convey that truth to the bitter man. It would be the hardest sermon he'd ever preached—and the riskiest. Faith told John he'd be eating breakfast with Abbie and the kids tomorrow, but beneath his black coat he was scared spitless.

Shortly after dawn, he set the letters to his family back on the kitchen table. He refused to let himself think the words "just in case." Doubt went against his nature, but so did being unprepared. He'd written words of love that he wanted each of them to have—if not today then in the future.

After strapping on the Colt Lightning, he strode across the yard to the stable. The morning sun splashed gold across the horizon and reminded him of the ring he'd put on Abbie's finger. Just above the glow he saw a slash of pink that made him think of Susanna and the baby yet to come.

He wanted to hold that child...and he would.

He wanted to see Susanna become a doctor...and he would.

And most of all, he wanted to ask Abbie to forgive him for his pride and unkind words.

John saddled his black mare and led her into the yard. Silas and Lawton were waiting on livery horses, one a gray and the other nearly white. Without a word, the three men rode down the trail he'd taken with Susanna two days ago.

John took strength from the picture they made. The preacher was wearing black, and so was the judge. The freed slave was wearing black, too, but only on his skin. The Book of Revelation talked about the Four Horsemen of the Apocalypse, but John figured three would have to do today. Grace, justice and freedom—they were riding side by side, yet someone was missing. John knew who it was. The fourth rider should have been Abbie, mounted on a snow-white horse and dressed in red—the color of love.

As soon as they reached the canyon, John reined in the mare. The moment called for a prayer that he said for them all. Silas and Lawton answered with their eyes and then rode off to take their places. When he was sure the two men had reached their positions, he rode alone down the trail. About thirty feet from the shack he dismounted and called out to Gantry.

"Ben, I'm here. Let's talk."

A rifle barrel poked out the window. "Say goodbye to your family, Leaf. It's a privilege I never had, but I'm feeling merciful today."

With the sun warm on his brow, John stared at the window. He needed to throw Gantry off balance, but there was a fine line between gaining the man's interest and lighting fire to his hate. John prayed for wisdom and then spoke from his heart. "I wrote you a letter, Ben. I never mailed it, but I should have. I owe you more amends than I can ever make."

The rifle wavered but then steadied. "I don't give a crap about your goddamned conscience. You killed my boys!"

If he'd been alone, John would have walked up to Ben with his hands in the air and taken his chances. But he couldn't do that with Abbie and the kids in danger. He had to lure Ben outside. "Come outside so you can see me. There's something you need to know about that day."

"What are you saying?"

"Come on out and I'll tell you."

"Just speak your piece."

"They were heroes, Ben. They died trying to save each other. You can be proud." Praying his words would be enough to draw the man outside, John kept his hand loose and ready.

"I don't want to hear this crap!"

Before John could reply, the gun barrel disappeared and the door flew open. He saw Abbie sitting on the floor. Their gazes locked, but then Gantry stepped between them with his arm hooked around Susanna's waist and a pistol at her temple. Muttering curses, he dragged her into the yard. Standing still while his daughter kicked at her captor took all of John's resolve, but he didn't have a shot.

"Let her go, Ben. Shoot me dead, but don't hurt a child. No matter what you think right now, you'll hate yourself for it."

Ben's eyes flickered like chards of a mirror, giving John hope that he was seeing both the monster he'd become and the father he'd been to his boys. Knowing that Lawton needed a clear shot and that Silas needed time, John kept talking. "Your boys are in heaven, Ben. They're with their ma and your folks. Even that old dog you had is with them. You're going to see them again. Let that knowledge bring you a comfort that my blood can't."

When Ben's pistol wavered, John prayed the man would lower the gun so they could all walk away. But a fresh burst of madness filled his eyes. "I want my boys *now*. Make that happen and I'll let her go."

"I'd take a bullet right now if it would bring them back, but it won't." John's voice cracked with the weight of the truth. "I hate myself for what I did to you, Ben. I don't know if anyone but God could forgive such a wrong, but I do know you'll hate yourself if you harm a child. Let her go, Ben. Your fight is with me."

Sweat beaded on the man's brow, but his hand stayed steady as he cocked the hammer.

"Papa!"

Like a stone skimming across a pond, Susanna's cry defied the laws of nature and gave John hope.

All that mattered was saving her life and protecting Abbie from a mother's deepest suffering.

Please God…give me words…

But there wasn't time for more talk. He needed to reach Ben now. Knowing he was playing a game of chicken he had to win, John whipped the Colt from his belt and pressed the barrel to his own temple. "I don't want to die, Ben, but I'm a father just like you. There's no way I'll let you hurt my daughter to get back at me. I'll pull this trigger if I have to."

Through a dreamlike haze, John saw Ben's agony—the misery of smelling his own hate and finally the truth that killing another man's child wouldn't bring back his boys. But it wasn't enough to make him lower the gun.

With sweat dripping down his temple, John felt the trigger hard against his finger. Life and death—it wasn't his call and neither was it Ben's. Praying for them all, John was willing him to feel a father's love in place of the hate when a cry tore from the man's throat. For no reason John could see, he lost his grip on Susanna and stumbled back. The sudden spin revealed Abbie, pounding at him with a rock and calling him names. Staggering or not, Gantry was still gripping the gun and Abbie was in point-blank range. John charged across the gap between them.

Please God… Please God…

Ten more steps and he'd have a hand on Ben. Another second he could strip the man of his weapon and Abbie would be safe. His breath chafed in his ears, blocking out the scrape of Gantry's boots in the dirt, Abbie's shouts, Susanna's whimpers... everything except the blast of a bullet.

Abbie... His love... His heart...

As he charged forward, John begged God for mercy—for the call of Abbie's voice, even a cry of pain to tell him she was alive, but all he heard was an unearthly wailing. Had Ben shot Abbie, or had Lawton fired at Ben? Either way, Gantry had dropped his weapon and was howling like a wild animal.

Not until he crumpled to his knees, revealing Abbie standing upright and clutching the promise rock, did John find his voice. "Are you all right?" he said to his wife.

Abbie stared at him as if she couldn't believe he was alive. But then her green eyes flared. "I'm so damn mad at you I could scream!"

John had never seen a more beautiful sight than his very angry wife. With a small cry, she threw herself into his arms and sobbed. He hung on to her for dear life, treasuring the tears that were dampening his shirt and blinking back his own. "It's over," he said again and again. "It's really over."

Keeping one arm around Abbie, he looked for

his daughter and found her already at his side. John pulled her into a hug and called for Robbie. The boy ran out of the shack and straight into his family's arms. With their heads bent and their arms in a tangle, the four of them made a house of sorts, sheltering each other and the baby in Abbie's womb.

They were clinging to each other and talking all at once when Ben moaned. Stepping back, John saw that Lawton had hit the man in the leg. Silas was tending to the wound, but it looked to John as if the bullet had struck bone. Ben would live, but he'd limp for the rest of his life. John crouched at his side. "I meant every word, Ben. I'd bring them back if I could."

Gantry stared hard. "I believe you. I saw your eyes. You'd have pulled that trigger."

"Maybe, but mostly I was trusting you'd remember how much you love your sons." Knowing it offered only a pittance of comfort, John handed Ben the letter.

The older man took it and put it in his pocket. "I guess we're done."

"Yeah, I think so."

As John stood, he spotted Lawton riding down the canyon. The old man leaped off the gray and ran toward Abbie and the kids. He hugged Robbie first, but then he pulled Susanna to his chest and kissed the top of her head. With his arms around both kids, he smiled at Abbie with pride.

John owed these men a debt he could never repay, but he could try. He put his arm around Abbie's waist, touched her belly and looked into her eyes. "If it's a boy, I'd like to call him Silas Lawton. What do you think?"

"It's perfect," she said.

But John noted Lawton's scowl and Silas pushing to his feet and shaking his head no. The two men shared a glance and then leveled their gazes at John. The judge spoke for them both. "You name my grandson 'John Junior,' or you'll be answering to me."

Silas's eyes twinkled. "Name the next one after us."

For the first time, John Horatio Leaf liked the sound of his own name. Pulling Abbie into his arms, he kissed her temple. "Let's make Julio's ring come true."

She turned in his arms and put her hand over his heart. "I'll have to think about it. I'm still mad at you."

"Oh, yeah?" He quirked a grin. "Just how mad are you?"

With her eyes sparkling and her fingers knotted in his shirt, she replied, "I'm positively furious."

Win, lose or draw—there's wasn't anything John liked better than *that* kind of fight. Tipping his face to the heavens, he thanked God for the woman made just for him.

Epilogue

Midas, New Mexico
October 1897

My Dearest Husband,
  We've just returned from our first trip to Washington in ten years. I can smell the diesel from the train clinging to my hair, and my ears are ringing with the chatter of our three young sons. I'm so glad you insisted on visiting Robbie at college, but the trip was so much more. As our train chugged into the station, the autumn leaves were ablaze and so was my heart. Looking at you and our boys, I felt nothing but joy.
  When we visited the house that now belongs to Robbie, you were at my side, holding my hand. I hugged Maggie and laughed myself silly. I walked in the garden and marveled at the birds. I showed you the ravens and the cardinals, the flower beds I'd planted and the dogwood tree

that had grown taller than the house. Not surprisingly, the garden was lovely in spite of the season. Countless women have tended the flowers and listened to the birds just as I used to do. It's a place of healing now.

My own journey began in that spot, but it didn't end until I found you again. You're my protector, my friend, my lover…my hero. I tell you every day that I love you, but somehow that's not enough today. I want to give you a letter you can read over and over, just like I treasure the letter you wrote to me before you faced Ben.

You don't know this, but I've read parts of it to each of our sons.

John Jr. heard it first. He was a week old and squalling all the time. He had to be the hungriest baby I've ever had. In the middle of the night, I'd hold him against my chest, set your letter by the lamp and read it in a mother's hushed tone. He's ten years old now and so much like you it scares me. He's got your heart and your will—good things to be sure. He also has your quick wit. I suspect you two will tangle when he gets a little older…after all, it's the way of fathers and sons.

The twins heard the letter next. Silas and Law wore me out that first year—and you, too! Did we sleep at all while they were teething? Then there was that awful week when they had whooping cough and we nearly lost them. I read your letter over and over. Your confidence that our family will always be together—for now and eternity—gave me strength.

Robbie might be Bert to you, but he's still a boy to me. Someday I'll share your letter with him, too. Maybe on his wedding day, though it may not come for some time. He's far more interested in inventing things than he is in girls... or so it seems!

And that leaves Susanna. I'm going to share the letter with her tonight. She's in love, John. You don't like the man who has stolen her heart, but I do. Rafe looks at her with the same longing I still see in your eyes for me. And she looks at him the way I looked at you when I was seventeen...the way I still do and always will. Nothing can separate our hearts—not the petty annoyances that come with sharing a house, not the big problems that come with raising children. No matter what the future holds, I will always hear your voice in the rippling stream. I'll feel your strength when I stand beneath the oak. I'll imagine the dip of your head on our pillow and see your love in the faces of our children.

Beloved husband, you are mine!

Your loving wife,

Abbie

* * * * *

Discover Pure Reading Pleasure with

Visit the Mills & Boon website for all the latest in romance

Buy all the latest releases, backlist and eBooks

Find out more about our authors and their books

Join our community and chat to authors and other readers

Free online reads from your favourite authors

Win with our fantastic online competitions

Sign up for our free monthly eNewsletter

Tell us what you think by signing up to our reader panel

Rate and review books with our star system

www.millsandboon.co.uk

 Follow us at twitter.com/millsandboonuk

 Become a fan at facebook.com/romancehq